He looked up at the broad yellow moon
and thought that she looked at him.

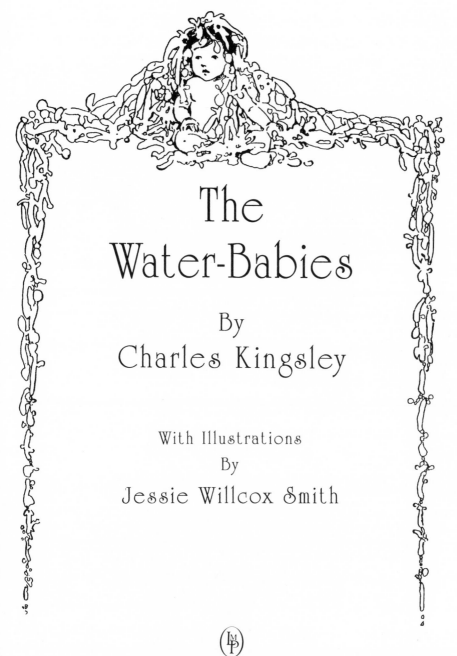

The
Water-Babies

By
Charles Kingsley

With Illustrations
By
Jessie Willcox Smith

LONGMEADOW PRESS
Children's Library
Stamford, Connecticut

Published by Longmeadow Press, 201 High Ridge Road, Stamford,
Connecticut 06904. All rights reserved. No part of this book may be reproduced
or utilized in any form or by any means, electronic or mechanical, including
photocopying, recording or by any information storage or retrieval system,
without permission in writing from the Publisher.

Longmeadow Press and the colophon are trademarks.

Interior Design by Pamela C. Pia

This Longmeadow Press edition is printed on archival quality paper. It is acid-
free and conforms to the guidelines established for permanence and
durability by the Council of Library Resources and the
American National Standards Institute. ∞™

Library of Congress Cataloging-in-Publication Data

Kingsley, Charles, 1819-1875.
    The water babies / by Charles Kingsley : with illustrations by Jessie
Wilcox Smith — 1st Longmeadow ed.
        p.   cm.
    Summary: The adventures of Tom, a sooty little chimney sweep with
a great longing to be clean, who is stolen by fairies and turned into a
water baby.
    ISBN: 0-681-00647-1 (acid-free paper) : $10.95
    [1. Fairy tales.   2. Chimney sweeps—Fiction.]   I. Smith, Jessie
Willcox, 1863-1935, ill.   II. Title.
PZ8.K619Wat   1994
[Fic]—dc20   94-15218
                                                            CIP
                                                            AC

Printed and bound in the United States of America.
First Longmeadow Press edition.
0 9 8 7 6 5 4 3 2 1

TO

MY YOUNGEST SON

GRENVILLE ARTHUR

AND

TO ALL OTHER GOOD LITTLE BOYS

Come read me my riddle, each good little man;
If you cannot read it, no grown-up folk can.

Illustrations

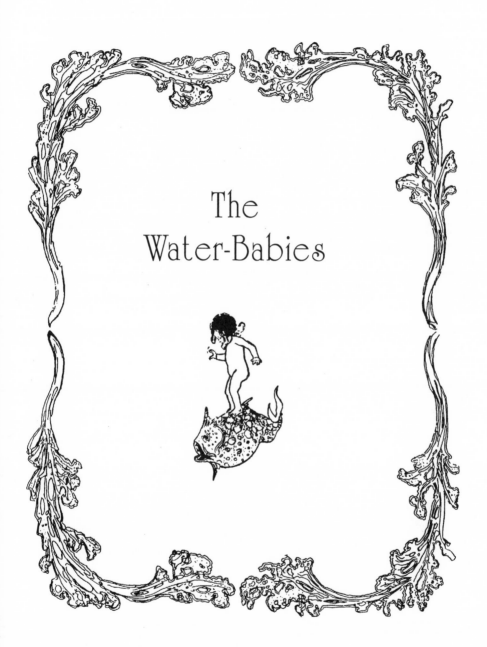

The Water-Babies

Chapter I

"I heard a thousand blended notes,
While in a grove I sate reclined,
In that sweet mood when pleasant thoughts
Bring sad thoughts to the mind.

To her fair works did Nature link
The human soul that through me ran;
And much it grieved my heart to think,
What man has made of man."

WORDSWORTH.

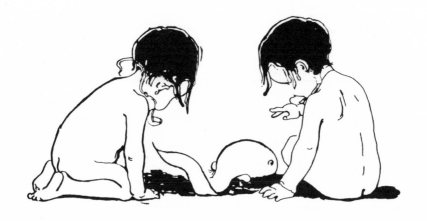

Chapter I

IS NAME was Tom. That is a short name, and you have heard it before, so you will not have much trouble in remembering it. He lived in a great town in the North country, where there were plenty of chimneys to sweep and plenty of money for Tom to earn and his master to spend. He could not read nor write, and did not care to do either; and he never washed himself, for there was no water up the court where he lived. He had never been taught to say his prayers. He never had heard of God, or of Christ, except in words which you never have heard, and which it would have been

well if he had never heard. He cried half his time, and laughed the other half. He cried when he had to climb the dark flues, rubbing his poor knees and elbows raw; and when the soot got into his eyes, which it did every day in the week; and when his master beat him, which he did every day in the week; and when he had not enough to eat, which happened every day in the week likewise. And he laughed the other half of the day, when he was tossing halfpennies with the other boys, or playing leapfrog over the posts, or bowling stones at the horses' legs as they trotted by, which last was excellent fun, when there was a wall at hand behind which to hide. As for chimney-sweeping, and being hungry, and being beaten, he took all that for the way of the world, like the rain and snow and thunder, and stood manfully with his back to it till it was over, as his old donkey did to a hailstorm; and then shook his ears and was as jolly as ever; and thought of the fine times coming when he would be a man, and a master sweep, and sit in the public-house with a quart of beer and a long pipe, and play cards for silver money, and wear velveteens and ankle-jacks, and keep a white bull dog with one grey ear, and carry her puppies in his pocket, just like a man. And he would have apprentices, one, two, three, if he could. How he would bully them, and knock them about, just as his master did to him; and make them carry home the soot sacks, while he rode before them on his donkey, with a pipe in his mouth and a flower in his buttonhole, like a king at the head of his army. Yes, there were good times coming; and, when his master let him have a pull at the leavings of his beer, Tom was the jolliest boy in the whole town.

One day a smart little groom rode into the court where

Tom lived. Tom was just hiding behind a wall, to heave half a

brick at his horse's legs, as is the custom of
that country when they welcome strangers;
but the groom saw him, and halloed to him
to know where Mr. Grimes, the chimney-
sweep, lived. Now, Mr. Grimes was Tom's
own master, and Tom was a good man of
business, and always civil to customers, so
he put the half-brick down quietly behind
the wall, and proceeded to take orders.

Mr. Grimes was to come up next morning
to Sir John Harthover's, at the Place, for his
old chimney-sweep was gone to prison, and
the chimneys wanted sweeping. And so he
rode away, not giving Tom time to ask what
the sweep had gone to prison for, which
was a matter of interest to Tom, as he had
been in prison once or twice himself.
Moreover, the groom looked so very neat
and clean, with his drab gaiters, drab
breeches, drab jacket, snow-white tie with
a smart pin in it, and clean round ruddy
face, that Tom was offended and disgusted
at his appearance, and considered him a
stuck-up fellow, who gave himself airs
because he wore smart clothes, and other
people paid for them; and went behind the
wall to fetch the half-brick after all; but did
not, remembering that he had come in the

way of business, and was, as it were, under a flag of truce.

His master was so delighted at his new customer that he knocked Tom down out of hand, and drank more beer that night than he usually did in two, in order to be sure of getting up in time next morning; for the more a man's head aches when he wakes, the more glad he is to turn out, and have a breath of fresh air. And, when he did get up at four the next morning, he knocked Tom down again, in order to teach him (as young gentlemen used to be taught at public schools) that he must be an extra good boy that day, as they were going to a very great house, and might make a very good thing of it, if they could but give satisfaction.

And Tom thought so likewise, and, indeed, would have done and behaved his best, even without being knocked down. For, of all places upon earth, Harthover Place (which he had never seen) was the most wonderful; and, of all men on earth, Sir John (whom he had seen, having been sent to gaol by him twice) was the most awful.

Harthover Place was really a grand-place, even for the rich North country; with a house so large that in the frame-breaking riots, which Tom could just remember, the Duke of Wellington, with ten thousand soldiers and cannon to match, were easily housed therein; at least, so Tom believed; with a park full of deer, which Tom believed to be monsters who were in the habit of eating children; with miles of game preserves, in which Mr. Grimes and the collier lads poached at times, on which occasions Tom saw pheasants and wondered what they tasted like; with a noble salmon river, in which Mr. Grimes and his friends would have liked to poach, but then they must have got into cold water, and that they did not like at all. In short, Harthover was a grand place, and Sir John a grand old man, whom even Mr. Grimes respected; for not only could he send Mr. Grimes to prison when he deserved it, as he did once or twice a week; not only did he own all the land about for miles; not only was he a jolly, honest, sensible squire as ever kept a pack of hounds, who would do what he thought right by his neighbours, as well as get what he thought right for himself; but, what was more, he weighed full fifteen stone, was nobody knew how many inches round the chest, and could have thrashed Mr. Grimes himself in fair fight, which very few folk round there could do, and which, my dear little boy, would not have been right for him to do, as a great many things are not which one both can do, and would like very much to do. So Mr. Grimes touched his hat to him when he rode through the town, and called him a "buirdly awd chap," and his young ladies "gradely lasses," which are two high compliments in the North country; and thought that that made up for his poaching Sir John's pheasants; whereby you may perceive that Mr. Grimes had not been to a properly inspected Government National School.

Now, I dare say you never got up at three o'clock on a midsummer morning. Some people get up then because they want to catch salmon; and some, because they want to climb Alps; and a great many more, because they must, like Tom. But I assure you that three o'clock on a midsummer morning is the pleasantest time of all the twenty-four hours, and all the three hundred and sixty-five days; and why everyone does not get up then, I never could tell, save that they are all determined to spoil their nerves and their complexions by doing all night what they might just as well do all day. But Tom, instead of going out to dinner at half-past eight at night, and to a ball at ten, and finishing off somewhere between twelve and four, went to bed at seven, when his

master went to the public-house, and slept like a dead pig; for which reason he was as pert as a game cock (who always gets up early to wake the maids), and just ready to get up when the fine gentlemen and ladies were just ready to go to bed.

So he and his master set out; Grimes rode the donkey in front, and Tom and the brushes walked behind—out of the court, and up the street, past the closed window shutters, and the winking, weary policemen, and the roofs all shining grey in the grey dawn.

They passed through the pigmen's village, all shut up and silent now; and through the turnpike; and then they were out in the real country, and plodding along the black dusty road, between black slag walls, with no sound but the groaning and thumping of the pit engine in the next field. But soon the road grew white, and the walls likewise; and at the wall's foot grew long grass and gay flowers, all drenched with dew; and instead of the groaning of the pit engine, they heard the skylark saying his matins high up in the air, and the pit bird warbling in the

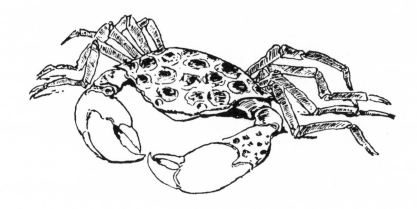

sedges, as he had warbled all night long.

All else was silent. For old Mrs. Earth was still fast asleep, and, like many pretty people, she looked still prettier asleep than awake. The great elm trees in the gold-green meadows were fast asleep above, and the cows fast asleep beneath them; nay, the few clouds which were about were fast asleep likewise, and so tired that they had lain down on the earth to rest, in long white flakes and bars, among the stems of the elm trees, and along the tops of the alders by the stream, waiting for the sun to bid them rise and go about their day's business in the clear blue overhead. On they went; and Tom looked, and looked, for he never had been so far into the country before, and longed to get over a gate, and pick buttercups, and look for birds' nests in the hedge; but Mr. Grimes was a man of business, and would not have heard of that.

Soon they came up with a poor Irishwoman, trudging along with a bundle at her back. She had a grey shawl over her head, and a crimson madder petticoat; so you may be sure she came from Galway. She had neither shoes nor stockings, and limped along as if she were tired and footsore; but she was a very tall, handsome woman, with bright grey eyes, and heavy black hair hanging about her cheeks. And she took Mr. Grimes' fancy so much, that when he came alongside he called out to her:

"This is a hard road for a gradely foot like that. Will ye up, lass, and ride behind me?"

But perhaps she did not admire Mr. Grimes's look and voice, for she answered quietly:

"No, thank you; I'd sooner walk with your little lad here."

"You may please yourself," growled Grimes, and went on smoking.

So she walked beside Tom, and talked to him, and asked

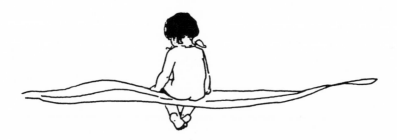

him where he lived, and what he knew, and all about himself, till Tom thought he had never met such a pleasant-spoken woman. And she asked him, at last, whether he said his prayers, and seemed sad when he told her that he knew no prayers to say.

Then he asked her where she lived; and she said far away by the sea. And Tom asked her about the sea; and she told him how it rolled and roared over the rocks in winter nights, and lay still in the bright summer days, for the children to bathe and play in it; and many a story more, till Tom longed to go and see the sea, and bathe in it likewise.

At last, at the bottom of a hill, they came to a spring: not such a spring as you see here, which soaks up out of a white gravel in the bog, among red fly-catchers, and pink bottle-heath, and sweet white orchis; nor such a one as you may see, too, here, which bubbles up under the warm sandbank in the hollow lane, by the great tuft of lady ferns, and makes the sand dance reels at the bottom, day and night, all the year round; not such a spring as either of those; but a real, North country limestone fountain, like one of those in Sicily or Greece where the old heathen fancied the nymphs sat cooling themselves the hot summer's day, while the shepherds peeped at them from behind the bushes. Out of a low cave of rock, at the foot of a limestone crag, the great fountain rose, quelling and bubbling and gurgling so clear that you could not tell where the water ended and the air began, and ran away under the road, a stream large enough to turn a mill, among blue geranium, and golden globe-flower, and wild raspberry, and the bird-cherry with its tassels of snow.

And there Grimes stopped and looked; and Tom looked too. Tom was wondering whether anything lived in that dark cave, and came out at night to fly in the meadows. But Grimes was not wondering at all. Without a word, he got off his donkey, and clambered over the low road wall, and knelt down, and began dipping his ugly head into the spring—and very dirty he made it.

Tom was picking the flowers as fast as he could. The Irish-woman helped him, and showed him how to tie them up; and a very pretty nosegay they had made between them. But when he saw Grimes actually wash, he stopped, quite astonished; and when Grimes had finished, and began shaking his ears to dry them, he said:

"Why, Master, I never saw you do that before."

"Nor will again, most likely. 'Twasn't for cleanliness I did it, but for coolness. I'd be ashamed to want washing every week or so, like any smutty collier lad."

"I wish I might go and dip my head in," said poor little Tom. "It must be as good as putting it under the town pump; and there is no beadle here to drive a chap away."

"Thou come along," said Grimes; "what dost want with washing thyself? Thou did not drink half a gallon of beer last night, like me."

"I don't care for you," said naughty Tom, and ran down to the stream and began washing his face.

Grimes was very sulky, because the woman preferred Tom's company to his; so he dashed at him with horrid words, and tore him up from his knees, and began beating him. But Tom was accustomed to that, and got his head safe between Mr. Grimes's legs, and kicked his shins with all his might.

"Are you not ashamed of yourself, Thomas Grimes?" cried the Irishwoman over the wall.

Grimes looked up, startled at her knowing his name: but all he answered was, "No; nor never was yet;" and went on beating Tom.

"True for you. If you ever had been ashamed of yourself, you would have gone over into Vendale long ago."

"What do you know about Vendale?" shouted Grimes; but he left off beating Tom.

"I know about Vendale, and about you too. I know, for instance, what happened in Aldermire Copse, by night, two

years ago come Martinmas."

"You do?" shouted Grimes, and leaving Tom, climbed up over the wall and faced the woman. Tom thought he was going to strike her; but she looked him too full and fierce in the face for that.

"Yes; I was there," said the Irishwoman quietly.

"You are no Irishwoman by your speech," said Grimes, after many bad words.

"Never mind who I am. I saw what I saw; and if you strike that boy again, I can tell what I know."

Grimes seemed quite cowed, and got on his donkey without another word.

"Stop!" said the Irishwoman. "I have one more word for you both; for you will both see me again, before all is over. Those that wish to be clean, clean they will be; and those that wish to be foul, foul they will be. Remember."

And she turned away, and through a gate into the meadow. Grimes stood still a moment, like a man who had been stunned. Then he rushed after her, shouting, "You come back." But when he got into the meadow the woman was not there.

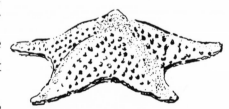

Had she hidden away? There was no place to hide

in. But Grimes looked about, and from also, for he was as puzzled as Grimes himself at her disappearing so suddenly; but look where they would, she was not there.

Grimes came back again, as silent as a post, for he was a little frightened; and getting on his donkey, filled a fresh pipe, and smoked away, leaving Tom in peace.

And now they had gone three miles and more, and came to Sir John's lodge gates.

Very grand lodges they were, with very grand iron gates,

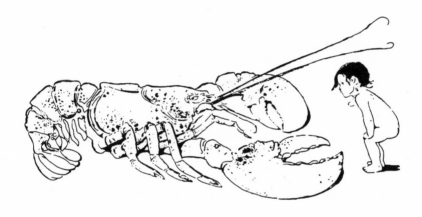

and stone gate-posts, and on the top of each a most dreadful bogey, all teeth, horns, and tail, which was the crest which Sir John's ancestors wore in the Wars of the Roses; and very prudent men they were to wear it, for all their enemies must have run for their lives at the very first sight of them.

Grimes rang at the gate, and out came a keeper on the spot, and opened.

"I was told to expect thee," he said. "Now, thou'lt be so good as to keep to the main avenue, and not let me find a hare or a rabbit on thee when thou comest back. I shall look sharp for one, I tell thee."

"Not if it's in the bottom of the soot-bag," quoth Grimes, and at that he laughed; and the keeper laughed and said:

"If that's thy sort, I may as well walk up with thee to the hall."

"I think thou best had. It's thy business to see after thy game, man, and not mine."

So the keeper went with them, and, to Tom's surprise, he and Grimes chatted together all the way quite pleasantly. He did not know that a keeper is only a poacher turned outside in, and a poacher a keeper turned inside out.

They walked up a great lime avenue, a full mile long, and between their stems Tom peeped trembling at the horns of the sleeping deer, which stood up among the ferns. Tom had never seen such enormous trees, and as he looked up he fancied that the blue sky rested on their heads. But he was puzzled very much by a strange murmuring noise, which followed them all the way. So much puzzled, that at last he took courage to ask the keeper what it was.

He spoke very civilly, and called him Sir, for he was horribly afraid of him, which pleased the keeper, and he told him that they were the bees about the time flowers.

"What are bees?" asked Tom.

"What make honey."

"What is honey?" asked Tom.

"Thou hold thy noise," said Grimes.

"Let the boy be," said the keeper. "He's a civil young chap now, and that's more than he'll be long, if he bides with thee."

Grimes laughed, for he took that for a compliment.

"I wish I were a keeper," said Tom, "to live in such a beautiful place, and wear green velveteens, and have a real dog-whistle at my button, like you."

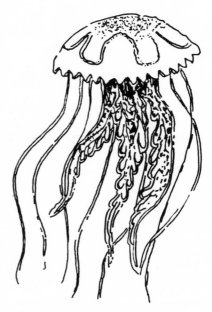

The keeper laughed; he was a kind-hearted fellow enough.

"Let well alone, lad, and ill too at times. Thy life's safer than mine at all events, eh, Mr. Grimes?"

And Grimes laughed again, and then the two men began talking quite low. Tom could hear, though, that it was about some poaching fight—and at last Grimes said surlily—

"Hast thou anything against me?"

"Not now."

"Then don't ask me any questions till thou hast, for I am a man of honour."

And at that they both laughed again, and thought it a very good joke.

And by this time they were come up to the great iron gates

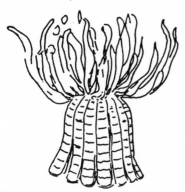

in front of the house; and Tom stared through them at the rhododendrons and azaleas, which were all in flower; and then at the house itself, and wondered how many chimneys there were in it, and how long ago it was built, and what was the man's name that built it, and whether he got much money for his job?

These last were very difficult questions to answer. For Harthover had been built at ninety different times, and in nineteen different styles, and looked as if somebody had built a whole street of houses of every imaginable shape, and then stirred them together with a spoon.

For the attics were Anglo-Saxon.

The third floor, Norman.

The second, Cinque-cento.

The first floor, Elizabethan.

The right wing, Pure Doric.

The centre, Early English, with a huge portico, copied from the Parthenon.

The left wing, Pure Boeotian, which the country folk admired most of all, because it was just like the new barracks in the town, only three times as big.

The grand staircase was copied from the Catacombs at Rome.

The back staircase from the Tajmahal at Agra. This was built by Sir John's great-great-great uncle, who won, in Lord Clive's Indian wars, plenty of money, plenty of wounds, and no more taste than his betters.

The cellars were copied from the caves of Elephanta.

The offices from the Pavilion at Brighton.

And the rest from nothing in heaven, or earth, or under the earth.

So that Harthover House was a great puzzle to antiquarians, and a thorough Naboth's vineyard to critics, and architects, and all persons who like meddling with other men's business, and spending other men's money. So they were all setting upon poor Sir John, year after year, and trying to talk him into spending a hundred thousand pounds or so in building to please them and not himself. But he always put them off, like a canny North-countryman as he was. One wanted him to build a Gothic house, but he said he was no Goth; and another to build an Elizabethan, but he said he lived under good Queen Victoria, and not good Queen Bess; and another was bold enough to tell him that his house was ugly, but he said he lived inside it, and not outside; and another, that there was no unity in it; but he said that that was just why he liked the old place. For he liked to see how each Sir John, and Sir Hugh, and Sir Ralph, and Sir Randal, had left his mark upon the place, each after his own taste; and he had no more notion of disturbing his ancestors' work than of disturbing their graves. For now the house looked like a real live house, that had a history, and had grown and grown as the world grew; and that it was only an upstart fellow, who did not know who his own grandfather was, who

would change it for some spick and span new Gothic or Elizabethan thing, which looked as if it had been all spawned in a light, as mushrooms are. From which you may collect (if you have wit enough) that Sir John was a very sound-headed, sound-hearted squire, and just the man to keep the countryside in order, and show good sport with his hounds.

But Tom and his master did not go in through the great iron gates, as if they had been Dukes or Bishops, but round the back way, and a very long way round it was; and into a little back door, where the ash-boy let them in, yawning horribly; and then in a passage the housekeeper met them, in such a flowered chintz dressing-gown, that Tom mistook her for My Lady herself, and she gave Grimes solemn orders about "You will take care of this, and take care of that," as if he was going up the chimneys, and not Tom. And Grimes listened, and said every now and then, under his voice, "You'll mind that, you little beggar?" and Tom did mind, all at least that he could. And then the housekeeper turned them into a grand room, all covered up in sheets of brown paper, and bade them begin, in a lofty and tremendous voice; and so after a whimper or two,

and a kick from his master, into the grate Tom went, and up the chimney, while a housemaid stayed in the room to watch the furniture, to whom Mr. Grimes paid many playful and chivalrous compliments, but met with very slight encouragement in return.

How many chimneys he swept I cannot say; but he swept so many that he got quite tired, and puzzled too, for they were not like the town flues to which he was accustomed, but such as you would find—if you would only get up them and look, which perhaps you would not like to do—in old country houses, large and crooked chimneys, which had been altered again and again, till they ran one into another, anastomosing (as Professor Owen would say) considerably. So Tom fairly lost his way in them; not that he cared much for that, though

he was in pitchy darkness, for he was as much at home in a chimney as a mole is underground; but at last, coming down as he thought the right chimney, he came down the wrong one, and found himself standing on the hearth rug in a room the like of which he had never seen before.

Tom had never seen the like. He had never been in gentlefolks' rooms but when the carpets were all up, and the curtains down, and the furniture huddled together under a cloth, and the pictures covered with aprons and dusters; and he had often enough wondered what the rooms were like when they were all ready for the quality to sit in. And now he saw, and he thought the sight very pretty.

The room was all dressed in white: white window curtains, white bed curtains, white furniture, and white walls, with just a few lines of pink here and there. The carpet was all over gay little flowers; and the walls were hung with pictures in gilt frames, which amused Tom very much. There were pictures of ladies and gentlemen, and pictures of horses and dogs. The horses he liked; but the dogs he did not care for much, for there were no bull dogs among them, not even a

terrier. But the two pictures which took his fancy most were, one a man in long garments, with little children and their mothers round him, who was laying his hand upon the children's heads. That was a very pretty picture, Tom thought, to hang in a lady's room. For he could see that it was a lady's room by the dresses which lay about.

The other picture was that of a man nailed to a cross, which surprised Tom much. He fancied that he had seen something like it in a shop window. But why was it there? "Poor man," thought Tom, "and he looks so kind and quiet. But why should the lady have such a sad picture as that in her room? Perhaps it was some kinsman of hers, who had been murdered by the savages in foreign parts, and she kept it there for a remembrance." And Tom felt sad, and awed, and turned to look at something else.

The next thing he saw, and that too puzzled him, was a washing-stand, with ewers and basins, and soap and brushes, and towels; and a large bath, full of clean water—what a heap of things all for washing! "She must be a very dirty lady," thought Tom, "by my master's rule, to want as much scrubbing as all that. But she must be very cunning to put the dirt out of the way so well afterwards, for I don't see a speck about the room, not even on the very towels."

And then, looking toward the bed, he saw that dirty lady,

and held his breath with astonishment.

Under the snow-white coverlet, upon the snow-white pillow, lay the most beautiful little girl that Tom had ever seen. Her cheeks were almost as white as the pillow, and her hair was like threads of gold spread all about over the bed. She might have been as old as Tom, or maybe a year or two older; but Tom did not think of that. He thought only of her delicate skin and golden hair, and wondered whether she were a real live person, or one of the wax dolls he had seen in the shops. But when he saw her breathe, he made up his mind that she was alive, and stood staring at her, as if she had been an angel out of heaven.

No. She cannot be dirty. She never could have been dirty, thought Tom to himself. And then he thought, "And are all people like that when they are washed?" And he looked at his own wrist, and tried to rub the soot off, and wondered whether it ever would come off. "Certainly I should look much prettier then, if I grew at all like her."

And looking round, he suddenly saw, standing close to him,

"No. She cannot be dirty.
She never could have been dirty."

a little ugly, black, ragged figure, with bleared eyes and grinning white teeth. He turned on it angrily. What did such a little black ape want in that sweet young lady's room? And behold, it was himself, reflected in a great mirror, the like of which Tom had never seen before.

And Tom, for the first time in his life, found out that he was dirty; and burst into tears with shame and anger; and turned to sneak up the chimney again and hide, and upset the fender, and threw the fire-iron down, with a noise as of ten thousand tin kettles tied to ten thousand mad dogs' tails.

Up jumped the little white lady in her bed, and, seeing Tom, screamed as shrill as any peacock. In rushed a stout old nurse from the next room, and seeing Tom likewise, made up her mind that he had come to rob, plunder, destroy, and burn; and dashed at him, as he lay over the fender, so fast that she caught him by the jacket.

But she did not hold him. Tom had been in a police man's hands many a time, and out of them too, what is more; and he would have been ashamed to face his friends for ever if he had been stupid enough to be caught by an old woman: so he doubled under the good lady's arm, across the room, and out of the window in a moment.

He did not need to drop out, though he would have done so bravely enough. Nor even to let himself down a spout, which would have been an old game to him; for once he got up by a spout to the church roof, he said to take jackdaws' eggs, but the policemen said to steal lead; and when he was seen on high, sat there till the sun got too hot, and came down by another spout, leaving the policemen to go back to the station-house and eat their dinners.

But all under the window spread a tree, with great leaves, and sweet white flowers, almost as big as his head. It was a magnolia, I suppose; but Tom knew nothing about that, and cared less; for down the tree he went, like a cat, and across the garden lawn, and over the iron railings, and up the park towards the wood, leaving the old nurse to scream murder and fire at the window.

The under gardener, mowing, saw Tom, and threw down his scythe, caught his leg in it, and cut his shin open, whereby he kept his bed for a week; but in his hurry he never knew it, and

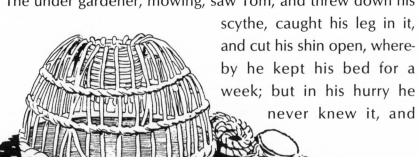

gave chase to poor Tom. The dairymaid heard the noise, got the churn between her knees, and tumbled over it, spilling all the cream; and yet she jumped up and gave chase to Tom. A groom cleaning Sir John's hack at the stables let him go loose, whereby he kicked himself lame in five minutes; but he ran out and gave chase to Tom. Grimes upset the soot-sack in the new-gravelled yard, and spoilt it all utterly; but he ran out and gave chase to Tom. The old steward

opened the park gate in such a hurry, that he hung up his pony's chin upon the spikes, and for aught I know it hangs there still; but he jumped off and gave chase to Tom. The ploughman left his horses at the headland, and one jumped over the fence, and pulled the other into the ditch, plough and all; but he ran on and gave chase to Tom. The keeper, who was taking a stoat out of a trap, let the stoat go, and caught his own finger; but he jumped up and ran after Tom, and considering what he said, and how he looked, I should have been sorry for Tom if he had caught him. Sir John looked out

of his study window (for he was an early old gentleman), and up at the nurse, and a marten dropt mud in his eye, so that he had at last to send for the doctor; and yet he ran out and gave chase to Tom. The Irishwoman, too, was walking up to the house to beg—she must have got round by some byway: but she threw away her bundle and gave chase to Tom likewise. Only my lady did not give chase; for when she had put her head out of the window, her night-wig fell into the garden, and she had to ring up her lady's maid, and send her down for it privately; which quite put her out of the running, so that she came in nowhere, and is consequently not placed.

In a word, never was there heard at Hall Place, not even when the fox was killed in the conservatory, among acres of broken glass and tons of smashed flower-pots, such a noise, row, hubbub, babel, shindy, hullabaloo, stramash, charivari, and total contempt of dignity, repose, and order, as that day, when Grimes, the gardener, the groom, the dairymaid, Sir John, the steward, the ploughman, the keeper, and the Irishwoman, all ran up the park, shouting, "Stop thief," in the belief that Tom had at least a thousand pounds' worth of jewels in his empty pockets; and the very magpies and jays followed Tom up, screaking and screaming, as if he were a hunted fox, beginning to droop his brush.

And all the while poor Tom paddled up the park with his little bare feet, like a small black gorilla fleeing to the forest. Alas for him! there was no big father gorilla therein to take his part; to scratch out the gardener's inside with one paw, toss the dairymaid into a tree with another, and wrench off Sir John's head with a third, while he cracked the keeper's skull with his teeth, as easily as if it had been a cocoa-nut or a paving-stone.

However, Tom did not remember ever having had a father; so he did not look for one, and expected to have to take care of himself; while, as for running, he could keep up for a couple of miles with any stagecoach, if there was the chance of a copper or a cigar-end, and turn coach wheels on his hands and feet ten times following, which is more than you can do. Wherefore his pursuers found it very difficult to catch him; and we will hope that they did not catch him at all.

Tom, of course, made for the woods. He had never been in a wood in his life; but he was sharp enough to know that he might hide in a bush, or swarm up a tree, and, altogether, had more chance there than in the open. If he had not known that, he would have been foolisher than a mouse or a minnow.

But when he got into the wood, he found it a very different

sort of place from what he had fancied. He pushed into a thick cover of rhododendrons, and found himself at once caught in a trap. The boughs laid hold of his legs and arms, poked him in his face and his stomach, made him shut his eyes tight (though that was no great loss, for he could not see at best a yard before his nose); and when he got through the rhododendrons, the hassockgrass and sedges tumbled him over, and cut his poor little fingers afterwards most spitefully; the birches birched him as soundly as if he had been a nobleman at Eton, and over the face too (which is not fair swishing, as all brave boys will agree), and the lawyers tripped him up, and tore his shins as if they had sharks' teeth—which lawyers are likely enough to have.

"I must get out of this," thought Tom, "or I shall stay here till somebody comes to help me—which is just what I don't want."

But how to get out was the difficult matter. And indeed I don't think he would ever have got out at all, but have stayed there till the cock-robins covered him with leaves, if he had not suddenly run his head against a wall.

Now running your head against a wall is not pleasant, especially if it is a loose wall, with the stones all set on edge, and a sharp-cornered one hits you between the eyes, and makes you see all manner of beautiful stars. The stars are very beautiful, certainly; but unfortunately they go in the twenty-thousandth part of a split second, and the pain which comes after them does not. And so Tom hurt his head; but he was a brave boy, and did not mind that a penny. He guessed that over the wall the cover would end; and up it he went, and over like a squirrel.

And there he was out on the great grouse moors, which the

country folk called Harthover Fell—heather and bog and rock, stretching away and up, up to the very sky.

Now, Tom was a cunning little fellow—as cunning as an old Exmoor stag. Why not? Though he was but ten years old, he had lived longer than most stags, and had more wits to start with into the bargain.

He knew as well as a stag, that if he backed he might throw the hounds out. So the first thing he did when he was over the wall, was to make the neatest double sharp to his right, and run along under the wall for nearly half a mile.

Whereby Sir John, and the keeper, and the steward, and the gardener, and the ploughman, and the dairymaid, and all the hue and cry together, went on ahead half a mile in the very opposite direction, and inside the wall, leaving him a mile off on the outside, while Tom heard their shouts die away in the wood, and chuckled to himself merrily.

At last he came to a dip in the land, and went to the bottom of it, and then he turned bravely away from the wall, and up the moor; for he knew that he had put a hill between him and his enemies, and could go on without their seeing him.

Charles Kingsley

But the Irishwoman, alone of them all, had seen which way Tom went. She had kept ahead of everyone the whole time; and yet she neither walked nor ran. She went along quite smoothly and gracefully, while her feet twinkled past each other so fast, that you could not see which was foremost; till everyone asked the other who the strange woman was, and all agreed, for want of anything better to say, that she must be in league with Tom.

But when she came to the plantation they lost sight of her; and they could do no less. For she went quietly over the wall

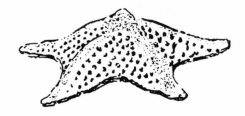

after Tom, and followed him wherever he went. Sir John and the rest saw no more of her; and out of sight was out of mind.

And now Tom was right away into the heather, over just such a moor as those in which you have been bred, except that there were rocks and stones lying about everywhere; and that instead of the moor growing flat as he went upwards, it grew more and more broken and hilly; but not so rough but that little Tom could jog along well enough, and find time, too, to stare about at the strange place, which was like a new world to him.

He saw great spiders there, with crowns and crosses marked on their backs, who sat in the middle of their webs, and when they saw Tom coming, shook them so fast that they became invisible. Then he saw lizards, brown, and grey, and green, and thought they were snakes, and would sting him: but they were as much frightened as he, and shot away into the heath. And then, under a rock, he saw a pretty sight—a great brown, sharp-nosed creature, with a white tag to her brush, and round her, four or five smutty little cubs, the funniest fellows Tom ever saw. She lay on her back, rolling about, and stretching out her legs, and head, and tail in the bright sunshine; and the cubs jumped over her, and ran round her, and nibbled her paws, and lugged her about by the tail; and she seemed to enjoy it mightily. But one selfish little fellow stole away from the rest to a dead crow close by, and dragged it off to hide it, though it was nearly as big as he was. Whereat all his little brothers set off after him in full cry, and saw Tom; and then all ran back, and up jumped Mrs. Vixen, and caught one up in her mouth, and the rest toddled after her, and into a dark crack in the rocks; and there was an end of the show.

And next he had a fright; for as he scrambled up a sandy brow—whirr-poof-poof-cock-cock-kick—something went off in his face with a most horrid noise. He thought the ground had blown up, and the end of the world come.

And when he opened his eyes (for he shut them very tight), it was only an old cock grouse, who had been washing himself in sand, like an Arab, for want of water, and who, when Tom had all but trodden on him, jumped up with a noise like the express train, leaving his wife and children to shift for themselves, like an old coward, and went off, screaming, "Cur-ru-u-uck, cur-ru-u-uck—murder, thieves, fire—cur-u-uck-cock-kick—the end of the world is come—kick-kick-cock-kick." He was always fancying that the end of the world was come, when anything happened which was farther off than the end of his own nose. But the end of the world was not come, any more than the twelfth of August was, though the old grouse cock was quite certain of it.

So the old grouse came back to his wife and family an hour afterwards, and said solemnly, "Cock-cock-kick, my dears, the end of the world is not quite come; but I assure you it is coming the day after tomorrow—cock." But his wife had heard that so often, that she knew all about it, and a little more. And beside, she was the mother of a family, and had seven little poults to wash and feed every day; and that made her very practical, and a little sharp-tempered; so all she answered was, "Kick-kick-kick—go and catch spiders, go and catch spiders—kick."

So Tom went on, and on, he hardly knew why; but he liked the great, wide, strange place, and the cool, fresh, bracing air. But he went more and more slowly as he got higher up the hill; for now the ground grew very bad indeed. Instead of soft turf and springy heather, he met great patches of flat limestone rock, just like ill-made pavements, with deep cracks between the stones and ledges filled with ferns; so he had to hop from stone to stone, and now and then he slipped in between, and hurt his little bare toes, though they were tolerably tough ones; but still he would go on and up, he could not tell why.

What would Tom have said, if he had seen, walking over the moor behind him, the very same Irishwoman who had taken his part upon the road? But whether it was that he looked too little behind him, or whether it was that she kept out of sight behind the rocks and knolls, he never saw her, though she saw him.

And now he began to get a little hungry, and very thirsty; for he had run a long way, and the sun had risen high in heaven, and the rock was as hot as an oven, and the air danced reels over it, as it does over a limekiln, till everything round seemed quivering and melting in the glare.

But he could see nothing to eat any-where, and still less to drink.

The heath was full of bilberries and whimberries; but they were only in flower yet, for it was June. And as for water, who can find that on the top of a limestone rock? Now and then he passed by a deep, dark swallow-hole, going down into the earth, as if it was the chimney of some dwarf's house underground, and more than once, as he passed, he could hear water falling, trickling, tinkling, many, many feet below. How he longed to get down to it, and cool his poor baked lips! But, brave little chimney-sweep as he was, he dared not climb down such chimneys as those.

So he went on, and on, till his head spun round with the heat, and he thought he heard church bells ringing a long way off.

"Ah!" he thought, "where there is a church, there will be houses and people; and, perhaps, someone will give me a bit and a sup." So he set off again to look for the church, for he was sure that he heard the bells quite plain.

And in a minute more, when he looked round, he stopped again, and said, "Why, what a big place the world is!"

And so it was; for, from the top of the mountain, he could see—what could he not see?

Behind him, far below, was Harthover, and the dark woods, and the shining salmon river; and on his left, far below, was the town, and the smoking chimneys of the collieries; and far, far away, the river widened to the shining sea, and little white specks, which were ships, lay on its bosom. Before him lay, spread out like a map, great plains, and farms, and villages, amid dark knots of trees. They all seemed at his very feet; but he had sense to see that they were long miles away.

And to his right rose moor after moor, hill after hill, till they faded away, blue into blue sky. But between him and those moors, and really at his very feet, lay something, to which, as soon as Tom saw it, he determined to go, for that was the place for him.

A deep, deep green and rocky valley, very narrow, and filled with wood; but through the wood, hundreds of feet below him, he could see a clear stream glance. Oh, if he could but get down to that stream! Then, by the stream he saw the roof of a little cottage, and a little garden set out in squares and beds. And there was a tiny little red thing moving in the garden no bigger than a fly. As Tom looked down, he saw that it was a woman in a red petticoat. Ah! perhaps she would give him something to eat. And there were the church bells ringing again. Surely there must be a village down there. Well, nobody would know him, or what had happened at the Place. The news could not have got there yet, even if Sir John had set all the policemen

in the county after him; and he could get down there in five minutes.

Tom was quite right about the hue and cry not having got thither, for he had come, without knowing it, the best part of ten miles from Harthover: but he was wrong about getting down in five minutes, for the cottage was more than a mile off, and a good thousand feet below.

However, down he went, like a brave little man as he was, though he was very footsore, and tired, and hungry, and thirsty; while the church bells rang so loud, he began to think that they must be inside his own head, and the river chimed and tinkled far below; and this was the song which it sang:—

Clear and cool, clear and cool,
By laughing shallow, and dreaming pool;
Cool and clear, cool and clear,
By shining shingle, and foaming wear;
Under the crag where the ouzel sings,
And the ivied wall where the church bell rings,
Undefiled, for the undefiled;
Play by me, bathe in me, mother and child.

Dank and foul, dank and foul,
By the smoky town in its murky cowl;
Foul and dank, foul and dank,
By wharf and sewer and slimy bank;
Darker and darker the further I go,
Baser and baser the richer I grow;
Who dare sport with the sin-defiled?
Shrink from me, turn from me, mother and child.

Strong and free, strong and free,
The floodgates are open, away to the sea.
Free and strong, free and strong,
Cleansing my streams as I hurry along,
To the golden sands, and the leaping bar,
And the taintless tide that awaits me afar,
As I lose myself in the infinite main,
Like a soul that has sinned and is pardoned again.
Undefiled, for the undefiled,
Play by me, bathe in me, mother and child.

So Tom went down; and all the while he never saw the Irish-woman going down behind him.

Chapter II

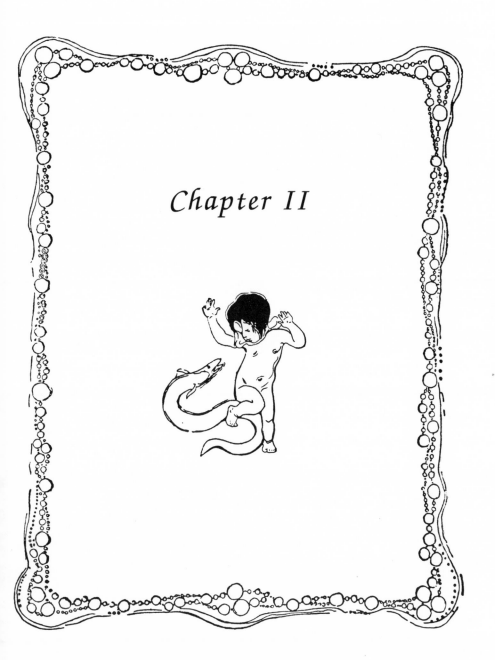

"And is there care in heaven? and is there love
In heavenly spirits to these creatures base
That may compassion of their evils move?
There is: — else much more wretched were the case
Of men than beasts: But oh! the exceeding grace
Of Highest God that loves His creatures so,
And all His works with mercy doth embrace,
That blessed Angels He sends to and fro,
To serve to wicked man, to serve His wicked foe!"

SPENCER.

Chapter II

 MILE off, and a thousand feet down. So Tom found it; though it seemed as if he could have chucked a pebble on to the back of the woman in the red petticoat who was weeding in the garden, or even across the dale to the rocks beyond.

For the bottom of the valley was just one field broad, and on the other side ran the stream; and above it, grey crag, grey down, grey stair, grey moor, walled up to heaven.

A quiet, silent, rich, happy place; a narrow crack cut deep into the earth; so deep, and so out of the way, that the bad bogeys can hardly find it out. The name of the place is Vendale; and if you want to see it for yourself, you must go up into the High Craven, and search by Bolland Forest north by Ingleborough, to the Nine Standards and Cross Fell; and if you have not found it, you must turn south, and search the Lake Mountains, down to Scaw Fell and the sea; and then if you have not found it, you must go northward again by merry Carlisle, and search the Cheviots all across, from Annan Water to Berwick Law; and then, whether you have found Vendale or not, you will have found such a country, and such a people, as ought to make you proud of being a British boy.

So Tom went to go down; and first he went down three hundred feet of steep heather, mixed up with loose brown gritstone, as rough as a file; which was not pleasant to his poor little heels as he came bump, stump, jump, down the steep. And still he thought he could throw a stone into the garden.

Then he went down three hundred feet of limestone terraces, one below the other, as straight as if Mr. George White had ruled them with his ruler and then cut them out with his chisel. There was no heath there, but—

First, a little grass slope, covered with the prettiest flowers, rockrose and saxifrage, and thyme and basil, and all sorts of sweet herbs.

Then bump down a two-foot step of limestone.

Then another bit of grass and flowers.

Then bump down a one-foot step.

Then another bit of grass and flowers for fifty yards, as steep as the house-roof, where he had to slide down on his dear little tail.

Then another step of stone, ten feet high; and there he had to stop himself, and crawl along the edge to find a crack; for if he had rolled over, he would have rolled right into the old woman's garden, and frightened her out of her wits.

Then, when he had found a dark narrow crack, full of green-stalked fern, such as hangs in the basket in the drawing-room, and had crawled down through it, with knees and elbows, as he would down a chimney, there was another grass slope, and another step, and so on, till—oh, dear me! I wish it was all

over; and so did he. And yet he thought he could throw a stone into the old woman's garden.

At last he came to a bank of beautiful shrubs—whitebeam with its great silver-backed leaves, and mountain-ash, and oak—and below them cliff and crag, cliff and crag, with great beds of crown-ferns and wood-sedge; while through the shrubs he could see the stream sparkling, and hear it murmur on the white pebbles. He did not know that it was three hundred feet below.

You would have been giddy, perhaps, at looking down; but Tom was not. He was a brave little chimney-sweep; and when he found himself on the top of a high cliff, instead of sitting down and crying for his baba (though he never had had any baba to cry for), he said—"Ah, this will just suit me!" though he was very tired; and down he went, by stock and stone, sedge and ledge, bush and rush, as if he had been born a jolly little black ape, with four hands instead of two.

And all the while he never saw the Irishwoman coming down behind him.

But he was getting terribly tired now. The burning sun on the fells had sucked him up; but the damp heat of the woody crag sucked him up still more; and the perspiration ran out of the ends of his fingers and toes, and washed him cleaner than he had been for a whole year. But, of course, he dirtied everything terribly as he went. There has been a great black smudge all down the crag ever since. And there have been more black beetles in Vendale since than ever were known before; all, of course, owing to Tom's having blacked the original papa of them all, just as he was setting off to be married, with a sky-blue coat and scarlet leggings, as smart as a gardener's dog with a polyanthus in his mouth.

At last he got to the bottom. But, behold, it was not the bottom—as people usually find when they are coming down a mountain. For at the foot of the crag were heaps and heaps of fallen lime-stone of

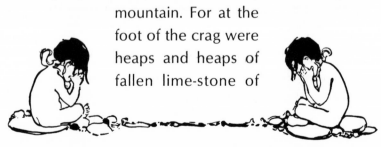

every size from that of your head to that of a stagewagon, with holes between them full of sweet heath-fern; and before Tom got through them, he was out in the bright sunshine again; and then he felt, once for all and suddenly, as people generally do, that he was b-e-a-t, beat.

You must expect to be beat a few times in your life, little man, if you live such a life as a man ought to live, let you be as strong and healthy as you may; and when you are, you will find it a very ugly feeling. I hope that that day you may have a stout, staunch friend by you who is not beat; for if you have not, you had best lie where you are, and wait for better times, as poor Tom did.

He could not get on. The sun was burning, and yet he felt chill all over. He was quite empty, and yet he felt quite sick. There was but two hundred yards of smooth pasture between him and the cottage, and yet he could not walk down it. He could hear the stream murmuring only one field beyond it, and yet it seemed to him as if it was a hundred miles off.

He lay down on the grass till the beetles ran over him, and the flies settled on his nose. I don't know when he would have got up again, if the gnats and the midges had not taken compassion on him. But the gnats blew their trumpets so loud in his ear, and the midges nibbled so at his hands and face wherever they could find a place free from soot, that at last he woke up, and stumbled away, down over a low wall, and into a narrow road, and up to the cottage door.

And a neat, pretty cottage it was, with clipped yew hedges all round the garden, and yews inside too, cut into peacocks and trumpets and teapots and all kinds of queer shapes. And out of the open door came a noise like that and the frogs on the Great-A, when they know that it is going to be scorching hot tomorrow—and how they know that I don't know, and you don't know, and nobody knows.

He came slowly up to the open door, which was all hung round with clematis and roses; and then peeped in, half afraid.

And there sat by the empty fireplace, which was filled with a pot of sweet herbs, the nicest old woman that ever was seen, in her red petticoat, and short dimity bedgown, and clean white cap, with a black silk handkerchief over it, tied under her chin. At her feet sat the grandfather of all the cats, and opposite her sat, on two benches, twelve or fourteen neat, rosy, chubby little children, learning their Chris-cross-row; and gabble enough they made about it.

Such a pleasant cottage it was, with a shiny clean stone floor, and curious old prints on the walls, and an old black oak sideboard full of bright pewter and brass dishes, and a cuckoo clock in the corner, which began shouting as soon as Tom appeared; not that it was frightened at Tom, but that it was just eleven o'clock.

All the children started at Tom's dirty black figure; the girls began to cry, and the boys began to laugh, and all pointed at him rudely

enough: but Tom was too tired
to care for that.

"What art thou, and what dost
want?" cried the old dame. "A
chimney-sweep! Away with thee.
I'll have no sweeps here."

"Water," said poor little Tom,
quite faint.

"Water? There's plenty i' the beck," she said,
quite sharply.

"But I can't get there; I'm most clemmed with
hunger and drought." And Tom sank down
upon the doorstep, and laid his head against
the post.

And the old dame looked at him through
her spectacles one minute, and two, and three;
and then she said, "He's sick; and a bairn's a
bairn, sweep or none."

"Water," said Tom.

"God forgive me!" and she put by her
spectacles, and rose, and came to Tom.
"Water's bad for thee; I'll give thee milk." And
she toddled off into the next room, and brought
a cup of milk and a bit of bread.

Tom drank the milk off at one draught, and
then looked up, revived.

"Where didst come from?" said the dame.

"Over Fell, there," said Tom, and pointed up
into the sky.

"Over Harthover? and down Lewthwaite

Crag? Art sure thou art not lying?"

"Why should I?" said Tom, and leant his head against the post.

"And how got ye up there?"

"I came over from the Place," and Tom was so tired and desperate, he had no heart or time to think of a story, so he told all the truth in a few words.

"Bless thy little heart! And thou hast not been stealing, then?"

"No."

"Bless thy little heart! and I'll warrant not. Why, God's guided the bairn, because he was innocent! Away from the Place, and over Harthover Fell, and down Lewthwaite Crag! Who ever heard the like, if God hadn't led him? Why dost not eat thy bread?"

"I can't."

"It's good enough, for I made it myself."

"I can't," said Tom, and he laid his head on his knees, and then asked—

"Is it Sunday?"

"No, then; why should it be?"

"Because I hear the church bells ringing so."

"Bless thy pretty heart! The bairn's sick. Come wi' me, and I'll hap thee up somewhere. If thou wert a bit cleaner I'd put thee in my own bed, for the Lord's sake. But come along here."

But when Tom tried to get up, he was so tired and giddy that she had to help him and lead him.

She put him in an outhouse upon soft sweet hay and an old rug, and bade him sleep off his walk, and she would come to him when school was over in an hour's time.

And so she went in again, expecting Tom to fall fast asleep

at once.

But Tom did not fall asleep.

Instead of it, he turned and tossed and kicked about in the strangest way, and felt so hot all over that he longed to get into the river and cool himself; and then he fell half asleep, and dreamt that he heard the little white lady crying to him, "Oh, you're so dirty; go and be washed;" and then that he heard the Irishwoman saying, "Those that wish to be clean, clean they will be." And then he heard the church bells ring so

loud, close to him, too, that he was sure it must be Sunday, in spite of what the old dame had said; and he would go to church, and see what a church was like inside, for he had never been in one, poor little fellow, in all his life. But the people would never let him come in, all covered soot and dirt like that. He must go to the river and wash first. And he said out loud again and again, though being half asleep he did not know it, "I must be clean, I must be clean."

And all of a sudden he found himself, not in the outhouse

on the hay, but in the middle of a meadow, over the road, with the stream just before him, saying continually, "I must be clean, I must be clean." He had got there on his own legs, between sleep and awake, as children will often get out of bed, and go about the room, when they are not quite well. But he was not a bit surprised, and went on to the bank of the brook, and lay down on the grass, and looked into the clear, clear limestone water, with every pebble at the bottom bright and clean, while the little silver trout dashed about in fright at the sight of his black face; and he dipped his hand in and found it so cool, cool, cool; and he said, "I will be a fish; I will swim in the water; I must be clean, I must be clean."

So he pulled off all his clothes in such haste that he tore some of them, which was easy enough with such ragged old things. And he put his poor, hot, sore feet into the water, and then his legs, and the farther he went in, the more the church bells rang in his head.

"Ah," said Tom, "I must be quick and wash myself; the

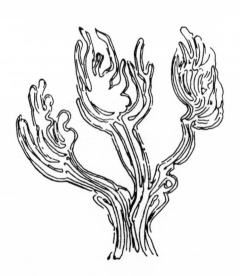

bells are ringing quite loud now; and they will stop soon, and then the door will be shut, and I shall never be able to get in at all."

Tom was mistaken, for in England the church doors are left open all service time for everybody who likes to come in, Churchman or Dissenter;

ay, even if he were a Turk or a Heathen; and if any man dared
to turn him out, as long as he be-haved quietly, the good old
English law would punish that man, as he deserved, for ordering
any peaceable person out of God's house, which belongs to
all alike. But Tom did not know that, any more than he knew
a great deal more which people ought to know.

And all the while he never saw the Irishwoman; not behind
him this time, but before.

For just before he came to the riverside she had stepped
down into the cool, clear water; and her shawl and her petticoat
floated off her, and the green waterweeds floated round her
sides, and the white water lilies floated round her head, and
the fairies of the stream came up from the bottom, and bore
her away and down upon their arms; for she was the Queen
of them all, and perhaps of more besides.

"Where have you been?" they asked her.

"I have been smoothing sick folk's pillows and whispering
sweet dreams into their ears; opening cottage casements to
let out the stifling air; coaxing little children away from gutters
and foul pools where fever breeds; turning women from the
gin-shop door, and staying men's hands as they were going to
strike their wives; doing all I can to help those that will not
help themselves: and little enough that is, and weary work for
me. But I have brought you a new little brother, and watched
him safe all the way here."

Then all the fairies laughed for joy at the thought that they
had a little brother coming.

"But mind, maidens, he must not see you, or know that you
are here. He is but a savage now, and like the beasts which
perish; and from the beasts which perish he must learn. So

you must not play with him, or speak to him, or let him see you; but only keep him from being harmed."

Then the fairies were sad, because they could not play with their new brother, but they always did what they were told.

And their Queen floated away down the river; and whither she went, thither she came. But all this Tom, of course, never saw or heard: and perhaps if he had, it would have made little difference in the story, for he was so hot and thirsty, and longed so to be clean for once, that he tumbled himself as quick as he could into the clear, cool stream.

And he had not been in it two minutes before he fell fast asleep, into the quietest, sunniest, cosiest sleep that ever he had in his life; and he dreamt about the green meadows by which he had walked that morning, and the tall elm-trees, and the sleeping cows; and after that he dreamt of nothing at all.

The reason of his falling into such a delightful sleep is very simple; and yet hardly anyone has found it out. It was merely that the fairies took him.

Some people think that there are no fairies. Cousin Cramchild tells little folks so in his Conversations. Well, perhaps there are none—in Boston, U.S., where he was raised. There are only a clumsy lot of spirits there, who can't make people hear without thumping on the table; but they get their living thereby, and I suppose that is all they want. And Aunt Agitate, in her Arguments on political economy, says there are none. Well, perhaps there are none—in her political economy. But it is a wide world, my little man—and thank heaven for it, for else, between crinolines and theories, some of us would get squashed—and plenty of room in it for fairies, without people seeing them; unless, of course, they look in the right place.

The most wonderful and the strongest things in the world, you know, are just the things which no one can see. There is life in you; and it is the life in you which makes you grow, and move, and think, and yet you can't see it. And there is steam in a steam engine; and that is what makes it move, and yet you can't see it; and so there may be fairies in the world, and they may be just what makes the world go round to the old tune of

C'est l'amour, l'amour, l'amour
Qui fait le monde à la ronde:

and yet no one may be able to see them except those whose hearts are going round to that same tune. At all events, we will make believe that there are fairies in the world. It will not be the last time by many a one that we shall have to make believe. And yet, after all, there is no need for that. There must be fairies—for this is a fairy tale; and how can one have a fairy tale if there are no fairies?

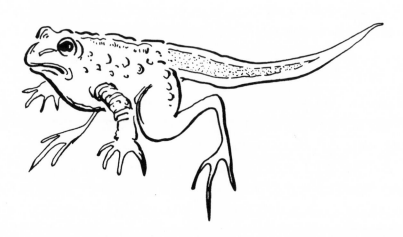

You don't see the logic of that? Perhaps not. Then please not to see the logic of a great many arguments exactly like it, which you will hear before your beard is grey.

The kind old dame came back at twelve, when school was over, to look at Tom; but there was no Tom there. She looked about for his footprints; but the ground was so hard that there was no slot, as they say in dear old North Devon. And if you grow up to be a brave, healthy man, you may know some day what no slot means, and know, too, I hope, what a slot does mean—a broad slot, with blunt claws, which makes a man put out his cigar, and set his teeth, and tighten his girths, when he sees it; and what his rights mean, if he has them, brow, bay, tray, and points; and see something worth seeing between Haddon Wood and Countisbury Cliff, with good Mr. Palk Coliyns to show you the way, and mend your bones as fast as you smash them. Only when that jolly day comes, please don't break your neck; stogged in a mire you never will be, I trust; for you are a heath-cropper bred and born.

So the old dame went in again quite sulky, thinking that little Tom had tricked her with a false story, and shammed ill and then run away again.

But she altered her mind the next day. For, when Sir John and the rest of them had run themselves out of breath, and lost Tom, they went back again, looking very foolish.

And they looked more foolish still when Sir John heard more

of the story from the nurse; and more foolish still, again, when they heard the whole story from Miss Ellie, the little lady in white. All she had seen was a poor little black chimney-sweep, crying and sobbing, and going to get up the chimney again. Of course, she was very much frightened; and no wonder. But that was all. The boy had taken nothing in the room; by the mark of his little sooty feet they could see that he had never been off the hearth rug till the nurse caught hold of him. It was all a mistake.

So Sir John told Grimes to go home, and promised him five shillings if he would bring the boy quietly up to him, without beating him, that he might be sure of the truth. For he took for granted, and Grimes too, that Tom had made his way home.

But no Tom came back to Mr. Grimes that evening; and he went to the police office to tell them to look out for the boy. But no Tom was heard of. As for his having gone over those great fells to Vendale, they no more dreamed of that than of his having gone to the moon.

So Mr. Grimes came up to Harthover next day with a very sour face; but when he got there, Sir John was over the hills and far away, and Mr. Grimes had to sit in the outer servants' hall all day and drink strong ale to wash away his sorrows; and they were washed away long before Sir John came back.

For good Sir John had slept very badly that night; and he

said to his lady, "My dear, the boy must have got over into the grouse moors and lost himself; and he lies very heavily on my conscience, poor little lad. But I know what I will do."

So at five the next morning up he got, and into his bath, and into his shooting jacket and gaiters, and into the stableyard, like a fine old English gentleman, with a face as red as a rose, and a hand as hard as a table, and a back as broad as a bullock's, and bade them bring his shooting pony, and the keeper to come on his pony, and the huntsman, and the first whip, and the second whip, and the under keeper with the bloodhound in a leash—a great dog as tall as a calf, of the colour of a gravel walk, with mahogany ears and nose, and a throat like a church bell. They took him up to the place where Tom had gone into the wood, and there the hound lifted up his mighty voice and told them all he knew.

Then he took them to the place where Tom had climbed the wall; and they shoved it down, and all got through.

And then the wise dog took them over the moor, and over the fells, step by step, very slowly; for the scent was a day old, you know, and very light from the heat and drought. But that was why cunning old Sir John started at five in the morning.

And at last he came to the top of Lewthwaite Crag, and there he bayed, and looked up in their faces, as much as to say, "I tell you he is gone down here!"

They could hardly believe that Tom would have gone so far; and when they looked at that awful cliff, they could never believe that he would have dared to face it. But if the dog said so, it must be true.

"Heaven forgive us!" said Sir John. "If we find him at all, we shall find him lying at the bottom." And he slapped his great

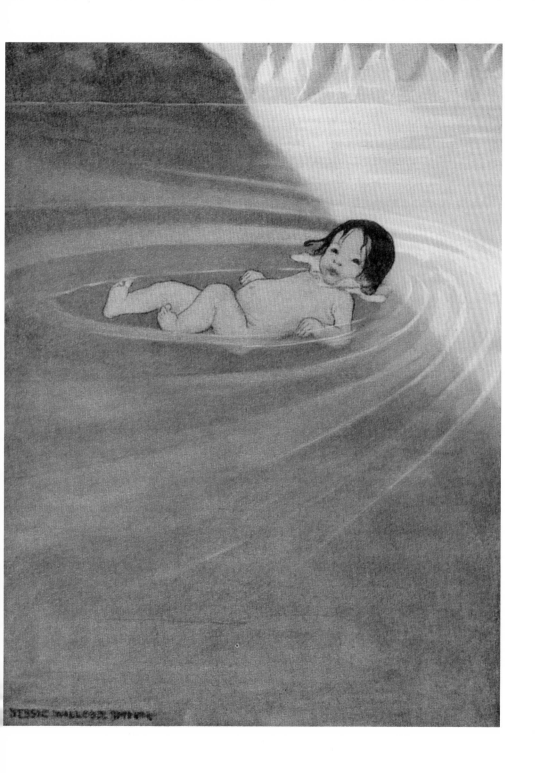

He felt how comfortable it was to have nothing
on him but himself.

hand upon his great thigh, and said:

"Who will go down over Lewthwaite Crag, and see if that boy is alive? Oh, that I were twenty years younger, and I would go down myself!" And so he would have done, as well as any sweep in the county. Then he said:

"Twenty pounds to the man who brings me that boy alive!" and as was his way, what he said he meant.

Now among the lot was a little groom-boy, a very little groom indeed; and he was the same who had ridden up the court, and told Tom to come to the Hall; and he said:

"Twenty pounds or none, I will go down over Lewthwaite Crag, if it's only for the poor boy's sake. For he was as civil a spoken little chap as ever climbed a flue."

So down over Lewthwaite Crag he went: a very smart groom

he was at the top, and a very shabby one at the bottom; for he tore his gaiters, and he tore his breeches, and he tore his jacket, and he burst his braces, and he burst his boots, and he lost his hat, and what was worst of all, he lost his shirt pin, which he prized very much, for it was gold, and he had won it in a raffle at Malton, and there was a figure at the top of it of t'ould mare, noble old Beeswing herself, as natural as life; so it was a really severe loss; but he never saw anything of Tom.

And all the while Sir John and the rest were riding round, full three miles to the right, and back again, to get into Vendale, and to the foot of the crag.

When they came to the old dame's school, all the children came out to see. And the old dame came out too; and when she saw Sir John she curtsied very low, for she was a tenant of his.

"Well, dame, and how are you?" said Sir John.

"Blessings on you as broad as your back, Harthover," says she—she didn't call him Sir John, but only Harthover for that is the fashion in the North country—"and welcome into Vendale; but you're no hunting the fox this time of year?"

"I am hunting, and strange game too," said he.

"Blessings on your heart, and what makes you look so sad the morn?"

"I'm looking for a lost child, a chimney-sweep, that is run away."

"Oh, Harthover, Harthover," says she, "ye were always a just man and a merciful; and ye'll no harm he poor little lad if I give you tidings of him?"

"Not I, not I, dame. I'm afraid we hunted him out of the

house all on a miserable mistake, and the hound has brought him to the top of Lewthwaite Crag, and—"

Whereat the old dame broke out crying, without letting him finish the story.

"So he told me the truth after all, poor little dear! Ah, first thoughts are best, and a body's heart'll guide them right, if they will but hearken to it." And then she told Sir John all.

"Bring the dog here, and lay him on," said Sir John, without another word, and he set his teeth very hard.

And the dog opened at once, and went away at the back of the cottage, over the road, and over the meadow, and through a bit of alder copse; and there, upon an alder stump, they saw Tom's clothes lying. And then they knew as much about it all as there was any need to know.

And Tom?

Ah, now comes the most wonderful part of this wonderful story. Tom, when he woke, for of course he woke—children always wake after they have slept exactly as long as is good for them—found himself swimming about in the stream, being about four inches, or—that I may be accurate—3.87902 inches long, and having round the parotid region of his fauces a set of external gills (I hope you understand all the big words), just like those of a sucking eft, which he mistook for a lace frill, till he pulled at them, found he hurt himself, and made up his mind that they were part of himself, and best left alone.

In fact, the fairies had turned him into a water-baby.

A water-baby? You never heard of a water-baby. Perhaps not. That is the very reason why this story was written. There are a great many things in the world which you never heard of, and a great many more which nobody ever heard of, and a great many things, too, which nobody will ever hear of, at least until the coming of the Cocqcigrues, when man shall be the measure of all things.

"But there are no such things as water-babies."

How do you know that? Have you been there to see? And if you had been there to see, and had seen none, that would not prove that there were none. If Mr. Garth does not find a fox in Eversley Wood—as folks sometimes fear he never will—that does not prove that there are no such things as foxes. And as is Eversley Wood to all the woods in England, so are the waters we know to all the waters in the world. And no one has a right to say that no water-babies exist, till they have seen no water-babies existing; which is quite a different thing, mind, from not seeing water-babies, and a thing which nobody ever did, or perhaps ever will do.

"But surely if there were water-babies, somebody would have caught one at least?"

Well. How do you know that somebody has not?

"But they would have put it into spirits, or into the *Illustrated News*, or perhaps cut it into two halves, poor dear little thing, and sent one to Professor Owen, and one to Professor Huxley, to see what they would each say about it."

Ah, my dear little man! that does not follow at all, as you will see before the end of the story.

"But a water-baby is contrary to nature."

Well, but, my dear little man, you must learn to talk about such things, when you grow older, in a very different way from that. You must not talk about "ain't" and "can't" when you speak of this great, wonderful world round you, of which the wisest man knows only the very smallest corner, and is, as the great Sir Isaac Newton said, only a child picking up pebbles on the shore of a boundless ocean.

You must not say that this cannot be, or that that is contrary to nature. You do not know what nature is, or what she can do; and nobody knows, not even Sir Roderick Murchison, or Professor Owen, or Professor Sedgwick, or Professor Huxley, or Mr. Darwin, or Professor Faraday, or Mr. Grove, or any other of the great men whom good boys are taught to respect. They are very wise men, and you must listen respectfully to all they say; but even if they should say, which I am sure they never would, "That cannot exist. That is contrary to nature," you must wait a little, and see; for perhaps even they may be wrong. It is only children who read Aunt Agitate's Arguments, or Cousin Cramchild's Conversations; or lads who go to popular lectures, and see a man pointing at a few big, ugly pictures on the wall, or making nasty smells with bottles and squirts, for an hour or two, and calling that anatomy or chemistry—who talk about "cannot exist," and "contrary to nature." Wise men are afraid to say that there is anything contrary to nature, except what is contrary to mathematical truth; for two and two cannot make five, and two straight lines cannot join twice and a part cannot be as great as the whole, and so on (at least, so it seems at present); but the wiser very rash, dangerous word, that "cannot;" and if people use it too often, the Queen of all the Fairies, who makes the clouds thunder and the fleas bite, and takes just as much trouble about one as about the other, is apt to astonish them suddenly by showing them, that though they say she cannot, yet she can, and what is more, will, whether they approve or not.

And therefore it is that there are dozens and hundreds of things in the world which we should certainly have said were contrary to nature, if we did not see them going on under our eyes all day long. If people had never seen little seeds grow into great plants and trees, of quite different shape from themselves, and these trees again produce fresh seeds, to grow into fresh trees, they would have said, "The thing cannot be; it is contrary to nature." And they would have been quite as right in saying so as in saying that most other things cannot be.

Or suppose again that you had come, like M. Du Chaillu, a traveller from unknown parts, and that no human being had ever seen or heard of an elephant. And suppose that you described him to people, and said, "This is the shape, and plan, and anatomy of the beast, and of his feet, and of his trunk, and of his grinders, and of his tusks, though they are not tusks at all, but two fore teeth run mad; and this is the section of his skull, more like a mushroom than a reasonable skull of a reasonable or unreasonable beast; and so forth, and so forth; and though the beast (which I assure you I have seen and shot) is first cousin to the little hairy coney of Scripture, second cousin to pig, and (I suspect) thirteenth or fourteenth cousin to a rabbit, yet he is the wisest of all beasts, and can do everything save read, write, and cast accounts." People would surely have said, "Nonsense your elephant is contrary to nature," and have thought you were telling stories—as the French thought of Le Vaillant when he came back to Paris and said that he had shot a giraffe; and as the king of the Cannibal Islands thought of the English sailor when he said that in his country water turned to marble, and rain fell as feathers. They would tell you, the more they knew of science, "Your elephant is an impossible monster, contrary to the laws of comparative anatomy, as far as yet known." To which you would answer the less, the more you thought.

Did not learned men, too, hold, till within the last twenty-five years, that a flying dragon was an impossible monster?

And do we not now know that there are hundreds of them found fossil up and down the world? People call them Pterodactyles; but that is only because they are ashamed to call them flying dragons, after denying so long that flying dragons could exist. And has not a German only lately discovered, what is most monstrous of all, that some of the flying dragons, lizards though they are, had feathers? And if that last is not contrary to what people mean by nature nowadays, one hardly knows what is the truth is, that folk's fancy that such and such things cannot be, simply because

they have not seen them is worth no more than a savage's fancy that there cannot be such a thing as a locomotive, because he never saw one running wild in the forest. Wise men know that their business is to examine what is, and not to settle what is not. They know that there are elephants; they know that there have been flying dragons; and the wiser they are, the less inclined they will be to say positively that there are no water-babies.

No water-babies, indeed? Why, wise men of old said that everything on earth had its double in the water; and you may see that that is, if not quite true, still quite as true as most other theories which you are likely to hear for many a day. There are land-babies—then why not water-babies? Are there not water-rats, water-flies, water-crickets, water-crabs, water-tortoises, water-scorpions, water-tigers and water-hogs, water-cats and water-dogs, sea-lions and sea-bears, sea-horses and sea-elephants, sea-mice and sea-urchins, sea-razors and sea-pens, sea-combs and sea-fans; and of plants, are there not water-grass, and water-crowfoot, water-milfoil, and so on, without end?

"But all these things are only nicknames; the water things are not really akin to the land things."

That's not always true. They are, in millions of cases, not only of the same family, but actually the same individual creatures. Do not even you know that a green drake, and an alder-fly, and a dragon-fly, live under water till they change their skins, just as Tom changed his? And if a water animal can continually change into a land animal, why should not a land animal sometimes change into a water animal? Don't be put down by any of Cousin Cramchild's arguments, but stand up to him like a man, and answer him (quite respectfully, of course) thus:—

If Cousin Cramchild says, that if there are water-babies, they must grow into water-men, ask him how he knows that they do not? and then, how he knows that they must, any more than the Proteus of the Adelsberg caverns grows into a perfect newt?

If he says that it is too strange a transformation for a land-baby to turn into a water-baby, ask him if he ever heard of the transformation of Syllis, or the Distomas, or the common jellyfish, of which M. Quatrefages says excellently well—"Who would noy exclaim that a miracle had come to pass, if he saw a reptile come out of the egg dropped by the hen in his poultry yard, and the reptile give birth at once to an indefinite number of fishes and birds? Yet the history of the jelly-fish is quite as wonderful as that would be." Ask him if he knows about all this; and if he does not, tell him to go and look for himself; and advise him (very respectfully, of course) to settle no more what strange things cannot happen, till he has seen what strange things do happen every day.

If he says that things cannot degrade, that is, change downwards into lower forms, ask him, who told him that water-babies were lower than land-babies? But even if they were, does he know about the strange degradation of the common goose-barnacles which one finds sticking on ships' bottoms, or the still stranger degradation of some cousins of theirs, of which one hardly likes to talk, so shocking and ugly it is?

And, lastly, if he says (as he most certainly will) that these transformations only take place in the lower animals, and not in the higher, say that that seems to little boys, and to some grown people, a very strange fancy. For if the changes of the lower animals are so wonderful, and so difficult to discover, why should not there be changes in the higher animals far more wonderful and far more difficult to discover? And may not man, the crown and flower of all things, undergo some change as much more wonderful than all the rest, as the Great Exhibition is more wonderful than a rabbit burrow? Let him answer that. And if he says (as he will) that not having seen such a change in his experience, he is not bound to believe it, ask him respectfully where his microscope has been? Does not each of us, in coming into this world, go through a transformation and does not reason and analogy, as well as Scripture, tell us that that transformation is not the last? and that though what we shall be we know not, yet we are here but as the crawling caterpillar, and shall be hereafter as the perfect fly. The old Greeks, heathens as they were, saw as much as that two thousand years ago, and I care very little for Cousin Cramchild, if he sees even less than they. And so forth, and so forth, till he is quite cross. And then tell him that if there are no water-babies, at least there ought to be; and that, at least, he cannot answer.

And meanwhile, my dear little man, till you know a great deal more about nature than Professor Owen and Professor Huxley put together, don't tell me about what cannot be, or fancy that anything is too wonderful to be true. "We are fearfully and wonderfully made," said old David; and so we are, and so is everything around us, down to the very deal table. Yes; much more fearfully and wonderfully made, already, is the table as it stands now, nothing but a piece of dead deal wood, than if, as foxes say and geese believe, spirits could make it dance, or talk to you by rapping on it.

Am I in earnest? Oh dear no. Don't you know that this is a fairy tale, and all fun and pretence; and that you are not to believe one word of it, even if it is true?

But at all events, so it happened to Tom. And, therefore, the keeper, and the groom, and Sir John, made a great mistake, and were very unhappy (Sir John, at least), without any reason, when they found a black thing in the water, and said it was Tom's body, and that he had been drowned. They were utterly mistaken. Tom was quite alive, and cleaner, and merrier, than he ever had been. The fairies had washed him, you see, in the swift river, so thoroughly, that not only his dirt, but his whole husk and shell, had been washed quite off him, and the pretty little real Tom was washed out of the inside of it, and swam away, as a caddis does when its case of stones and silk is bored through, and away it goes on its back, paddling to the shore, there to split its skin, and fly away as a caperer, on four fawn-coloured wings, with long legs and horns. They are foolish fellows, the caperers, and fly into the candle at night, if you leave the door open. We will hope Tom will be wiser, now he has got safe out of his sooty old shell.

But good Sir John did not understand all this, not being a fellow of the Linnoean Society; and he took it into his head that Tom was drowned. When they looked into the empty pockets of his shell, and found no jewels there, nor money—nothing but three marbles, and a brass button with a string to it—then Sir John did something as like crying as ever he did in his life, and blamed himself more bitterly than he need have done. So he cried, and the groom-boy cried, and the huntsman cried, and the dame cried, and the little girl cried, and the dairymaid cried, and the old nurse cried (for it was somewhat her fault), and my lady cried, for though people have wigs, there is no reason why they should not have hearts; but the keeper did not cry, though he had been so good-natured to Tom the morning before, for he was so dried up with running after poachers, that you could no more get tears out of him than milk out of leather, and Grimes did not cry, for Sir John gave him ten pounds, and he drank it all in a week. Sir John sent, far and wide, to find Tom's father and mother; but he might have looked till Doomsday for them, for one was dead, and the other was in Botany Bay. And the little girl would not play with her dolls for a whole week, and never forgot poor little Tom. And soon my lady put a pretty little tombstone over Tom's shell in the little churchyard in Vendale, where the old dalesmen all sleep side by side between the limestone crags. And the dame decked it with garlands every Sunday, till she grew so old that she could not stir abroad; then the little children decked it for her. And always she sung an old, old song, as she sat spinning what she called her wedding-dress. The children could not understand it, but they liked it none the less for that; for it was very sweet, and very sad; and that was enough for them. And these are the words of it:

> When all the world is young, lad,
> And all the trees are green;
> And every goose a swan, lad,
> And every lass a queen;
> Then hey for boot and horse, lad,
> And round the world away:
> Young blood must have its course, lad,
> And every dog his day.

> When all the world is old, lad,
> And all the trees are brown;
> And all the sport is stale, lad,
> And all the wheels run down;
> Creep home and take your place there,
> The spent and maimed among:
> God grant you find one face there,
> You loved when all was young.

Those are the words: but they are only the body of it: the soul of the song was the dear old woman's sweet face, and sweet voice, and the sweet old air to which she sang; and that, alas! one cannot put paper. And at last she grew so stiff and lame, that the angels were forced to carry her; and they helped her on with her wedding dress, and carried her up over Harthover Fells, and a long way beyond that too; and there was a new schoolmistress in Vendale, and we will hope that she was not certificated.

And all the while Tom was swimming about in the river, with a pretty little lace collar of gills about his neck, as lively as a grig, and as clean as a fresh-run salmon.

Now if you don't like my story, then go to the schoolroom and learn your multiplication-table, and see if you like that better. Some people, no doubt, would do so. So much the better for us, if not for them. It takes all sorts, they say, to make a world.

Chapter III

"He prayeth well who loveth well,
Both men and bird and beast;
He prayeth best who loveth best,
All things both great and small:
For the dear God who loveth us,
He made and loveth all. "

COLERIDGE.

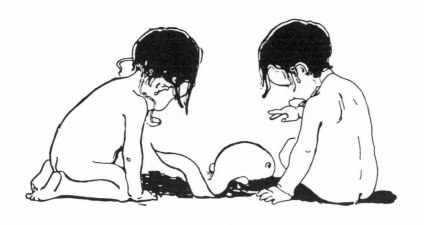

Chapter III

OM was now quite amphibious. You do not know what that means? You had better, then, ask the nearest Government pupil-teacher, who may possibly answer you smartly enough, thus: "Amphibious. Adjective, derived from two Greek words, *amphi*, a fish, and *bios*, a beast. An animal supposed by our ignorant ancestors to be compounded of a fish and a beast; which therefore, like the hippopotamus, can't live on the land, and dies in the water."

However that may be, Tom was amphibious; and what is better still, he was clean. For the first time in his life, he felt how comfortable it was to have nothing on him but himself. But he only enjoyed it: he did not know it, or think about it; just as you enjoy life and health, and yet never think about being alive and healthy; and may it be long before you have to think about it!

He did not remember having ever been dirty. Indeed, he did not remember any of his old troubles, being tired, or hungry, or beaten, or sent up dark chimneys. Since that sweet sleep, he had forgotten all about his master, and Harthover Place, and the little white girl, and, in a word, all that had happened to him when he lived before; and what was best of all, he had forgotten all the bad words which he had learnt from Grimes, and the rude boys with whom he used to play.

That is not strange; for you know, when you came into this world, and became a land-baby, you remembered nothing. So why should he, when he became a water-baby?

Then have you lived before?

My dear child, who can tell? One can only tell that by remembering something which happened where we lived before; and as we remember nothing, we know nothing about it; and no book, and no man, can ever tell us certainly.

There was a wise man once, a very wise man, and a very good man, who wrote a poem about the feelings which some children have about having lived before; and this is what he said—

> "Our birth is but a sleep and a forgetting;
> The soul that rises with us, our life's star,
> Hath elsewhere had its setting
> And cometh from afar:
> Not in entire forgetfulness,
> And not in utter nakedness,
> But trailing clouds of glory, do we come
> From God, who is our home."

There, you can know no more than that. But if I was you, I would believe that. For then the great fairy Science, who is likely to be queen of all the fairies for many a year to come, can only do you good, and never do you harm; and instead of fancying, with some people, that your body makes your soul, as if a steam engine could make its own coke; or, with some other people, that your soul has nothing to do with your body, but is only stuck into it like a pin into a pin cushion, to fall out with the first shake;—you will believe the one true,

orthodox,   *inductive,*
rational,   *deductive,*
philosophical,   *seductive,*
logical,   *productive,*
irrefragable,   *salutary,*
nominalistic,   *comfortable,*
realistic,
and on-all-accounts-to-be-received

doctrine of this wonderful fairy tale; which is, that your soul makes your body, just as a snail makes his shell. For the rest, it is enough for us to be sure that whether or not we lived before, we shall live again; though not, I hope, as poor little heathen Tom did. For he went downward into the water; but we, I hope, shall go upward to a very different place.

But Tom was very happy in the water. He had been sadly overworked in the land-world; and so now, to make up for that, he had nothing but holidays in the water-world for a long, long time to come. He had nothing to do now but enjoy himself, and look at all the pretty things which are to be seen in the cool, clear water-world, where the sun is never too hot, and the frost is never too cold.

And what did he live on? Water-cresses, perhaps; or perhaps water-gruel, and water-milk: too many land-babies do so likewise. But we do not know what one-tenth of the water things eat; so we are not answerable for the water-babies.

Sometimes he went along the smooth gravel waterways, looking at the crickets which ran in and out among the stones, as rabbits do on land; or he climbed over the ledges of rock, and saw the sand-pipes hanging in thousands, with every one of them a pretty little head and legs peeping out; or he went into a still corner, and watched the caddises eating dead sticks as greedily as you would eat plum-pudding, and building their houses with silk and glue. Very fanciful ladies they were; none of them would keep to the same materials for a day. One would begin with some pebbles; then she would stick on a piece of green weed; then she found a shell, and stuck it on too; and the poor shell was alive, and did not like at all being taken to build houses with: but the caddis did not let him have any voice in the matter, being rude and selfish, as vain people are apt to be; then she stuck on a piece of rotten wood, then a very smart pink stone, and so on, till she was patched all over like an Irishman's coat. Then she found a long straw, five times as long as herself, and said, "Hurrah! my sister has a tail, and I'll have one too;" and she stuck it on her back, and marched about with it quite proud, though it was very inconvenient indeed. And, at that, tails became all the fashion among the caddis-baits in that pool, as they were at the end of the Long Pool last May, and they all toddled about with long straws sticking out behind, getting between each other's legs, and tumbling over each other, and looking so ridiculous, that Tom laughed at them till he cried, as we did. But they were quite right, you know; for people must always follow the fashion, even if it be spoon bonnets.

Then sometimes he came to a deep still reach; and there he saw the water-forests. They would have looked to you only little weeds; but Tom, you must remember, was so little that everything looked a hundred times as big to him as it does to you, just as things do to a minnow, who sees and catches the little water-creatures which you can only see in a microscope.

And in the water-forest he saw the water-monkeys and water-squirrels (they had all six legs, though; everything almost has six legs in the water, except efts and water-babies), and nimbly enough they ran among the branches. There were water-flowers there, too, in thousands; and Tom tried to pick them; but as soon as he touched them, they drew themselves in and turned into knots of jelly: and then Tom saw that they were all alive— bells, and stars, and wheels, and flowers, of all beautiful shapes and colours; and all alive and busy, just as Tom was. So now he found that there was a great deal more in the world than he had fancied at first sight.

There was one won- derful little fellow, too, who peeped out of the top of a house built of round bricks. He had two big wheels, and one little one, all over teeth, spinning round and round like the wheels in a thrashing-machine; and Tom stood and stared at him, to see what he was going to make with his machinery. And what do you think he was doing? Brick-making. With his two big wheels he swept together all the mud which floated in the water: all that was nice in it he put into his stomach and ate, and all the mud he put into the little wheel on his breast, which really was a round hole set with teeth;

and there he spun it into a neat, hard, round brick; and then he took it and stuck it on the top of his house wall, and set to work to make another. Now was he not a clever little fellow?

Tom thought so; but when he wanted to talk to him, the brick-maker was much too busy and proud of his work to take notice of him.

Now you must know that all the things under the water talk, only not such a language as ours, but such as horses, and dogs, and cows, and birds talk to each other; and Tom soon learned to understand them and talk to them; so that he might have had very pleasant company if he had only been a good boy. But I am sorry to say he was too like some other little boys, very fond of hunting and tormenting creatures for mere sport. Some people say that boys cannot help it, that it is nature, and only a proof that we are all originally descended from beasts of prey. But whether it is nature or not, little boys can help it, and must help it. For if they have naughty, low, mischievous tricks in their nature, as monkeys have, that is no reason why they should give way to those tricks like monkeys, who know no better. And therefore they must not torment dumb creatures; for if they do, a certain old lady who is coming will surely give them exactly what they deserve.

But Tom did not know that; and he pecked and howked the poor water things about sadly, till they were all afraid of him, and got out of his way, or crept into their shells; so he had no one to speak to or play with.

The water-fairies, of course, were very sorry to see him so unhappy, and longed to take him, and tell him how naughty he was, and teach him to be good, and to play and romp with him too; but they had been forbidden to do that. Tom had to learn his lesson for himself by sound and sharp experience, as many another foolish person has to do, though there may be many a kind heart yearning over them all the while, and longing to teach them what they can only teach themselves.

At last one day he found a caddis, and wanted it to peep out of its house; but its house door was shut. He had never seen a caddis with a house door before; so what must he do, the meddlesome little fellow, but pull it open to see what the poor lady was doing inside. What a shame! How should you like to have anyone breaking your bedroom door in to see how you looked when you were in bed? So Tom broke to pieces the door, which was the prettiest little grating of silk, stuck all over with shining bits of crystal; and when he looked in the caddis poked out her head, and it had turned into just the shape of a bird's. But when Tom spoke to her she could not answer; for her mouth and face were tight tied up in a new nightcap of neat pink skin. However, if she didn't answer, all the other caddises did; for they held up their hands and shrieked like the cats in Struwwelpeter: "Oh, you nasty, horrid boy; there you are at it again! And she had just laid herself up for a fortnight's sleep, and then she would have come out with such beautiful wings and flown about, and laid such lots of eggs: and now you have broken her door, and she can't mend it because her mouth is tied up for a fortnight, and she will die. Who sent you here to worry us out of our lives?"

So Tom swam away. He was very much ashamed of himself, and felt all the naughtier; as little boys do when they have done wrong, and won't say so.

Then he came to a pool full of little trout, and began tormenting them, and trying to catch them; but they slipped through his fingers, and jumped clean out of water in their fright. But as Tom chased them, he came close to a great dark hover under an alder root, and out flushed a huge old brown trout ten times as big as he was, and ran right against him, and knocked all the breath out of his body; and I don't know which was the more frightened of the two.

Then he went on sulky and lonely, as he deserved to be; and under a bank he saw a very ugly dirty creature sitting, about half as big as himself, which had six legs, and a big stomach, and a most ridiculous head with two great eyes and a face just like a donkey's.

"Oh," said Tom, "you are an ugly fellow, to be sure!" and he began making faces at him; and put his nose close to him, and halloed at him, like a very rude boy.

When, hey presto! all the thing's donkey-face came off in a moment, and out popped a long arm with a pair of pincers at the end of it, and caught Tom by the nose. It did not hurt him much; but it held him quite tight.

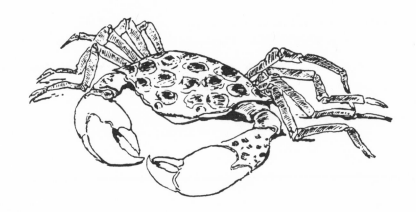

"Yah, ah! Oh, let me go!" cried Tom.

"Then let me go," said the creature. "I want to be quiet. I want to split."

Tom promised to let him alone, and he let go. "Why do you want to split?" said Tom.

"Because my brothers and sisters have all split, and turned into beautiful creatures with wings; and I want to split too. Don't speak to me. I am sure I shall split. I will split!"

Tom stood still and watched him. And he swelled himself,

and puffed, and stretched himself out stiff, and at last—crack, puff, bang—he opened all down his back, and then up to the top of his head.

And out of his inside came the most slender, elegant, soft creature, as soft and as smooth as Tom; but very pale and weak, like a little child who has been ill a long time in a dark room. It moved its legs very feebly; and looked about it half ashamed, like a girl when she goes for the first time into a ballroom; and then it began walking slowly up a grass stem to the top of the water.

Tom was so astonished that he never said a word but he stared with all his eyes. And he went up to the top of the water too, and peeped out to see what would happen.

And as the creature sat in the warm bright sun, wonderful change came over it. It grew strong and firm; the most lovely colours began to show on its body, blue and yellow and black, spots and bars and rings; out of its back rose four great wings bright brown gauze; and its eyes grew so large that they filled all its head, and shone like ten thousand diamonds.

"Oh, you beautiful creature!" said Tom; and he put out his hand to catch it.

But the thing whirred up into the air, and hung poised on its wings a moment, and then settled down again by Tom quite fearless.

"No!" it said, "you cannot catch me. I am dragon-fly now, the king of all the flies; and I shall dance in the sunshine, and hawk over the river, and catch gnats, and have a beautiful wife like myself. I know what I shall do. Hurrah!" And he flew away into the air, and began catching gnats.

"Oh! come back, come back," cried Tom, "you beautiful

creature. I have no one to play with and am so lonely here. If you will but come back I will never try to catch you."

"I don't care whether you do or not," said the dragon-fly;

"for you can't. But when I have had my dinner, and looked a little about this pretty place, I will come back; and have a little chat about all I have seen in my travels. Why, what a huge tree this is! and what huge leaves on it!"

It was only a big dock: but you know the dragon-fly had never seen any but little water-trees; starwort, and milfoil, and water-crowfoot, and such like; so it did look very big to him. Besides, he was very short-sighted, as all dragon-flies are; and never could see a yard before his nose, any more than a great many other folks, who are not half as handsome as he.

The dragon-fly did come back, and chatted away with Tom. He was a little conceited about his fine colours and his large wings; but you know, he had been a poor dirty creature all his life before; so there were great excuses for him. He was very fond of talking about all the wonderful things he saw in the trees and the meadows; and Tom liked to listen to him, for he had forgotten all about them. So in a little while they became great friends.

And I am very glad to say, that Tom learnt such a lesson that day, that he did not torment creatures for a long time after. And then the caddises grew quite tame, and used to tell him strange stories about the way they built their houses, and changed their skins, and turned at last into winged flies; till Tom began to long to change his skin, and have wings like them some day.

And the trout and he made it up (for trout very soon forget, if they have been frightened and hurt). So Tom used to play with them at hare and hounds, and great fun they had; and he used to try to leap out of the water, head over heels, as they did before a shower came on; but somehow he never could manage it. He liked most, though, to see them rising at the flies as they sailed round and round under the shadow of the great oak, where the beetles fell flop into the water, and the green caterpillars let themselves down from the boughs by silk ropes for no reason at all; and then changed their foolish minds for no reason at all either; and hauled themselves up again into the tree, rolling up the rope in a ball between their paws; which is a very clever rope-dancer's trick, and neither Blondin nor Leotard could do it: but why they should take so much trouble about it no one can tell; for they cannot get their living, as Blondin and Leotard do, by trying to break their necks on a string.

And very often Tom caught them just as they touched the water; and caught the alder-flies, and the caperers, and the

cock-tailed duns and spinners, yellow, and brown, and claret, and grey, and gave them to his friends the trout. Perhaps he was not quite kind to the flies; but one must do a good turn to one's friends when one can.

And at last he gave up catching even the flies; for he made acquaintance with one by accident, and found him a very merry little fellow. And this was the way it happened; and it is all quite true.

He was basking at the top of the water one hot day in July, catching duns and feeding the trout, when he saw a new sort, a dark grey little fellow with a brown head. He was a very little fellow indeed, but he made the most of himself, as people ought to do. He cocked up his head, and he cocked up his wings, and he cocked up his tail, and he cocked up the two whisks at his tail-end, and, in short, he looked the cockiest little man of all little men. And so he proved to be; for instead of getting away, he hopped upon Tom's finger, and sat there as bold as nine tailors; and he cried out in the tiniest, shrillest, squeakiest little voice you ever heard.

"Much obliged to you, indeed; but I don't want it yet."

"Want what?" said Tom, quite taken aback by his impudence.

"Your leg, which you are kind enough to hold out for me to sit on. I must just go and see after my wife for a few minutes. Dear me! what a troublesome business a family is!" (though the idle little rogue did nothing at all, but left his poor wife to lay all the eggs by herself). "When I come back, I shall be glad of it, if you'll be so good as to keep it sticking out just so;" and off he flew.

Tom thought him a very cool sort of personage; and still more so, when in five minutes he came back, and said—"Ah, you were tired waiting? Well, your other leg will do as well."

And he popped himself down on Tom's knee, and began chatting away in his squeaking voice.

"So you live under the water? It's a low place. I lived there for some time; and was very shabby and dirty. But I didn't choose that that should last. So I turned respectable, and came

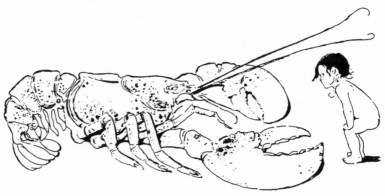

up to the top, and put on this grey suit. It's a very business-like suit, you think, don't you?"

"Very neat and quiet indeed," said Tom.

"Yes, one must be quiet, and neat, and respectable, and all that sort of thing for a little, when one becomes a family man. But I'm tired of it, that's the truth. I've done quite enough business, I consider, in the last week, to last me my life. So I shall put on a ball dress, and go out and be a smart man, and see the gay world, and have a dance or two. Why shouldn't one be jolly if one can?"

"Oh! she is a very plain, stupid creature, and that's the truth; and thinks about nothing but eggs. If she chooses to come, why she may; and if not, why I go without her;—and here I go."

And, as he spoke, he turned quite pale, and then quite white.

"Why, you're ill!" said Tom. But he did not answer.

"You're dead," said Tom, looking at him as he stood on his knee as white as a ghost.

"No I ain't!" answered a little squeaking voice over his head. "This is me up here, in my ball dress; and that's my skin. Ha, ha! you could not do such a trick as that!"

And no more Tom could, nor Houdin, nor Robin, nor Frikell, nor all the conjurers in the world. For the little rogue had jumped clean out of his own skin, and left it standing on Tom's knee, eyes, wings, legs, tails exactly as if it had been alive.

"Ha, ha!" he said, and he jerked and skipped up and down, never stopping an instant, just as if he had St. Vitus's dance. "Ain't I a pretty fellow now?"

And so he was; for his body was white, and his tail orange, and his eyes all the colours of a peacock's tail. And what was the oddest of all, the whisks at the end of his tail had grown five times as long as they were before.

"Ah!" said he, "now I will see the gay world. My living won't cost me much, for I have no mouth, you see, and no inside; so I can never be hungry, nor have the stomach-ache neither."

No more he had. He had grown as dry and hard and empty as a quill, as such silly, shallow-hearted fellows deserve to grow. But, instead of being ashamed of his emptiness, he was quite proud of it, as a good many fine gentlemen are, and began flirting and flipping up and down, and singing:

"My wife shall dance, and I shall sing,
So merrily pass the day;
For I hold it one of the wisest things,
To drive dull care away. "

And he danced up and down for three days and three nights, till he grew so tired, that he tumbled into the water, and floated down. But what became of him Tom never knew, and he himself never minded; for Tom heard him singing to the last, as he floated down:

"To drive dull care away-ay-ay!"

And if he did not care, why nobody else cared either.

But one day Tom had a new adventure. He was sitting on a water-lily leaf, he and his friend the dragon-fly, watching the gnats dance. The dragon-fly had eaten as many as he wanted, and was sitting quite still and sleepy, for it was very hot and bright. The gnats (who did not care the least for their poor brothers' death) danced a foot over his head quite happily, and a large black fly settled within an inch of his nose, and began washing his own face and combing his hair with his paws; but the dragon-fly never stirred, and kept on chatting to Tom about the times when he lived under the water.

Suddenly, Tom heard the strangest noise up the stream; cooing, and grunting, and whining, and squeaking, as if you had put into a bag two stock-doves, nine mice, three guinea-pigs, and a blind puppy, and left them there to settle themselves and make music.

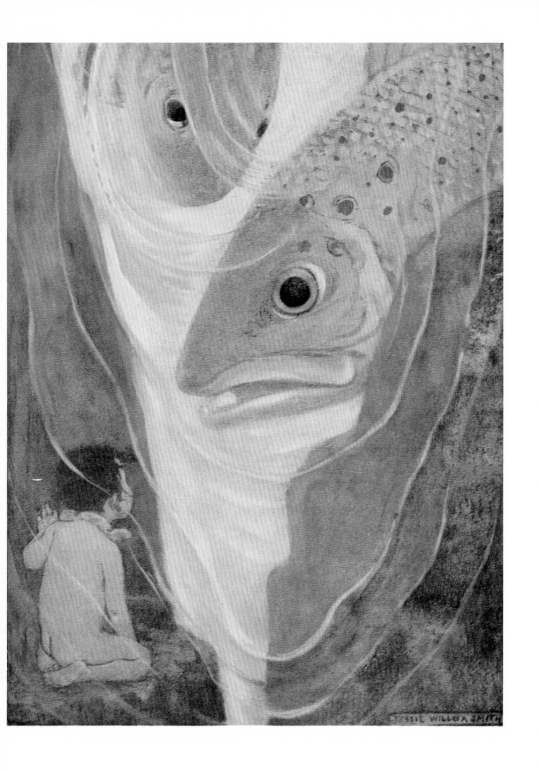

"Oh, don't hurt me!" cried Tom. "I only want
to look at you; you are so handsome."

He looked up the water, and there he saw a sight as strange as the noise; a great ball rolling over and over down the stream, seeming one moment of soft brown fur, and the next of shining glass: and yet it was not a ball; for sometimes it broke up and streamed away in pieces, and then it joined again; and all the while the noise came out of it louder and louder.

Tom asked the dragon-fly what it could be; but, of course, with his short sight, he could not even see it, though it was not ten yards away. So he took the neatest little header into the

water, and started off to see for himself; and, when he came near, the ball turned out to be four or five beautiful creatures, many times larger than Tom, who were swimming about, and rolling, and diving, and twisting, and wrestling, and cuddling, and kissing, and biting, and scratching, in the most charming fashion that ever was seen. And if you don't believe me, you may go to the Zoological Gardens (for I am afraid that you won't see it nearer, unless, perhaps, you get up at five in the morning, and go down to Cordery's Moor, and watch by the great withy pollard which hangs over the backwater, where

the otters breed sometimes), and then say, if otters at play in the water are not the merriest, lithest, gracefullest creatures you ever saw.

But, when the biggest of them saw Tom, she darted out from the rest, and cried in the water-language sharply enough, "Quick, children, here is something to eat, indeed!" and came at poor Tom, showing such a wicked pair of eyes, and such a set of sharp teeth in a grinning mouth, that Tom, who had thought her very handsome, said to himself, "Handsome is that handsome does," and slipped in between the water-lily roots as fast as he could, and then turned round and made faces at her.

"Come out," said the wicked old otter, "or it will be worse for you."

But Tom looked at her from between two thick roots, and shook them with all his might, making horrible faces all the while, just as he used to grin through the railings at the old woman, when he lived before. It was not quite well-bred, no doubt; but you know, Tom had not finished his education yet.

"Come away, children," said the Otter in disgust, "it is not worth eating, after all. It is only a nasty eft, which nothing eats, not even those vulgar pike in the pond."

"I am not an eft!" said Tom; "efts have tails."

"You are an eft," said the otter very positively; I see your two hands quite plain, and I know you have a tail."

"I tell you I have not," said Tom. "Look here!" and he turned his pretty little self quite round; and sure enough, he had no more tail than you.

The otter might have got out of it by saying that Tom was a frog; but, like a great many other people, when she had once said a thing, she stood to it, right or wrong; so she answered:

"I say you are an eft, and therefore you are, and not fit food for gentlefolk like me and my children. You may stay there till the salmon eat you" (she knew the salmon would not, but she wanted to frighten poor Tom). "Ha! ha! they will eat you, and we will eat them;" and the otter laughed such a wicked, cruel laugh—as you may hear them do sometimes: and the first time that you hear it you will probably think it is bogeys.

"What are salmon?" asked Tom.

"Fish, you eft, great fish, nice fish to eat. They are the lords of the fish, and we are the lords of the salmon;" and she laughed again. "We hunt them up and down the pools, and drive them up into a corner, the silly things; they are so proud, and bully the little trout, and the minnows, till they see us coming, and then they are so meek all at once: and we catch them, but we disdain to eat them all; we just bite out their soft throats and suck their sweet juice—Oh, so good!"—(and she licked her wicked lips)—"and

then throw them away, and go and catch another. They are coming soon, children, coming soon; I can smell the rain coming up off the sea, and then hurrah for a the salmon, and plenty of eating all day long."

And the otter grew so proud that she turned head over heels twice, and then stood upright half out of the water, grinning like a Cheshire cat.

"And where do they come from?" asked Tom, who kept himself very close, for he was considerably frightened.

"Out of the sea, eft, the great wide sea, where they might stay and be safe if they liked. But out of the sea the silly things come, into the great river down below, and we come up to watch for them; and when they go down again we go down and follow them. And there we fish for the bass and the pollock, and have jolly days along the shore, and toss and roll in the breakers, and sleep snug in the warm dry crags. Ah, that is a merry life too, children, if it were not for those horrid men."

"What are men?" asked Tom; but somehow he seemed to know before he asked.

"Two-legged things, eft; and, now I come to look at you, they are actually something like you, if you had not a tail," (she was determined that Tom should have a tail), "only a great deal bigger, worse luck for us; and they catch the fish with hooks and lines which get into out feet sometimes, and set pots along the rocks to catch lobsters. They speared my poor dear husband as he went out to find something for me to eat. I was laid up among the crags then, and we were very low in the world, for the sea was so rough that no fish would come in shore. But they speared him, poor fellow, and I saw them carrying him away upon a pole. Ah, he lost his life for your sakes, my children, poor dear obedient creature that he was."

And the otter grew so sentimental (for otters can be very sentimental when they choose, like a good many people who are both cruel and greedy, and no good to anybody at all), that she sailed solemnly away down the burn, and Tom saw her no more for that time. And lucky it was for her that she did so; for no sooner was she gone, than down the bank came seven little rough terrier dogs, snuffing and yapping, and grubbing and splashing, in full cry after the otter. Tom hid among the water-lilies till they were gone; for he could not guess that they were the water-fairies come to help him.

But he could not help thinking of what the otter had said about the great river and the broad sea. And, as he thought, he longed to go and see them. He could not tell why; but the more he thought, the more he grew discontented with the narrow little stream in which he lived, and all his companions there; and wanted to get out

into the wide wide world, and enjoy all the wonderful sights of which he was sure it was full.

And once he set off to go down the stream. But the stream was very low: and when he came to the shallows he could not keep under water, for there was no water left to keep under. So the sun burnt his back and made him sick; and he went back again and lay quiet in the pool for a whole week more.

And then, on the evening of a very hot day, he saw a sight.

He had been very stupid all day, and so had the trout; for they would not move an inch to take a fly, though there were thousands on the water, but lay dozing at the bottom under the shade of the stones; and Tom lay dozing too, and was glad to cuddle their smooth cool sides, for the water was quite warm and unpleasant.

But towards evening it grew suddenly dark, and Tom looked up and saw a blanket of black clouds lying right across the valley above his head, resting on the crags right and left. He felt not quite frightened, but very still; for everything was still.

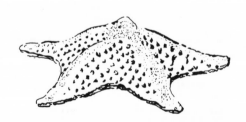

There was not a whisper of wind, nor a chirp of a bird to be heard; and next a few great drops of rain fell plop into the water, and one hit Tom on the nose and made him pop his head down quickly enough.

And then the thunder roared, and the lightning flashed, and leapt across Vendale and back again, from cloud to cloud, and cliff to cliff, till the very rocks in the stream seemed to shake; and Tom looked up at it through the water, and thought it the finest thing he ever saw in his life.

But out of the water he dared not put his head; for the rain came down by the bucketsful, and the hail hammered like shot on the stream, and churned it into foam; and soon the stream rose, and rushed down, higher and higher, and fouler and fouler, full of beetles, and sticks, and straws, and worms, and addle-eggs, and wood-lice, and leeches, and odds and ends, and omnium-gatherums, and this, that, and the other, enough to fill nine museums.

Tom could hardly stand against the stream, and hid behind a rock. But the trout did not; for out they rushed from among the stones, and began gobbling the beetles and leeches in the most greedy and quarrelsome way, and swimming about with great worms hanging out of their mouths, tugging and kicking to get them away from each other.

And now, by the flashes of the lightning, Tom saw a new sight—all the bottom of the stream alive with great eels, turning and twisting along, all down stream and away. They had been hiding for weeks past in the cracks of the rocks, and in burrows in the mud, and Tom had hardly ever seen them, except now and then at night: but now they were all out, and went hurrying past him so fiercely and wildly that he was quite frightened.

And as they hurried past he could hear them say to each other, "We must run, we must run. What a jolly thunderstorm! Down to the sea, down to the sea!"

And then the otter came by with all her brood, wining and sweeping along as fast as the eels themselves; and she spied Tom as she came by, and said:

"Now is your time, eft, if you want to see the world. Come along, children, never mind those nasty eels: we shall breakfast on salmon tomorrow. Down to the sea, down to the sea!"

Then came a flash brighter than all the rest, and by the light

of it—in the thousandth part of a second they were gone again—but he had seen them, he was certain of it—three beautiful little white girls, with their arms twined round each other's necks, floating down the torrent, as they sang, "Down to the sea, down to the sea!"

"Oh stay! Wait for me!" cried Tom; but they were gone: yet he could hear their voices clear and sweet through the roar of thunder and water and wind, singing as they died away, "Down to the sea!"

"Down to the sea;" said Tom; "everything is going to the

sea, and I will go too. Good-bye, trout." But the trout were so busy gobbling worms that they never turned to answer him; so that Tom was spared the pain of bidding them farewell.

And now, down the rushing stream, guided by the bright flashes of the storm; past tall birch-fringed rocks, which shone out one moment as clear as day, and the next were dark as night; past dark hovers under swirling banks, from which great trout rushed out on Tom, thinking him to be good to eat, and turned back sulkily, for the fairies sent them home again with a tremendous scolding, for daring to meddle with a water-baby; on through narrow strids and roaring cataracts, where Tom was deafened and blinded for a moment by the rushing waters; along deep reaches, where the white water-lilies tossed and flapped beneath the wind and hail; past sleeping villages; under dark bridge arches, and away and away to the sea. And Tom could not stop, and did not care to stop; he would see the great world below, and the salmon, and the breakers, and the wide, wide sea.

And when the daylight came, Tom found himself out in the salmon river.

And what sort of a river was it? Was it like an Irish stream, winding through the brown bogs, where the wild ducks squatter up from among the white water-lilies, and the curlews flit to and fro, crying, "Tullie-wheep, mind your sheep;" and Dennis tells you strange stories of the Peishtamore, the great bogey-snake which lies in the black peat pools, among the old pine stems, and puts his head out at night to snap at the cattle as they come down to drink?—But you must not believe all that Dennis tells you, mind; for if you ask him, "Is there a salmon here, do you think, Dennis?"

"Is it salmon, thin, your honour names? Salmon? Cartloads it is of thim, thin, an' ridgmens, shouldthering ache other out of water, av' ye'd but the luck to see thim."

Then you fish the pool all over, and never get a rise.

"But there can't be a salmon here, Dennis! and, if you'll but think, if one had come up last tide, he'd be gone to the higher pools by now."

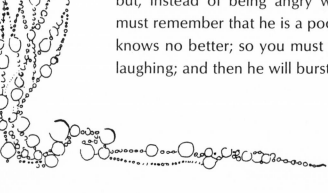

"Shure thin, and your honour's the thrue fisherman, and understands it all like a book. Why, ye spake as if ye'd known the wather a thousand years! As I said, how could there be a fish here at all, just now?"

"But you said just now they were shouldering each other out of water?"

And then Dennis will look up at you with his handsome, sly, soft, sleepy, good-natured, untrustable, Irish grey eye, and answer with the prettiest smile:

"Shure, and didn't I think your honour would like a pleasant answer?"

So you must not trust Dennis, because he is in the habit of giving pleasant answers: but, instead of being angry with him, you must remember that he is a poor Paddy, and knows no better; so you must just burst out laughing; and then he will burst out laughing too and slave for you, and trot about after you, and show you good sport if he can—for he is an affectionate fellow, and as fond of sport as you are—and if he can't, tell you fibs instead, a hundred an hour; and wonder all the while why poor ould Ireland does not prosper like England and Scotland, and some other places, where folk have taken up a ridiculous fancy that honesty is the best policy.

Or was it like a Welsh salmon river, which is remarkable chiefly (at least, till this last year) for containing no salmon, as they have been all poached out by the enlightened peasantry, to prevent the *Cythrawl Sassenach* (which means you, my little dear, your kith and kin, and signifies much the same as the Chinese *Fan Quei*) from coming bothering into Wales, with good tackle, and ready money, and civilization, and common honesty, and other like things of which the Cyrmry stand in no need whatsoever?

Or was it such a salmon stream as I trust you will see among the Hampshire water-meadows before your hairs are grey, under the wise new fishing laws?—when Winchester apprentices shall covenant, as they did three hundred years ago, not to be made to eat salmon more than three days a week; and fresh-run fish shall be as plentiful under Salisbury spire as they are in Hollyhole at Christchurch; in the good time coming, when folks shall see that, of all Heaven's gifts of food, the one to be protected most carefully is that worthy gentleman salmon, who is generous enough to go down to the sea weighing five ounces, and to come back next year weighing five pounds, without having cost the soil or the state one farthing?

Or was it like a Scotch stream, such as Arthur Clough drew in his *"Bothie"*:—

"Where over a ledge of granite
Into a granite basin the amber torrent descended. . .
Beautiful there for the colour derived from green rocks under;
Beautiful most of all, where beads of foam uprising
Mingle their clouds of white with the delicate hue of the stillness. . .
Cliff over cliff for its sides, with rowan and pendant birch boughs.". . .

Ah, my little man, when you are a big man, and fish such a stream as that, you will hardly care, I think whether she be roaring down in full spate, like coffee covered with scald cream, while the fish are swirling at your fly as an oar-blade swirls in a boat-race, or flashing up the cataract like silver arrows, out of the fiercest of the foam; or whether the fall be dwindled to a single thread, and the shingle below be as white and dusty as a turnpike road, while the salmon huddle together in one dark cloud in the clear amber pool, sleeping away their time till the rain creeps back again off the sea. You will not care much, if you have eyes and brains; for you will lay down your rod contentedly, and drink in at your eyes the beauty of that glorious place; and listen to the water-ouzel piping on the stones, and watch the yellow roes come down to drink, and look up at you with their great, soft, trustful eyes, as much as to say, "You could not have the heart to shoot at us?" And then, if you have sense, you will turn and talk to the great giant of a gilly who lies basking on the stone beside you. He will tell you no fibs, my little man; for he is a Scotchman, and fears God, and not the priest; and, as you talk with him, you will be surprised more and more at his knowledge, his sense, his humour, his courtesy; and you will find out—unless you have found it out before—that a man may learn from his Bible to be a more thorough gentleman than if he had been brought up in all the drawing-rooms in London.

No. It was none of these, the salmon stream at Harthover. It was such a stream as you see in dear old Bewick; Bewick, who was born and bred upon them. A full hundred yards broad it was, sliding on from broad pool to broad shallow, and broad shallow to broad pool, over great fields of shingle, under oak

and ash coverts, past low cliffs of sandstone, past green meadows, and fair parks, and a great house of grey stone, and brown moors above, and here and there against the sky the smoking chimney of a colliery. You must look at Bewick to see just what it was like, for he has drawn it a hundred times with the care and the love of a true north countryman; and, even if you do not care about the salmon river, you ought, like all good boys, to know your Bewick.

At least, so old Sir John used to say, and very sensibly he put it too, as he was wont to do:

"If they want to describe a finished young gentleman in France, I hear, they say of him, '*Il sait son Rabelais.*' But if I want to describe one in England, I say, 'He knows his Bewick.' And I think that is the higher compliment."

But Tom thought nothing about what the river was like. All his fancy was, to get down to the wide, wide sea.

And after a while he came to a place where the river spread out into broad, still, shallow reaches, so wide that little Tom, as he put his head out of the water, could hardly see across.

And there he stopped. He got a little frightened. "This must be the sea," he thought. "What a wide place it is. If I go on into it I shall surely lose my way, or some strange thing will bite me. I will stop here and look out for the otter, or the eels, or some one to tell me where I shall go."

So he went back a little way, and crept into a crack of the rock, just where the river opened out into the wide shallows, and watched for someone to tell him his way; but the otter and the eels were gone on miles and miles down the stream.

There he waited, and slept too, for he was quite tired with his night's journey; and, when he woke, the stream was clearing to a beautiful amber hue, though it was still very high. And after a while he saw a sight which made him jump up; for he knew in a moment it was one of the things which he had come to look for.

Such a fish! ten times as big as the biggest trout, and a hundred times as big as Tom, sculling up the stream past him, as easily as Tom had sculled down.

Such a fish! shining silver from head to tail, and here and there a crimson dot; with a grand hooked nose, and grand curling lip, and a grand bright eye, looking round him as proudly as a king, and surveying the water right and left as if it all belonged to him. Surely he must be the salmon, the king of all the fish.

Tom was so frightened that he longed to creep into a hole; but he need not have been; for salmon are all true gentlemen, and, like true gentlemen, they look noble and proud enough, and yet, like true gentlemen, they never harm or quarrel with anyone, but go about their own business, and leave rude fellows to themselves.

The salmon looked him full in the face, and then went on without minding him, with a swish or two of his tail which made the stream boil again. And in a few minutes came another, and then four or five, and so on; and all passed Tom, rushing and plunging up the cataract with strong strokes of their silver tails, now and then leaping clean out of water and up over a rock, shining gloriously for a moment in the bright sun; while Tom was so delighted that he could have watched them all day long.

And at last one came up bigger than all the rest; but he came slowly, and stopped, and looked back, and seemed very anxious and busy. And Tom saw that he was helping another salmon, an especially handsome one, who had not a single spot upon it, but was clothed in pure silver from nose to tail.

"My dear," said the great fish to his companion, "you really look dreadfully tired, and you must not over-exert yourself at first. Do rest yourself behind this rock;" and he shoved her gently with his nose to the rock where Tom sat.

You must know that this was the salmon's wife. For salmon, like other true gentlemen, always choose their lady, and love her, and are true to her, and take care of her, and work for her, and fight for her, as every true gentleman ought; and are not like vulgar chub and roach and pike, who have no high feelings, and take no care of their wives.

Then he saw Tom, and looked at him very fiercely one moment, as if he was going to bite him.

Tom sat upon the buoy long days, long weeks,
looking out to sea.

"What do you want here?" he said very fiercely.

"Oh, don't hurt me!" cried Tom. "I only want to look at you; you are so handsome."

"Ah," said the salmon, very stately but very civilly, "I really beg your pardon; I see what you are, my little dear. I have met one or two creatures like you before, and found them very agreeable and well-behaved. Indeed, one of them showed me a great kindness lately, which I hope to be able to repay. I hope we shall not be in your way here. As soon as this lady is rested, we shall proceed on our journey."

What a well-bred old salmon he was!

"So you have seen things like me before?" asked Tom.

"Several times, my dear. Indeed, it was only last night that one at the river's mouth came and warned me and my wife of some new stake-nets which had got into the stream, I cannot tell how, since last winter, and showed us the way round them in the most charmingly obliging way."

"So there are babies in the sea?" cried Tom, and clapped his little hands. "Then I shall have someone to play with there? How delightful!"

"Were there no babies up this stream?" asked the lady salmon.

"No; and I grew so lonely. I thought I saw three last night; but they were gone in an instant, down to the sea. So I went too; for I had nothing to play with but caddises and dragon-flies and trout."

"Ugh!" cried the lady, "what low company!"

"My dear, if he has been in low company, he has certainly not learnt their low manners," said the salmon.

"No, indeed, poor little dear; but how sad for him to live among such people as caddises, who have actually six legs, the nasty things; and dragon-flies, too! why, they are not even good to eat; for I tried them once, and they are all hard and empty; and, as for trout, everyone knows what they are." Whereupon she curled up her lip, and looked dreadfully scornful, while her husband curled up his too, till he looked as proud as Alcibiades.

"Why do you dislike the trout so?" asked Tom.

"My dear, we do not even mention them, if we can help it; for I am sorry to say they are relations of ours who do us no credit. A great many years ago they were just like us; but they were so lazy, and cowardly, and greedy, that instead of going down to the sea every year to see the world and grow strong and fat, they chose to stay and poke about in the little streams and eat worms and grubs: and they are very properly punished for it; for they have grown ugly and brown and spotted and small; and are actually so degraded in their tastes, that they will eat our children."

"And then they pretend to scrape acquaintance with us again," said the lady. "Why, I have actually known one of them propose to a lady salmon, the little impudent little creature."

"I should hope," said the gentleman, "that there are very few ladies of our race who would degrade themselves by listening to such a creature for an instant. If I saw such a thing happen, I should consider it my duty to put them both to death upon the spot." So the old salmon said, like an old blue-blooded hidalgo of Spain; and what is more, he would have done it too. For you must know, no enemies are so bitter against each other as those who are of the same race; and a salmon looks on a trout, as some folks look on some little folks, as something just too much like himself to be tolerated.

Chapter IV

"Sweet is the lore which Nature brings;
Our meddling intellect
Mis-shapes the beauteous forms of things
We murder to dissect.

Enough of science and of art:
Close up these barren leaves;
Come forth, and bring with you a heart
That watches and receives."

WORDSWORTH.

Chapter IV

o the salmon went up, after Tom had warned them of the wicked old otter; and Tom went down, but slowly and cautiously, coasting along the shore. He was many days about it, for it was many miles down to the sea: and perhaps he would never have found his way, if the fairies had not guided him, without his seeing their fair faces, or feeling their gentle hands.

And, as he went, he had a very strange adventure.

It was a clear, still September night, and the moon shone so brightly down through the water, that he could not sleep, though he shut his eyes as tight as possible. So at last he came up to the top, and sat upon a little point of rock, and looked up at the broad, yellow moon, and wondered what she was, and thought that she looked at him. And he watched the moonlight on the rippling river, and the black heads of the firs, and the silver-frosted lawns, and listened to the owl's hoot, and the snipe's bleat, and the fox's bark, and the otter's laugh; and smelt the soft perfume of the birches, and the wafts of heather honey off the grouse moor far above; and felt very happy, though he could not well tell why. You, of course, would have been very cold sitting there on a September night, without the least bit of clothes on your wet back; but Tom was a water-baby, and therefore felt cold no more than a fish.

Suddenly, he saw a beautiful sight. A bright red light moved along the riverside, and threw down into the water a long tap-root of flame. Tom, curious little rogue that he was, had to go and see what it was; so he swam to the shore, and met the light as it stopped over a shallow run at the edge of a low rock.

And there, underneath the light, lay five or six great salmon, looking up at the flame with their great goggle eyes, and wagging their tails, as if they were very much pleased at it.

Tom came to the top, to look at this wonderful light nearer, and made a splash.

And he heard a voice say:

"There was a fish rose."

He did not know what the words meant; but he seemed to know the sound of them, and to know the voice which spoke them; and he saw on the bank three great two-legged creatures, one of whom held the light, flaring and sputtering, and another a long pole. And he knew that they were men, and was frightened, and crept into a hole in the rock, from which he could see what went on.

The man with the torch bent down over the water, and looked earnestly in; and then he said:

"Tak that muckle fellow, lad; he's ower fifteen punds; and haud your hand steady."

Tom felt that there was some danger coming, and longed to warn the foolish salmon, who kept staring up at the light as if

he was bewitched. But, before he could make up his mind, down came the pole through the water; there was a fearful splash and struggle, and Tom saw that the poor salmon was speared right through, and was lifted out of the water.

And then, from behind, there sprung on these three men three other men; and there were shouts, and blows, and words which Tom recollected to have heard before; and he shuddered and turned sick at them now, for he felt somehow that they were strange, and ugly, and wrong, and horrible. And it all began to come back to him. They were men; and they were fighting; savage, desperate, up-and-down fighting, such as Tom had seen too many times before.

And he stopped his little ears, and longed to swim away; and was very glad that he was a water-baby, and had nothing to do any more with horrid dirty men, with foul clothes on their backs, and foul words on their lips; but he dared not stir out of his hole; while the rock shook over his head with the trampling and struggling of the keepers and the poachers.

All of a sudden there was a tremendous splash, and a frightful flash, and a hissing, and all was still.

For into the water, close to Tom, fell one of the men; he who held the light in his hand. Into the swift river he sank, and rolled over and over in the current. Tom heard the men above run along, seemingly looking for him; but he drifted down into the deep hole below, and there lay quite still, and they could not find him.

Tom waited a long time, till all was quiet; and then he peeped out, and saw the man lying. At last he screwed up his courage, and swam down to him. "Perhaps," he thought, "the water has made him fall asleep, as it did me."

Then he went nearer. He grew more and more curious, he could not tell why. He must go and look at him. He would go very quietly, of course; so he swam round and round him, closer and closer; and, as he did

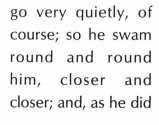

not stir, at last he came quite close and looked him in the face.

The moon shone so bright that Tom could see every feature; and, as he saw, he recollected bit by bit. It was his old master, Grimes.

Tom turned tail, and swam away as fast as he could.

"Oh dear me!" he thought, "now he will turn into a water-baby. What a nasty, troublesome one he will be! And perhaps he will find me out, and beat me again."

So he went up the river again a little way, and lay here the rest of the night under an alder root; but, when morning came, he longed to go down again to the big pool, and see whether Mr. Grimes had turned into a water-baby yet.

So he went very carefully, peeping round all the rocks, and hiding under all the roots. Mr. Grimes lay there still; he had not turned into a water-baby. In the afternoon Tom went back again. He could not rest till he had found out what had become of Mr. Grimes. But this time Mr. Grimes was gone; and Tom made up his mind that he was turned into a water-baby.

He might have made himself easy, poor little man; Mr. Grimes did not turn into a water-baby, or anything like one at all. But he did not make himself easy; and a long time he was fearful lest he should meet Grimes suddenly in some deep pool. He could not know that the fairies had carried him away, and put him, where they put everything which falls into the water, exactly where it ought to be. But, do you know, what had happened to Mr. Grimes had such an effect on him, that he never poached salmon any more. And it is quite certain that, when a man becomes a confirmed poacher, the only way to cure him is to put him under water for twenty-four hours, like Grimes. So, when you grow to be a big man, do you behave as all honest fellows should; and never touch a fish or a head of game which belongs to another man without his express leave; and then people will call you a gentleman, and treat you like one; and perhaps give you good sport; instead of hitting you into the river, or calling you a poaching snob.

Then Tom went on down, for he was afraid of staying near Grimes; and as he went, all the vale looked sad. The red and yellow leaves showered down into the river; the flies and beetles were all dead and gone; the chill autumn fog lay low upon the hills, and sometimes spread itself so thickly on the river, that he could not see his way. But he felt his way instead, following the flow of the stream, day after day, past great bridges, past boats and barges, past the great town, with its wharfs, and mills, and tall smoking chimneys, and ships which rode at anchor in the stream; and now and then he ran against their hawsers, and wondered what they were, and peeped out, and saw the sailors lounging on board, smoking their pipes; and ducked under again, for he was terribly afraid of being caught by man and turned into a chimney-sweep once more. He did not know that the fairies were close to him always, shutting the sailors' eyes lest they should see him, and turning him aside from millraces, and sewer-mouths, and all foul and dangerous things. Poor little fellow, it was a dreary journey for him; and more than once he longed to be back in Vendale, playing with the trout in the bright summer sun. But it could not be. What has been once can never come over again. And people can be little babies, even water-babies, only once in their lives.

Besides, people who make up their minds to go and see the world, as Tom did, have to find it a weary journey. Lucky for them if they do not lose heart and stop halfway, instead of going on bravely to the end as Tom did. For then they will remain neither boys nor men, neither fish, flesh, nor good red herring; having learnt a great deal too much, and yet not enough; and own their wild oats, without having the advantage of reaping them.

But Tom was always a brave, determined little English bull dog, who never knew when he was beaten; and on and on he held, till he saw a long way off the red buoy through the fog. And then he found, to his surprise, the stream turned round, and running up inland.

It was the tide, of course; but Tom knew nothing of the tide. He only knew that in a minute more the water, which had been fresh, turned salt all round him. And then there came a change over him. He felt as strong, and light, and fresh, as if his veins had run champagne; and gave, he did not know why, three skips out of the water, a yard high, and head over heels, just as the salmon do when they first touch the noble, rich, salt water, which, as some wise men tell us, is the mother of all living things.

He did not care now for the tide being against him. The red buoy was in sight, dancing in the open sea; and to the buoy he would go, and to it he went. He passed great shoals of bass and mullet, leaping and rushing in after the shrimps,

but he never heeded them, or they him; and once he passed
a great black shining seal, who was coming in after the mullet.
The seal put his head and shoulders out
of water, and stared at him, looking
exactly like a fat old greasy negro with
a grey pate. And Tom, instead of being
frightened, said, "How d'ye do, sir; what
a beautiful place the sea is!" And the
old seal, instead of trying to bite him,
looked at him with his soft, sleepy, winking eyes,
and said, "Good tide to you, my little man; are
you looking for your brothers and sisters? I passed
them all at play outside."

"Oh, then," said Tom, "I shall have playfellows
at last!" and he swam on to the buoy, and got
upon it (for he was quite out of breath) and sat
there, and looked round for water-babies; but
there were none to be seen.

The sea breeze came in freshly with the tide,
and blew the fog away; and the little waves
danced for joy around the buoy, and the old buoy
danced with them. The shadows of the clouds
ran races over the bright blue bay, and yet never
caught each other up; and the breakers plunged
merrily upon the wide white sands, and jumped
up over the rocks, to see what the green fields
inside were like, and tumbled down and broke
themselves all to pieces, and never minded it a
bit, but mended themselves and jumped up again.
And the terns hovered over Tom like huge white

dragon-flies with black heads, and the gulls laughed like girls at play, and the sea-pies, with their red bills and legs, flew to and fro from shore to shore, and whistled sweet and wild. And Tom looked and looked, and listened; and he would have been very happy, if he could only have seen the water-babies. Then, when the tide turned, he left the buoy, and swam round and round in search of them, but in vain. Sometimes he thought he heard them laughing; but it was only the laughter of the ripples. And sometimes he thought he saw them at the bottom; but it

was only white and pink shells. And once he was sure he had found one, for he saw two bright eyes peeping out of the sand. So he dived down, and began scraping the sand away, and cried, "Don't hide; I do want someone to play with so much!" And out jumped a great turbot, with his ugly eyes and mouth all awry, and flopped away along the bottom, knocking poor Tom over. And he sat down at the bottom of the sea, and cried salt tears from sheer disappointment.

To have come all this way, and faced so many dangers, and

yet to find no water-babies! How hard! Well, it did seem hard: but people, even little babies, cannot have all they want without waiting for it, and working for it too, my little man, as you will find out some day.

And Tom sat upon the buoy long days, long weeks, looking out to sea, and wondering when the water-babies would come back; and yet they never came.

Then he began to ask all the strange things which came in out of the sea if they had seen any; and some said, "Yes," and some said nothing at all.

He asked the bass and the pollock; but they were greedy after the shrimps that they did not care to answer him a word.

Then there came in a whole fleet of purple sea-snails, floating along each on a sponge full of foam, and Tom said, "Where do you come from, you pretty creatures? and have you seen the water-babies?"

And the sea-snails answered, "Whence we come we know not; and whither we are going, who can tell? We float out our little life in the mid-ocean, with the warm sunshine above our heads, and the warm gulf stream below; and that is enough for us. Yes, perhaps we have seen the water-babies. We have seen many strange things as we sailed along." And they floated away, the happy, stupid things, and all went ashore upon the sands.

Then there came in a great lazy sunfish, as big as a fat pig cut in half; and he seemed to have been cut in half too, and squeezed in a clothes-press till he was flat; but to all his big body and big fins he had only a little rabbit's mouth, no bigger than Tom's; and, when Tom questioned him, he answered in a little squeaky, feeble voice:

"I'm sure I don't know, I've lost my way. I meant to go to

He felt the net very heavy; and lifted it out quickly,
with Tom all entangled in the meshes.

the Chesapeake, and I'm afraid I've got wrong, somehow. Dear me! it was all by following that pleasant warm water. I'm sure I've lost my way."

And, when Tom asked him again, he could only answer, "I've lost my way. Don't talk to me, I want to think."

But, like a good many other people, the more he tried to think the less he could think; and Tom saw him blundering about all day, till the coast-guardsmen saw his big fin above the water, and rowed out, and struck a boat-hook into him, and took him away. They took him up to the town and showed him for a penny a head, and made a good day's work of it. But of course Tom did not know that.

Then there came by a shoal of porpoises, rolling as they went—papas, and mammas, and little children—and all quite smooth and shiny, because the fairies French-polish them every morning; and they sighed so softly as they came by, that Tom took courage to speak to them; but all they answered was, "Hush, hush, hush," for that was all they had learnt to say.

And then there came a shoal of basking sharks, some of them as long as a boat, and Tom was frightened by them. But they were very lazy, good-natured fellows, not greedy tyrants, like white sharks and blue sharks and ground sharks and hammer-heads, who eat men, or saw-fish and threshers and ice-sharks, who hunt the poor old whales. They came and

rubbed their great sides against the buoy, and lay basking in the sun with their backfins out of water; and winked at Tom; but he never could get them to speak. They had eaten so many herrings that they were quite stupid; and Tom was glad when a collier brig came by, and frightened them all away; for they did smell most horribly, certainly, and he had to hold his nose tight as long as they were there.

And then there came by a beautiful creature, like a ribbon of pure silver with a sharp head and very long teeth; but it seemed very sick and sad. Sometimes it rolled helpless on its side; and then it dashed away glittering like white fire; and then it lay sick again and motionless.

"Where do you come from?" asked Tom. "And why are you so sick and sad?"

"I come from the warm Carolinas, and the sandbanks fringed with pines; where the great owl-rays leap and flap, like giant bats, upon the tide. But I wandered north and north, upon the treacherous warm gulf stream, till I met with the cold icebergs afloat in the mid-ocean. So I got tangled among the icebergs, and chilled with their frozen breath. But the water-babies helped me from among them, and set me free again. And now I am mending every day; but I am very sick and sad; and perhaps I shall never get home again to play with the owl-rays any more."

"Oh!" cried Tom. "And you have seen water-babies? Have you seen any near here?"

"Yes, they helped me again last night, or I should have been eaten by a great black porpoise."

How vexatious! The water-babies close to him, and yet he could not find one.

And then he left the buoy, and used to go along the sands and round the rocks, and come out in the night—like the forsaken Merman in Mr. Arnold's beautiful, beautiful poem, which you must learn by heart some day—and sit upon a point of rock, among the shining seaweeds, in the low October tides, and cry and call for the water-babies; but he never heard a voice call in return. And, at last, with his fretting and crying, he grew quite lean and thin.

But one day among the rocks he found a playfellow. It was not a water-baby, alas! but it was a lobster; and a very distinguished lobster he was; for he had live barnacles on his claws, which is a great mark of distinction in lobsterdom, and no more to be bought for money than a good conscience or the Victoria Cross.

Tom had never seen a lobster before; and he was mightily taken with this one; for he thought him the most curious, odd ridiculous creature he had ever seen; and there he was not far wrong; for all the ingenious men, and all the scientific men, and all the fanciful men, in the world, with all the old German bogey-painters into the bargain, could never invent, if all their wits were boiled into one, anything so curious, and so ridiculous, as a lobster.

He had one claw knobbed and the other jagged; and Tom delighted in watching him hold on to the seaweed with his knobbed claw, while he cut up salads with his jagged one, and then put them into his mouth, after smelling at them, like a monkey. And always the little barnacles threw out their casting nets and swept the water, and came in for their share of whatever there was for dinner.

But Tom was most astonished to see how he fired himself off—snap! like the leap-frogs which you make out of a goose's breast bone. Certainly he took the most wonderful shots, and backwards, too. For, if he wanted to go into a narrow crack, ten yards off, what do you think he did? If he had gone in head foremost, of course, he could not have turned round. So he used to turn his tail to it, and lay his long horns, which carry his sixth sense in their tips (and nobody knows what that sixth sense is), straight down his back to guide him, and twist his eyes back till they almost came out of their sockets, and then make ready, present, fire, snap!—and away he went, pop into the hole; and peeped out and twiddled his whiskers, as much as to say, "You couldn't do that."

Tom asked him about water-babies. "Yes," he said. He had seen them often. But he did not think much of them. They were meddlesome little creatures, that went about helping fish and shells which got into scrapes. Well, for his part, he should be ashamed to be helped by little soft creatures that had not even a shell on their backs. He had lived quite long enough in the world to take care of himself.

He was a conceited fellow, the old lobster, and not very civil to Tom; and you will hear how he had to alter his mind before he was done, as conceited people generally have. But he was so funny, and Tom so lonely, that he could not quarrel with him; and then used to sit in holes in the rocks, and chat for hours.

And about this time there happened to Tom a very strange and important adventure—so important, indeed, that he was very near never finding the water-babies at all, and I am sure you would have been sorry for that.

I hope that you have not forgotten the little white lady all this while. At least, here she comes, looking like a clean, white, good little darling, as she always was, and always will be. For it occurred in the pleasant, short December days, when the wind always blows from the south-west, till Old Father Christmas comes and spreads the great white tablecloth, ready for little boys and girls to give the birds their Christmas dinner of

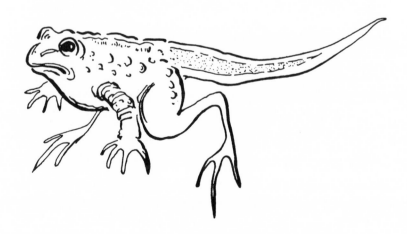

crumbs—it befel (to go on) in the pleasant December days that Sir John was so busy hunting that nobody at home could get a word out of him. Four days a week he hunted, and very good sport he had; and the other two he went to the bench and the board of guardians, and very good justice he did; and when he got home in time, he dined at five; for he hated this absurd new fashion of dining at eight in the hunting season,

which forces a man to make interest with the footman for cold beef and beer as soon as he comes in, and so spoil his appetite, and then sleep in an armchair in his bedroom, all stiff and tired, for two or three hours before he can get his dinner like a gentleman. And do you be like Sir John, my dear little man, when you are your own master; and, if you want either to read hard or ride hard, stick to the good old Cambridge hours of breakfast at eight and dinner at five, by which you may get two days' work out of one. But, of course, if you find a fox at three in the afternoon and run him till dark, and leave off twenty miles from home, why you must wait for your dinner till you can get it, as better men than you have done. Only see that, if you go hungry, your horse does not; but give him his warm gruel and beer, and take him gently home, remembering that good horses don't grow on the hedge like blackberries.

It befel (to go on a second time) that Sir John hunting all day and dining at five, fell asleep every evening and snored so terribly that all the windows in Harthover shook, and the soot fell down the chimneys. Whereon My Lady, being no more able to get conversation out of him than a song out of a dead nightingale, determined to go off and leave him, and the doctor, and Captain Swinger the agent, to snore in concert every evening to their hearts' content. So she started for the seaside with all the children, in order to put herself and them into condition by mild applications of iodine. She might as well have stayed at home and used Parry's liquid horse-blister, for there was plenty of it in the stables; and then she would have saved her money, and saved the chance, also, of making all the children ill instead of well (as hundreds are made), by taking them to some nasty smelling, undrained lodging, and then wondering how they caught scarlatina and diphtheria; but people won't be wise enough to understand that till they are all dead of bad smells, and then it will be too late; besides, you see, Sir John did certainly snore very loud.

But where she went to nobody must know, for fear young ladies should begin to fancy that there are water-babies there; and so hunt and howk after them (besides raising the price of lodgings), and keep them in aquariums, as the ladies of Pompeii (as you may see by the paintings) used to keep Cupids in cages. But nobody ever heard that they starved the Cupids, or let them die of dirt and neglect, as English young ladies do by the poor sea-beasts. So nobody must know where My Lady went. Letting water-babies die is as bad as taking singing-birds' eggs; for though there are thousands, ay, millions, of both of them in the world, yet there is not one too many.

Now, it happened that, on the very shore, and over the very rocks, where Tom was sitting with his friend the lobster, there walked one day the little white lady, Ellie herself, and with her a very wise man indeed—Professor Ptthmllnsprts.

His mother was a Dutchwoman, and therefore he was born at Curaçao (of course you have learnt your geography, and therefore know why); and his father a Pole, and therefore he was brought up at Petropaulowski (of course you have learnt your modern politics, and therefore know why): but for all that he was as thorough an Englishman as ever coveted his neighbour's goods. And his name, as I said, was Professor Ptthmllnsprts, which is a very ancient and noble Polish name.

He was, as I said, a very great naturalist, and chief professor of Necrobioneopalaeonthydrochthonanthropopithekology in the new university which the king of the Cannibal Islands had founded; and, being a member of the Acclimatization Society, he had come here to collect all the nasty things which he

could find on the coast of England, and turn them loose round the Cannibal Islands, because they had not nasty things enough there to eat what they left.

But he was a very worthy, kind, good-natured, little, old gentleman; and very fond of children (for he was not the least a cannibal himself); and very good to all the world as long as it was good to him. Only one fault he had, which cock-robins have likewise, as you may see if you look out of the nursery window—that, when anyone else found a curious worm, he would hop round them, and peck them, and set up his tail, and bristle up his feathers, just as a cock-robin would; and declare that he found the worm first; and that it was his worm; and, if not, that then it was not a worm at all. He had met Sir John at Scarborough, or Fleetwood, or somewhere or other (if you don't care where, nobody else does), and had made acquaintance with him, and become very fond of his children. Now, Sir John knew nothing about sea-cockyolybirds, and cared less, provided the fishmonger sent him good fish for dinner; and My Lady knew as little; but she thought it proper that the children should know something. For in the stupid old times, you must understand, children were taught to know one thing, and to know it well; but in these enlightened new times they are taught to know a little about everything, and to know it all ill; which is a great deal pleasanter and easier, and therefore quite right.

So Ellie and he were walking on the rocks, and he was showing her about one in ten thousand of all the beautiful and curious things which are to be seen there. But little Ellie was not satisfied with them at all. She liked much better to play with live children, or even with dolls, which she could pretend were alive; and at last she said honestly, "I don't care about all these things, because they can't play with me, or talk to me. If there were little children now in the water, as there used to be, and I could see them, I should like that."

"Children in the water, you strange little duck?" said the professor.

"Yes," said Ellie, "I know there used to be children in the water, and mermaids too, and mermen. I saw them all in a picture at home, of a beautiful lady sailing in a car drawn by

dolphins, and babies flying round her, and one sitting in her lap; and the mermaids swimming and playing, and the mermen trumpeting on conch-shells; and it is called The Triumph of Galatea; and there is a burning mountain in the picture behind. It hangs on the great staircase, and I have looked at it ever since I was a baby, and dreamt about it a hundred times; and it is so beautiful, that it must be true."

Ah, you dear little Ellie, fresh out of heaven! when will people understand that one of the deepest and wisest speeches which can come out of a human mouth is that—"It is so beautiful that it must be true."

Not till they give up believing that Mr. John Locke (good man and honest though he was) was the wisest man that ever lived on earth; and recollect that a wiser man than he lived long before him; and that his name was Plato, the son of Ariston.

But the professor was not in the least of that opinion. He held very strange theories about a good many things. He had even got up once at the British Association, and declared that apes had hippopotamus majors in their brains just as men have. Which was a shocking thing to say; for, if it were so, what would become of the faith, hope, and charity of immortal millions? You may think that there are other more important differences between you and an ape, such as being able to speak, and make machines, and know right from wrong, and say your prayers, and other little matters of that kind; but that is a child's fancy, my dear. Nothing is to be depended on but the great hippopotamus test. If you have a hippopotamus major in your brain, you are no ape, though you had four hands, no feet, and were more apish than the apes of all aperies. But, if a hippopotamus major is ever discovered in one single ape's brain, nothing will save your great-great-great-great-great-great-great-great-great-great-great-greater-greatest-grandmother from having been an ape too. No, my dear little man; always remember that the one true, certain, final, and all-important difference between you and an ape is, that you have a hippopotamus major in your brain, and it has none; and that, therefore, to discover one in its brain will be a very wrong and dangerous thing, at which everyone will be very much shocked, as we may suppose they were at the professor—Though really, after all, it don't much matter because—as Lord Dundreary and others would put it—nobody but men have hippopotamuses in their brains, so, if a hippopotamus was discovered in an ape's brain, why it would not be one, you know, but something else.

But the professor had gone, I am sorry to say, even further than that; for he had read at the British Association at Melbourne, Australia, in the year 1999 a paper, which assured every one who found himself the better or wiser for the news, that there were not, never had been, and could not be, any rational or half-rational beings except men anywhere, anywhen, or anyhow; that nymphs, satyrs, fauns, inui, dwarfs, trolls, elves, gnomes, fairies, brownies, nixes, wilis, kobolds, leprechauns, cluricaunes, banshees, will-o'-the-wisps, follets, lutins, magots, goblins, afrits, marids, jinns, ghouls, peris, deevs, angels, archangels, imps, bogies, or worse, were nothing at all, and pure bosh and wind. And he had to get up very early in the morning to prove that, and to eat his breakfast overnight; but he did it, at least to his own satisfaction. Whereon a certain great divine, and a very clever divine was he, called him a regular Sadducee; and probably he was quite right. Whereon the professor, in return, called him a regular Pharisee; and probably he was quite right too. But they did not quarrel in the least; for, when men are men of the world, hard words run off them like water off a duck's back. So the professor and the divine met at dinner that evening, and sat together on the sofa afterwards for an hour, and talked over the state of female labour on the antarctic continent (for nobody talks shop after his claret), and each vowed that the other was the best company he ever met in his life. What an advantage it is to be men of the world!

From all of which you may guess that the professor was not the least of little Ellie's opinion. So he gave her a succinct compendium of his famous paper at the British Association, in a form suited for the youthful mind. But as we have gone over his arguments against water-babies once already, which is once too often, we will not repeat them here.

Now, little Ellie was, I suppose, a stupid little girl; for instead of being convinced by Professor Ptthmllnsprts' arguments, she only asked the same question over again.

"But why are there not water-babies?"

I trust and hope that it was because the professor trod at that moment on the edge of a very sharp mussel, and hurt one of his corns sadly, that he answered quite sharply, forgetting that he was a scientific man, and therefore ought to have known that he couldn't know; and that he was a logician, and therefore ought to have known that he could not prove an universal negative—I say, I trust and hope it was because the mussel hurt his corn, that the professor answered quite sharply—

"Because there ain't."

Which was not even good English, my dear little boy; for, as you must know from Aunt Agitate's Arguments, the professor ought to have said, if he was so angry as to say anything of the kind— Because there are not; or are none; or are none of them; or (if he had been reading

Aunt Agitate too), because they do not exist.

And he groped with his net under the weeds so violently, that, as it happened, he caught poor little Tom.

He felt the net very heavy; and lifted it out quickly, with Tom all entangled in the meshes.

"Dear me!" he cried. "What a large pink Holothurian; with hands, too! It must be connected with Synapta."

And he took him out.

"It has actually eyes!" he cried. "Why, it must be a Cephalopod! This is most extraordinary!"

"No, I ain't!" cried Tom, as loud as he could; for he did not like to be called bad names.

"It is a water-baby!" cried Ellie; and of course it was.

"Water-fiddlesticks, my dear!" said the professor, and he turned away sharply.

There was no denying it. It was a water-baby; and he had said a moment ago that there were none. What was he to do?

He would have liked, of course, to have taken Tom home in a bucket. He would not have put him in spirits. Of course not. He would have kept him alive and petted him (for he was a very kind old gentleman), and written a book about him, and given him two long names, of which the first would have said a little about Tom, and the second all about himself; for of course he would have called him Hydrotecnon Ptthmllnsprtsianum, or some other long name like that; for they are forced to call everything by long names now, because they have used up all the short ones, ever since they took to making nine species out of one. But—what would all the learned men say to him after his speech at the British Association? And what would Ellie say, after what he had just told her?

There was a wise old heathen once, who said, "Maxima debetur pueris reverentia"—The greatest reverence is due to children; that is, that grown people should never say or do anything wrong before children, lest they should set them a bad example.—Cousin Cramchild says it means, "The greatest respectfulness is expected from little boys." But he was raised in a country where little boys are not expected to be respectful, because all of them are as good as the president:—Well, everyone knows his own concerns best; so perhaps they are. But poor cousin Cramchild, to do him justice, not being of that opinion, and having a moral mission, and being no scholar to speak of, and hard up for an authority—why, it was a very great temptation for him. But some people, and I am afraid the professor was one of them, interpret that in a more strange, curious, one-sided, left-handed, topsy-turvy, inside-out, behind-before fashion, than even Cousin Cramchild; for they make it mean, that you must show your respect for children, by never confessing yourself in the wrong to them, even if you know that you are so, lest they should lose confidence in their elders.

Now, if the professor had said to Ellie, "Yes, my darling, it is a water-baby, and a very wonderful thing it is; and it shows how little I know of the wonders of nature, in spite of forty years' honest labour. I was just telling you that there could be no such creatures: and, behold! here is one come to confound my conceit and show me that Nature can do, and has done, beyond all that man's poor fancy can imagine. So, let us thank the Maker, and Inspirer and Lord of Nature for all His wonderful and glorious works, and try and find out something about this one:"—I think that, if the professor had said that, little Ellie would have believed him more firmly, and respected him more deeply and loved him better, than ever she had done before. But he was of a very different opinion. He hesitated a moment. He longed to keep Tom, and yet he half wished he never had caught him; and, at last, he quite longed to get rid of him. So he turned away, and poked Tom with his finger, for want of anything better to do; and said carelessly, "My dear little maid, you must have dreamt of water-babies last night, your head is so full of them."

Now Tom had been in the most horrible and unspeakable fright all the while; and had kept as quiet as he could, though he was called a Holothurian and a Cephalopod; for it was fixed in his little head that if a man with clothes on caught him, he might put clothes on him too, and make a dirty black chimney-sweep of him again. But when the professor poked him, it was more than he could bear; and, between fright and rage, he turned to bay as valiantly as a mouse in a corner, and bit the professor's finger till it bled.

"Oh! ah! yah!" cried he; and, glad of an excuse to be rid of Tom, dropped him on to the seaweed, and thence he dived into the water, and was gone in a moment.

"But it was a water-baby, and I heard it speak!" cried Ellie. "Ah, it is gone!" And she jumped down off the rock to try and catch Tom before he slipped into the sea.

Too late! and what was worse, as she sprang down, she slipped, and fell some six feet, with her head on a sharp rock, and lay quite still.

The professor picked her up, and tried to waken her, and called to her, and cried over her, for he loved her very much; but she would not waken at all. So he took her up in his arms, and carried her to her governess, and they all went home; and

Tom reached and clawed down the hole after him . . .
the clumsy lobster pulled him in head-foremost.

little Ellie was put to bed, and lay there quite still, only now and then she woke up, and called out about the water-baby; but no one knew what she meant and the professor did not tell, for he was ashamed to tell.

And, after a week, one moonlight night, the fairies came flying in at the window, and brought her such a pretty pair of wings, that she could not help putting them on; and she flew with them out of the window, and over the land, and over the sea, and up through the clouds, and nobody heard or saw anything of her for a very long while.

And this is why they say that no one has ever yet seen a water-baby. For my part, I believe that the naturalists get dozens of them when they are out dredging; but they say nothing about them, and throw them overboard again, for fear of spoiling their theories. But, you see the professor was found out, as everyone is in due time. A very terrible old fairy found the professor out; she felt his bumps, and cast his nativity, and took the lunars of him carefully inside and out; and so she knew what he would do as well as if she had seen it in a print book, as they say in the dear old west country; and he did it; and so he was found out beforehand, as everybody always is; and the old fairy will find out the naturalists some day, and put them in *The Times*; and then on whose side will the laugh be?

So the old fairy took him in hand very severely there and then. But she says she is always most severe with the best people, because there is most chance of curing them, and therefore they are the patients who pay her best; for she has to work on the same salary as the Emperor of China's physicians (it is a pity that all do not), no cure, no pay.

So she took the poor professor in hand: and because he

was not content with things as they are, she filled his head with things as they are not, to try if he would like them better; and because he did not choose to believe in a water-baby when he saw it, she made him believe in worse things than water-babies—in unicorns, fire-drakes, manticoras, basilisks, amphisboenas, griffins, phoenixes, rocs, orcs, dog-headed men, three-headed dogs, three-bodied geryons, and other pleasant creatures, which folks think never existed yet, and which folks hope never will exist, though they know nothing about the matter, and never will; and these creatures so upset, terrified, flustered, aggravated, confused, astounded, horrified, and totally flabbergasted the poor professor, that the doctors said that he was out of his wits for three months; and, perhaps, they were right, as they are now and then.

So all the doctors in the county were called in, to make a report on his case; and of course every one of them flatly contradicted the other: else what use is there in being men of science? But at last the majority agreed on a report, in the true medical language, one half bad Latin, the other half worse Greek, and the rest what might have been English, if they had only learnt to write it. And this is the beginning thereof—

"The subanhypaposupernal anastomoses of peritomic diacellurite in the encephalo digital region of the distinguished individual of whose symptomatic phaenomena we had the melancholy honour (subsequently to a preliminary diagnostic inspection) of making an inspectorial diagnosis, presenting the interexclusively quadrilateral and antinomian diathesis known as Bumpsterhausen's blue follicles, we proceeded—"

But what they proceeded to do my lady never knew; for she was so frightened at the long words that she ran for her life, and locked herself into her bedroom, for fear of being squashed by the words and strangled by the sentence. A boa constrictor, she said, was bad company enough: but what was a boa constrictor made of paving-stones?

"It was quite shocking! What can they think is the matter with him?" said she to the old nurse.

"That his wit's just addled; may be wi' unbelief and heathenry," quoth she.

"Then why can't they say so?"

And the heaven, and the sea, and the rocks, and the vales re-echoed—"Why indeed?" But the doctors never heard them.

So she made Sir John write to *The Times* to command the Chancellor of the Exchequer for the time being to put a tax on long words;—

A light tax on words over three syllables, which are necessary evils, like rats: but like them, must be kept down judiciously.

A heavy tax on words over four syllables, as heterdoxy, spontancity, spiritualism, spuriosity, etc.

And on words over five syllables (of which I hope no one will wish to see any examples), a totally prohibitory tax.

And a similar prohibitory tax on words derived from three or more languages at once; words derived from two languages having become so common, that there was no more hope of rooting out them than of rooting out peth-winds.

The Chancellor of the Exchequer, being a scholar and a man of sense, jumped at the notion; for he saw in it the one and

only plan for abolishing Schedule D: but when he brought in his bill, most of the Irish members, and (I am sorry to say) some of the Scotch likewise, opposed it most strongly, on the ground that in a free country no man was bound either to understand himself or to let others understand him. So the bill fell through on the first reading; and the Chancellor, being a philosopher, comforted himself with the thought, that it was not the first time that a woman had hit off a grand idea, and the men turned up their stupid noses at it.

Now the doctors had it all their own way, and to work they went in earnest, and they gave the poor Professor divers and sundry medicines, as prescribed by the ancients and moderns, from Hippocrates to Feuchtersleben, as below, viz.:—

1. Hellebore, to wit—
Hellebore of Æta.
Hellebore of Galatia.
Hellebore of Sicily
And all other Hellebores, after the method of the Hellebor-
izing Helleborists of the Helleboric era. But that would not
do. Bumpsterhausen's bluefollicles would not stir an inch out
of his encephalo digital region.

2. Trying to find out what was the matter with him, after the
method of—
Hippocrates.
Aretaeus.
Celsus.
Coelius Aurelianus.
And Galen: but they found that a great deal too much trouble,
as most people have since; and so had recourse to—

3. Borage.

Cauteries.

Boring a hole in his head to let out fumes, which (says Gordonius) "will, without doubt, do much good." But it didn't.

Bezoar stone.

Diamargaritum.

A ram's brain boiled in spice.

Oil of wormwood

Water of Nile.

Capers.

Good wine (but there was none to be got.)

The water of a smith's forge.

Hops.

Ambergris.

Mandrake pillows.

Dormouse' fat.

Hares' ears.

Starvation.

Camphor.

Salts and Senna.

Musk.

Opium.

Strait-waistcoats.

Bullyings.

Bumpings.

Blisterings.

Bleedings.

Bucketings with cold water.

Knockings down.

Kneeling on his chest till they broke it in, etc., etc.; after the *mediaeval method: but that would not do. Bumpsterhausen's blue follicles stuck there still. Then—*

4. Coaxing.
Kissing.
Champagne and turtle.
Red herrings and soda water.
Good advice.
Gardening.
Croquet.
Musical soirées.
Aunt Sally.
Mild tobacco.
The Saturday Review.
A carriage with outriders, etc. etc., after the modern method. But that would not do.
And if he had but been a convict lunatic, and had shot at the Queen, killed all his creditors to avoid paying them, or indulged in any other little amiable eccentricity of that kind, they would have given him in addition—
The healthiest situation in England, on East Hampstead Plain. Free run of Windsor Forest.
The Times every morning.
A double-barrelled gun and pointers, and leave to shoot three Wellington College boys a week (not more) in case black game were scarce.
But as he was neither mad enough nor bad enough to be allowed such luxuries, they grew desperate, and fell into bad ways, viz.:—

5. *Suffumigations of sulphur.*

Heerwiggius his "Incomparable drink for madmen," only they could not find out what it was.

*Suffumigation of the liver of the fish * * * only they had forgotten its name, so Dr. Gray could not well procure them a specimen.*

Metallic tractors.

Holloway's Ointment.

Electro-biology.

Valentine Greatrakes his Stroking Cure.

Spirit-rapping.

Holloway's Pills.

Table-turning.

Morrison's Pills.

Homoeopathy.

Parr's Life Pills.

Mesmerism.

Pure Bosh.

Exorcisms, for which they read Malleus Maleficarurn, Nideri Formicarium, Delrio, Wierus, etc., but could not get one that mentioned water-babies.

Hydropathy.

Madame Rachel's Elixir of Youth.

The Poughkeepsie Seer his Prophecies.

The distilled liquor of addle eggs.

Pyropathy, as successfully employed by the old inquisitors to cure the malady of thought, and now by the Persian Mollahs to cure that of rheumatism.

Geopathy, or burying him.

Atmopathy, or steaming him.

Sympathy, after the method of Basil Valentine his Triumph of Antimony, and Kenelm Digby his Weapon-salve, which some call a hair of the dog that bit him.

Hermopathy, or pouring mercury down his throat, to move the animal spirits.

Meteoropathy, or going up to the moon to look for his lost wits, as Ruggiero did for Orlando Furioso's: only, having no hippogriff, they were forced to use a balloon; and, falling into the North Sea, were picked up by a Yarmouth herring-boat, and came home much the wiser, and all over scales.

Antipathy, or using him like "a man and a brother."

Apathy, or doing nothing at all.

With all other ipathies and opathies which Noodle has invented, and Foodle tried, since blackfellows chipped flints at Abbeville—which is a considerable time ago, to judge by the Great Exhibition.

But nothing would do; for he screamed and cried all day for a water-baby to come and drive away the monsters; and of course they did not try to find one, because they did not believe in them, and were thinking of nothing but Bumpsterhausen's blue follicles, having, as usual, set the cart before the horse, and taken the effect for the cause.

So they were forced at last to let the poor professor ease his mind by writing a great book, exactly contrary to all his old opinions; in which he proved that the moon was made of green cheese, and that all the mites in it (which you may see sometimes quite plain through a telescope, if you will only keep the lens dirty enough, as Mr. Weekes kept his voltaic battery) are nothing in the world but little babies, who are hatching and swarming up there in millions, ready to come down into this world whenever children want a new little brother or sister.

Which must be a mistake, for this one reason: that, there being no atmosphere round the moon (though someone or other says there is, at least on the other side, and that he has been round at the back of it to see, and found that the moon was just the shape of a Bath bun, and so wet that the man in the moon went about on Midsummer-day in Macintoshes and Cording's boots, spearing ells and sneezing); that therefore, I say, there being no atmosphere, there can be no evaporation; and, therefore, the dew-point can never fall below 71.5 below zero of Fahrenheit; and, therefore, it cannot be cold enough there about four o'clock in the morning to condense the babies' mesenteric apophthegms into their left ventricles; and, therefore, they can never catch the hooping-cough; and if they do not have hooping-cough, they cannot be babies at all; and, therefore, there are no babies in the moon.—Q.E.D.

Which may seem a roundabout reason; and so, perhaps, it is: but you will have heard worse ones in your time, and from better men than you are.

But one thing is certain; that, when the good old doctor got his book written, he felt considerably relieved from Bumpsterhausen's blue follicles, and a few things infinitely worse; to wit, from pride and vainglory, and from blindness and hardness of heart; which are the true causes of Bumpsterhausen's blue follicles, and of a good many other ugly things beside. Whereon the foul flood-water in his brains ran down, and cleared to a fine coffee colour, such as fish like to rise in, till very fine, clean, fresh-run fish did begin to rise in his brains; and he caught two or three of them (which is exceedingly fine sport, for brain rivers), and anatomized them carefully, and never mentioned what he found out from them, except to little children; and became ever after a sadder and a wiser man; which is a very good thing to become, my dear little boy, even though one has to pay a heavy price for the blessing.

Chapter V

"Stern Lawgiver! yet thou dost wear
The Godhead's most benignant grace;
Nor know we anything so fair
As is the smile upon thy face:
Flowers laugh before thee on their beds;
And fragrance in thy footing treads;
Thou dost preserve the stars from wrong;
And the most ancient Heavens,
through Thee are fresh and strong."

WORDSWORTH—Ode to Duty.

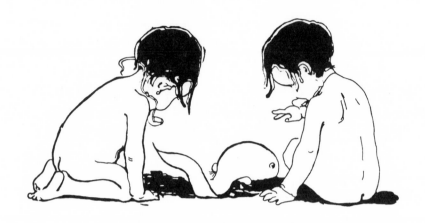

Chapter V

BUT what became of little Tom?

He slipped away off the rocks into the water, as I said before. But he could not help thinking of little Ellie. He did not remember who she was; but he knew that she was a little girl, though she was a hundred times as big as he. That is not surprising: size has nothing to do with kindred. A tiny weed may be first cousin to a great tree; and a little dog like Vick knows that Lioness is a dog too, though she is twenty times larger than herself. So Tom knew that Ellie was a little girl, and thought about her all that day, and longed to have had her to play with; but he had very soon to think of something else. And here is the account of what happened to him, as it was published next morning in the *Waterproof Gazette*, on the finest watered paper, for the use of the great fairy, Mrs. Bedonebyasyoudid, who reads the news very carefully every morning, and especially the police cases, as you will hear very soon.

He was going along the rocks in three-fathom water, watching the pollock catch prawns, and the wrasses nibble barnacles off the rocks, shells and all, when he saw a round cage of green withes; and inside it, looking very much ashamed of himself, sat his friend the lobster, twiddling his horns, instead of thumbs.

"What, have you been naughty, and have they put you in the lockup?" asked Tom.

The lobster felt a little indignant at such a notion, but he was too much depressed in spirits to argue; so he only said, "I can't get out."

"Why did you get in?"

"After that nasty piece of dead fish." He had thought it looked and smelt very nice when he was outside, and so it did, for a lobster; but now he turned round and abused it because he was angry with himself.

"Where did you get in?"

"Through that round hole at the top."

"Then why don't you get out through it?"

"Because I can't," and the lobster twiddled his horns more fiercely than ever, but he was forced to confess.

"I have jumped upwards, downwards, backwards, and sideways, at least four thousand times; and I can't get out: I always get up underneath there, and can't find the hole."

Tom looked at the traps and having more wit than the lobster, he saw plainly enough what was the matter; as you may if you will look at a lobster-pot.

"Stop a bit," said Tom. "Turn your tail up to me, and I'll pull you through hind-foremost, and then you won't stick in the spikes."

But the lobster was so stupid and clumsy that he couldn't hit the hole. Like a great many fox-hunters, he was very sharp as long as he was in his own country: but as soon as they get out of it they lose their heads; and so the lobster, so to speak, lost its tail.

Tom reached and clawed down the hole after him, till he caught hold of him; and then, as was to be expected, the clumsy lobster pulled him in head foremost.

"Hullo! here is a pretty business," said Tom. "Now take your great claws, and break the points of those spikes, and then we shall both get out easily."

"Dear me, I never thought of that," said the lobster; "and after all the experience of life that I have had!"

You see, experience is of very little good unless a man, or a lobster, has wit enough to make use of it. For a good many people, like old Polonius, have seen all the world, and yet remain little better than children after all.

But they had not got half the spikes away, when they saw a great dark cloud over them; and lo and behold, it was the otter.

How she did grin and grin when she saw Tom. "Yar!" said she, "you little meddlesome wretch, I have you now! I will serve you out for telling the salmon where I was!" And she crawled all over the pot to get in.

Tom was horribly frightened, and still more frightened when

she found the hole in the top, and squeezed herself right down through it, all eyes and teeth. But no sooner was her head inside than valiant Mr. Lobster caught her by the nose, and held on.

And there they were all three in the pot, rolling over and over, and very tight packing it was. And the lobster tore at the otter, and the otter tore at the lobster, and both squeezed and thumped poor Tom till he had no breath left in his body; and I don't know what would have happened to him if he had not at last got on the otter's back, and safe out of the hole.

He was right glad when he got out, but he would not desert his friend who had saved him; and the first time he saw his tail uppermost he caught hold of it, and pulled with all his might. But the lobster would not let go.

"Come along," said Tom; "don't you see she is dead?" And so she was, quite drowned and dead.

And that was the end of the wicked otter.

But the lobster would not let go.

"Come along, you stupid old stick-in-the-mud," cried Tom, "or the fisherman will catch you!" And that was true, for Tom felt someone above beginning to haul up the pot.

But the lobster would not let go.

Tom saw the fisherman haul him up to the boatside, and thought it was all up with him. But when Mr. Lobster saw the fisherman, he gave such a furious and tremendous snap, that he snapped out of his hand, and out of the pot, and safe into the sea. But he left his knobbed claw behind him; for it never came into his stupid head to let go after all, so he just shook his claw off as the easier method. It was something of a bull, that; but you must know the lobster was an Irish Lobster, and

They hugged and kissed each other for ever so long,
they did not know why.

was hatched off Island Magee at the mouth of Belfast Lough.

Tom asked the lobster why he never thought of letting go. He said very determinedly that it was a point of honour among lobsters. And so it is, as the Mayor of Plymouth found out once to his cost—eight or nine hundred years ago, of course; for if it had happened lately it would be personal to mention it.

For one day he was so tired with sitting on a hard chair, in a grand furred gown, with a gold chain round his neck, hearing one policeman after another come in and sing, "What shall we do with the drunken sailor, so early in the morning?" and

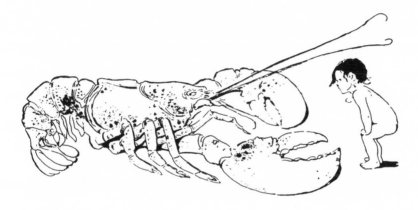

"Put him in the round house till he gets sober, so early in the morning."

That, when it was over, he jumped up, and played leapfrog with the town clerk, till he burst his buttons, and then had his luncheon, and burst some more buttons, and then said: "It is a low spring tide; I shall go out this afternoon and cut my capers."

Now he did not mean to cut such capers as you eat with boiled mutton. It was the commandant of artillery at Valetta who used to amuse himself with cutting them, and who stuck upon one of the bastions a notice, "No one allowed to cut capers here but me," which greatly edified the midshipmen in port, and the Maltese on the Nix Mangiare stairs. But all that the mayor meant was that he would go and have an afternoon's fun, like any schoolboy, and catch lobsters with an iron hook.

So to the Mewstone he went, and for lobsters he looked. And when he came to a certain crack in the rocks, he was so excited, that, instead of putting in his hook, he put in his hand; and Mr. Lobster was at home, and caught him by the finger, and held on.

"Yah!" said the mayor, and pulled as hard as he dared: but the more he pulled the more the lobster pinched, till he was forced to be quiet.

Then he tried to get his hook in with his other hand; but the hole was too narrow.

Then he pulled again; but he could not stand the pain.

Then he shouted and bawled for help: but there was no one nearer him than the men-of-war inside the breakwater.

Then he began to turn a little pale; for the tide flowed, and still the lobster held on.

Then he turned quite white; for the tide was up to his knees, and still the lobster held on.

Then he thought of cutting off his finger; but he wanted two things to do it with—courage and a knife; and he had got neither.

Then he turned quite yellow; for the tide was up to his waist, and still the lobster held on.

Then he thought over all the naughty things he ever had done: all the sand which he had put in the sugar, and the sloe-leaves in the tea, and the water in the treacle, and the salt in the tobacco (because his brother was a brewer, and a man must help his own kin).

Then he turned quite blue; for the tide was up to his breast, and still the lobster held on.

Then, I have no doubt, he repented fully of all the said naughty things which he had done, and promised to mend his life, as too many do when they think they have no life left to mend. Whereby, as they fancy, they make a very cheap bargain. But the old fairy with the birch rod soon undeceives them.

And then he grew all colours at once, and turned up his eyes like a duck in thunder; for the water was up to his chin, and still the lobster held on.

And then came a man-of-war's boat round the Mewstone, and saw his head sticking up out of the water. One said it was a keg of brandy, and another that it was a cocoanut, and another that it was a buoy loose, and another that it was a black diver, and wanted to fire at it. which would not have been Pleasant for the mayor: but just then such a yell came out of a great hole in the middle of it, that the midshipman in charge guessed what it was, and bade pull up to it as fast as they could. So somehow or other the Jack-tars got the lobster out, and set the mayor free, and put him ashore at the Barbican. He never went lobster-catching again and we will hope he put no more salt in the tobacco, not even to sell his brother's beer.

And that is the story of the Mayor of Plymouth which has two advantages—first, that of being quite true; and second, that of having (as folks say all good stories ought to have) no moral whatsoever: no more, indeed, has any part of this book, because it is a fairy tale, you know.

And now happened to Tom a most wonderful thing; for he

had not left the lobster five minutes before he came upon a water-baby.

A real live,water-baby, sitting on the white sand, very busy about a little point of rock. And when it saw Tom it looked up for a moment, and then cried, "Why, you are not one of us. You are a new baby! Oh, how delightful!"

And it ran to Tom, and Tom ran to it, and they hugged and kissed each other for ever so long, they did not know why. But they did not want any introductions there under the water.

At last Tom said, "O, where have you been all this while, I

have been looking for you so long, and I have been so lonely."

"We have been here for days and days. There are hundreds of us about the rocks. How was it you did not see us or hear us when we sing and romp every evening before we go home?"

Tom looked at the baby again, and then he said:

"Well, this is wonderful! I have seen things just like you again and again, but I thought you were shells, or sea-creatures. I never took you for water-babies like myself."

Now, was not that very odd? So odd, indeed, that you will, no doubt, want to know how it happened and why Tom could never find a water-baby till after he had got the lobster out of the pot. And if you will read this story nine times over, and then think for yourself, you will find out why. It is not good for little boys to be told everything and never to be forced to use their own wits. They would learn, then, no more than they do at Dr. Dulcimer's famous suburban establishment for the idler members of the youthful aristocracy, where the masters learn the lessons, and the boys hear them—which saves a great deal of trouble—for the time being.

"Now," said the baby, "come and help me, or I shall not have finished before my brothers and sisters come, and it is time to go home."

"What shall I help you at?"

"At this poor dear little rock; a great clumsy boulder came rolling by in the last storm, and knocked all its head off, and rubbed off all its flowers. And now I must plant it again with seaweeds, and coralline, and anemones, and I will make it the prettiest little rockgarden on all the shore."

So they worked away at the rock, and planted it, and smoothed the sand down round it, and capital fun they had till the tide began to turn. And then Tom heard all the other babies coming, laughing and singing and shouting and romping; and the noise they made was just like the noise of the ripple. So he knew that he had been hearing and seeing the water-babies all along; only he did not know them, because his eyes and ears were not opened.

And in they came, dozens and dozens of them, some bigger than Tom and some smaller, all in the neatest little white bathing dresses; and when they found that he was a new baby they hugged him and kissed him, and then put him in the middle and danced round him on the sand, and there was no one ever so happy as poor little Tom.

"Now then," they cried all at once, "we must come away home, we must come away home, or the tide will leave us dry. We have mended all the broken seaweed, and put all the rock pools in order, and planted all the shells again in the sand, and nobody will see where the ugly storm swept in last week."

And that is the reason why the rock pools are always so neat and clean; because the water-babies come inshore after every storm, to sweep them out, and comb them down, and put them all to rights again.

Only where men are wasteful and dirty, and let sewers run into the sea, instead of putting the stuff upon me fields like thrifty, reasonable souls; or throw herrings' heads, and dead dog-fish, or any other refuse into the water; or in any way make a mess upon the clean shore, there the water-babies will not come, sometimes not for hundreds of years (for they cannot abide anything smelly or foul); but leave tbe sea-anemones and the crabs to clear away everything, till the good tidy sea has covered up all the dirt in soft mud and clean sand, where the water-babies can plant live cockles and whelks and razor shells and sea-cucumbers and golden-combs, and make a pretty live garden again, after man's dirt is cleared away. And that, I suppose, is the reason why there are no water-babies at any watering-place which I have ever seen.

And where is the home of the water-babies? In St. Brandan's fairy isle.

Did you never hear of the blessed St. Brandan, how he preached to the wild Irish, on the wild wild Kerry coast; he and five other hermits, till they were weary, and longed to rest? For the wild Irish would not listen to them, or come to confession and to mass, but liked better to brew potheen, and dance the pater o'pee, and knock each other over the bead with shillelaghs, and shoot each other from behind turf-dykes, and steal each other's cattle, and burn each other's homes; till St. Brandan and his friends were weary of them, for they would not learn to be peaceable Christians at all.

So St. Brandan went out to the point of old Dunmore, and looked over the tideway roaring round the Blasquets, at the end of all the world, and away into the ocean, and sighed—"Ah that I had wings as a dove!" And far away, before the setting sun, he saw a blue fairy sea, and golden fairy islands, and he said, "Those are the islands of the blest." Then he and his friends got into a hooker, and sailed away and away to the westward, and were never heard of more. But the people who would not hear him were changed into gorillas, and gorillas they are until this day.

And when St. Brandan and the hermits came to that fairy isle, they found it overgrown with cedars, and full of beautiful birds; and he sat down under the cedars, and preached to all the birds in the air. And they liked his sermons so well that they told the fishes in the sea; and they came, and St. Brandan preached to them; and the fishes told the water-babies, who live in tbe caves under the isle; and they came up by hundreds every Sunday, and St. Brandan got quite a neat little Sunday school. And there he taught the water-babies for a great many hundred years, till his eyes grew too dim to see, and his beard grew so long that be dared not walk for fear of treading on it, and then he might have tumbled down. And at last he and the five hermits fell fast asleep under the cedar shades, and there they sleep unto this day. But the fairies took to the water-babies, and taught them their lessons themselves.

And some say that St. Brandan will awake, and begin to teach the babies once more: but some think that he will sleep on, for better for worse, till the coming of the Cocqcigrues. But, on still, clear summer evenings, when the sun sinks down into the sea, among golden cloud-capes and cloud-islands, and locks and friths of azure sky, the sailors fancy that they see, away to westward, St. Brandan's fairy isle.

But whether men can see it or not, St. Brandan's Isle once actually stood there; a great land out in the ocean, which has sunk and sunk beneath the waves. Old Plato called it Atlantis, and told strange tales of the wise men who lived therein, and of the wars they fought in the old times. And from off that island came strange flowers, which linger still about this land: the Cornish heath, and Cornish moneywort, and the delicate Venus's hair, and the London-pride which covers the Kerry mountains, and the little pink butterwort of Devon, and the great blue butterwort of Ireland, and the Connemara heath, and the bristlefern of the Turk waterfall, and many a strange plant more; all fairy tokens left for wise men and good children from off St. Brandan's Isle.

Now when Tom got there, he found that the isle stood all on pillars and that its roots were full of caves. There were pillars of black basalt, like Staffa; and pillars of green and

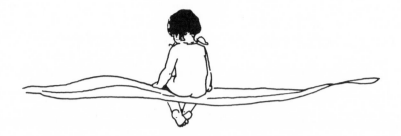

crimson serpentine, like Kynance; and pillars ribboned with red and white and yellow sandstone, like Livermead; and there were blue grottoes, like Capri; and white grottoes, like Adelsberg; all curtained and draped with seaweeds, purple and crimson, green and brown; and strewn with soft white sand, on which the water-babies sleep every night. But, to keep the place clean and sweet, the crabs picked up all the scraps off the floor, and ate them like so many monkeys; while the rocks were covered with ten thousand sea-anemones, and corals and madrepores, who scavenged the water all day long, and kept it nice and pure. But, to make up to them for having to do such nasty work, they were not left black and dirty, as poor chimney-sweeps and dustmen are. No; the fairies are more considerate and just than that; and have dressed them all in the most beautiful colours and patterns, till they look like vast flower-beds of gay blossoms. If you think I am talking nonsense, I can only say that it is true; and that an old gentleman named Fourier used to say that we ought to do the same by chimney-sweeps and dustmen, and honour them instead of despising them; and he was a very clever old gentleman: but unfortunately for him and the world, as mad as a March hare.

And, instead of watchmen and policemen to keep out nasty

things at night, there were thousands and thousands of water-snakes, and most wonderful creatures they were. They were all named after the Nereids, the sea fairies who took care of them, Eunice and Polynoe, Phyllodoce and Psamathe, and all the rest of the pretty darlings who swim round their Queen Amphitrite, and her car of cameo shell. They were dressed in green velvet, and black velvet, and purple velvet; and were all jointed in rings; and some of them had three hundred brains apiece, so that they must have been uncommonly shrewd detectives; and some had eyes in their tails; and some had eyes in every joint, so that they kept a very sharp look-out; and when they wanted a baby-snake, they just grew one at the end of their own tails, and when it was able to take care of itself it dropped off; so that they brought up their families very cheaply. But if any nasty thing came by, out they rushed upon it; and then out of each of their hundreds of feet there sprang a whole cutler's shop of

Scythes,	Javelins,
Billhooks,	Lances
Pickaxes,	Halberts,
Forks,	Gisarines,
Penknives,	Poleaxes,
Rapiers,	Fishhooks,
Sabres,	Brawdawls,
Yataghans,	Gimlets,
Creeses,	Corkscrews,
Ghoorka swords,	Pins,
Tucks,	Needles,

And so forth,

which stabbed, shot, poked, pricked, scratched, ripped, pinked, and crimped those naughty beasts so terribly, that they had to run for their lives, or else be chopped into small pieces and be eaten afterwards. And, if that is not all, every word, true, then there is no faith in microscopes, and all is over with the Linnaean Society.

And there were the water-babies in thousands, more than Tom, or you either, could count. All the little children whom the good fairies take to, because their cruel mothers and fathers will not; all who are untaught and brought up heathens, and all who come to grief by ill-usage or ignorance or neglect, all the little children who are overlaid, or given gin when they are young, or are let to drink out of hot kettles, or to fall into the fire; all the little children in alleys and courts, and tumble-down cottages, who die by fever, and cholera, and measles, and scarlatina, and nasty complaints which no one has any business to have, and which no one will have some day, when folks have common sense; and all the little children who have been killed by cruel masters, and wicked soldiers; they were all there, except, of course, the babes of Bethlehem who were killed by wicked King Herod; for they were taken straight to heaven long ago, as everybody knows, and we call them the Holy Innocents.

But I wish Tom had given up all his naughty tricks, and left off tormenting dumb animals, now that he had plenty of playfellows to amuse him. Instead of that, I am sorry to say, he would meddle with the creatures, all but the water-snakes, for they would stand no nonsense. So he tickled the madrepores, to make them shut up; and frightened the crabs, to make them hide in the sand and peep out at him with the tips of their eyes; and put stones into the anemones' mouths to make them fancy that their dinner was coming.

The other children warned him, and said, "Take care what you are at Mrs. Bedonebyasyoudid is coming." But Tom never heeded them, being quite riotous with high spirits and good luck, till, one Friday morning early, Mrs. Bedonebyasyoudid came indeed.

A very tremendous lady she was; and when the children saw her, they all stood in a row, very upright indeed, and smoothed down their bathing dresses, and put their hands behind them, just as if they were going to be examined by the inspector.

And she had on a black bonnet, and a black shawl, and no crinoline at all; and a pair of large green spectacles, and a great hooked nose, hooked so much that the bridge of it stood quite up above her eyebrows; and under her arm she carried a great birch rod. Indeed, she was so ugly, that Tom was tempted to make faces at her: but did not; for he did not admire the look of the birch rod under her arm.

And she looked at the children one by one, and seemed very much pleased with them, though she never asked them one question about how they were behaving; and then began giving them all sorts of nice sea-things—sea-cakes, sea-apples, sea-oranges, sea-bulls'eyes, sea-toffee; and to the very best of all she gave sea-ices, made out of sea-cows' cream, which never melts under water.

And, if you don't quite believe me, then just think—What is more cheap and plentiful than sea-rock? Then, why should there not be sea-toffee as well? And everyone can find sea-lemons (ready quartered too) if they will look for them at low tide;

and sea-grapes too sometimes, hanging in bunches; and, if you will go to Nice, you will find the fish-market full of sea-fruit, which they call "frutta di mare"; though I suppose they call them "fruits de mer" now, out of compliment to that most successful, and therefore most immaculate, potentate who is seemingly desirous of inheriting the blessing pronounced on those who remove their neighbours' landmark. And, perhaps, that is the very reason why the place is called Nice, because there are so many nice things in the sea there: at least, if it is not, it ought to be.

Now little Tom watched all these sweet things given away, till his mouth watered, and his eyes grew as round as an owl's. For he hoped that his turn would come at last; and so it did. For the lady called him up, and held out her fingers with something in them, and popped it into his mouth; and, lo and behold, it was a nasty, cold, hard pebble.

"You are a very cruel woman," said he, and began to

whimper.

"And you are a very cruel boy; who puts pebbles into the sea-anemones' mouths, to take them in, and make them fancy that they had caught a good dinner. As you did to them, so I must do to you."

"Who told you that?" said Tom.

"You did yourself, this very minute."

Tom had never opened his lips; so he was very much taken aback indeed.

"Yes; everyone tells me exactly what they have done wrong; and that without knowing it themselves. So there is no use trying to hide anything from me. Now go, and be a good boy, and I will put no more pebbles in your mouth, if you put none in other creatures."'

"I did not know there was any harm in it," said Tom.

"Then you know now. People continually say that to me: but I tell them, if you don't know that fire burns, that is no reason that it should not burn you; and if you don't know that dirt breeds fever, that is no reason why the fevers should not kill you. The lobster did not know that there was any harm in getting into the lobster pot; but it caught him all the same."

"Dear me," thought Tom, "she knows everything!" And so she did, indeed.

"And so, if you do not know that things are wrong, that is no reason why you should not be punished for them; though not as much, not as much, my little man" (and the lady looked very kindly after all), "as if you did know."

"Well, you are a little hard on a poor lad," said Tom.

"Not at all; I am the best friend you ever had in all your life. But I will tell you; I cannot help punishing people when they do wrong. I like it no more than they do; I am often very, very sorry for them, poor things: but I cannot help it. If I tried not to do it, I should do it all the same. For I work by machinery, just like an engine; and am full of wheels and springs inside; and am wound up very carefully, so that I cannot help going."

"Was it long ago since they wound you up?" asked Tom. For he thought, the cunning little fellow, "She will run down some day: or they may forget to wind her up, as old Grimes used to forget to wind up his watch when he came in from the public-house: and then I shall be safe."

"I was wound up once and for all, so long ago that I forget all about it."

"Dear me," said Tom, "you must have been made a long time!"

"I never was made, my child: and I shall go for ever and ever; for I am as old as Eternity, and yet as young as Time."

And there came over the lady's face a very curious expression—very solemn, and very sad; and yet very, very sweet. And she looked up and away, as if she were gazing through the sea, and through the sky, at something far, far off; and as she did so, there came such a quiet, tender, patient, hopeful smile over her face, that Tom thought for the moment that she did not look ugly at all. And no more she did; for she was like a great many people who have not a pretty feature in their faces, and yet are lovely to behold, and draw little children's hearts to them at once; because, though the house is plain enough, yet from the windows a beautiful and good spirit is looking forth.

And Tom smiled in her face, she looked so pleasant for the moment. And the strange fairy smiled too, and said:

"Yes. You thought me very ugly just now, did you not?"

Tom hung down his head, and got very red about the ears.

"And I am very ugly. I am the ugliest fairy in the world; and I shall be, till people behave themselves as they ought to do. And then I shall grow as handsome as my sister, who is the loveliest fairy in the world; and her name is Mrs. Doasyouwouldbedoneby. So she begins where I end, and I begin where she ends; and those who will not listen to her must listen to me, as you will see. Now, all of you run away, except Tom; and he may stay and see what I am going to do. It will be a very good warning for him to begin with, before he goes to school."

"Now, Tom, every Friday I come down here and call up all who have ill-used little children, and serve them as they served the children."

And at that Tom was frightened, and crept under a stone; which made the two crabs who lived there very angry, and frightened their friend the butter-fish into flapping hysterics: but he would not move for them.

And first she called up all the doctors who give little children so much physic (they were most of them old ones; for the young ones have learnt better, all but a few army surgeons, who still fancy that a baby's inside is much like a Scotch

Mrs. Be-done-by-as-you-did. "Little boys who are only fit
to play with sea-beasts cannot go there," she said.

grenadier's), and she set them all in a row; and very rueful they looked; for they knew what was coming.

And first she pulled all their teeth out; and then she bled them all round: and then she dosed them with calomel, and jalap, and salts and senna, and brimstone and treacle; and horrible faces they made; and then she gave them a great emetic of mustard and water, and no basins; and began all over again; and that was the way she spent the morning.

And then she called up a whole troop of foolish ladies, who pinch up their children's waists and toes; and she laced them all up in tight stays, so that they were choked and sick, and their noses grew red, and their hands and feet swelled; and then she crammed their poor feet into the most dreadfully tight boots, and made them all dance, which they did most clumsily indeed; and then she asked them how they liked it; and when they said not at all, she let them go: because they had only done it out of foolish fashion, fancying it was for their children's good, as if wasps waists and pigs' toes could be pretty, or wholesome, or of any use to anybody.

Then she called up all the careless nurserymaids, and stuck pins into them all over, and wheeled them about in perambulators with tight straps across their stomachs and their heads and arms hanging over the side, till they were quite sick and stupid, and would have had sunstrokes: but, being under the water, they could only have water-strokes; which, I assure you, are nearly as bad, as you will find if you try to sit under a mill wheel. And mind—when you hear a rumbling at the

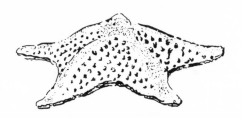

bottom of the sea, sailors will tell you that it is a ground-swell: but now you know better. It is the old lady wheeling the maids about in perambulators.

And by that time she was so tired, she had to go to luncheon.

And after luncheon she set to work again, and called up all the cruel schoolmasters—whole regiments and brigades of them; and, when she saw them, she frowned most terribly, and set to work in earnest, as if the best part of the day's work was to come. More than half of them were nasty, dirty, frowzy, grubby, smelly old monks, who, because they dare not hit a man of their own size, amused themselves with beating little children instead; as you may see in the picture of old Pope Gregory (good man and true though he was, when he meddled with things which he did understand), teaching children to sing their fa-fa-mi-fa, with a cat-o'nine-tails under his chair: but, because they never had any children of their own, they took into their heads (as some folks do still) that they were the only people in the world who knew how to manage children; and they first brought into England, in the old Anglo-Saxon times, the fashion of treating free boys, and girls too, worse than you would treat a dog or a horse: but Mrs. Bedonebyasyoudid has caught them all long ago; and given them many a taste of their own rods; and much good may it do them.

And she boxed their ears, and thumped them over the head with rulers, and pandied their hands with canes, and told them that they told stories, and were this and that bad sort of people; and the more they were very indignant, and stood upon their honour, and declared they told the truth, the more she declared they were not, and that they were only telling lies; and at last she birched them all round soundly with her great birch rod, and set them each an imposition of three hundred thousand lines of Hebrew to learn by heart before she came back next Friday. And at that they all cried and howled so, that their breaths came all up through the sea like bubbles out of soda-water; and that is one reason of the bubbles in the sea. There are others: but that is the one which principally concerns little boys. And by that time she was so tired that she was glad to stop; and, indeed, she had done a very good day's work.

Tom did not quite dislike the old lady: but he could not help thinking her a little spiteful—and no wonder if she was, poor old soul; for, if she has to wait to grow handsome till people do as they would be done by, she will have to wait a very long time.

Poor old Mrs. Bedonebyasyoudid! she has a great deal of hard work before her, and had better have been born a washerwoman, and stood over a tub all day: but, you see, people cannot always choose their own profession.

But Tom longed to ask her one question; and after all, whenever she looked at him, she did not look cross at all; and now and then there was a funny smile in her face, and she chuckled to herself in a way which gave Tom courage, and at last he said:

"Pray, ma'am, may I ask you a question?"

"Certainly, my little dear."

"Why don't you bring all the bad masters here, and serve them out too? The butties that knock about the poor collier-boys; and the nailers that file off their lads' noses and hammer their fingers; and all the master sweeps, like my master Grimes? I saw him fall into the water long ago; so I surely expected he would have been here. I'm sure he was bad enough to me."

Then the old lady looked so very stern that Tom was quite frightened, and sorry that he had been so bold. But she was not angry with him. She only answered, "I look after them all the week round; and they are in a very different place from this, because they knew that they were doing wrong."

She spoke very quietly; but there was something in her voice which made Tom tingle from head to foot, as if he had got into a shoal of sea-nettles.

"But these people," she went on, "did not know that they were doing wrong; they were only stupid and impatient; and therefore I only punish them till they become patient, and learn to use their common sense like reasonable beings. But as for chimney-sweeps, and collier-boys, and nailer lads, my sister has set good people to stop all that sort of thing; and very much obliged to her I am; for if she could only stop the cruel masters from ill-using poor children, I should grow handsome at least a thousand years sooner. And now do you be a good boy, and do as you would be done by, which they did not; and then, when my sister, Madame Doasyouwouldbedoneby, comes on Sunday, perhaps she will take notice of you, and teach you how to behave. She understands that better than I do." And so she went.

Tom was very glad to hear that there was no chance of meeting Grimes again, though he was a little sorry for him, considering that he used sometimes to give him the leavings of the beer; but he determined to be a very good boy all Saturday; and he was; for he never frightened one crab, nor tickled any live corals, nor put stones into the sea-anemones' mouths, to make them fancy they had got a dinner; and, when Sunday morning came, sure enough, Mrs. Doasyouwouldbedoneby came too. Whereat all the little children began dancing and clapping their hands, and Tom danced too with all his might.

And as for the pretty lady, I cannot tell you what the colour of her hair was, or of her eyes: no more could Tom; for, when anyone looks at her, all they can think of is, that she has the sweetest, kindest, tenderest, funniest, merriest face they ever saw, or want to see. But Tom saw that she was a very tall woman, as tall as her sister; but instead of being gnarly, and horny, and scaly, and prickly, like her, she was the most nice,

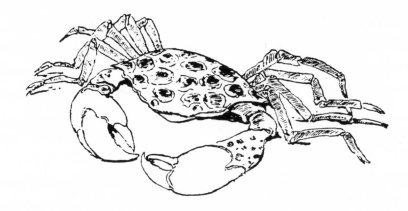

soft, fat, smooth, pussy, cuddly, delicious creature who ever nursed a baby; and she understood babies thoroughly, for she had plenty of her own, whole rows and regiments of them, and has to this day. And all her delight was, whenever she had a spare moment, to play with babies, in which she showed herself a woman of sense; for babies are the best company, and the pleasantest playfellows, in the world; at least, so all the wise people in the world think. And therefore when the children saw her, they naturally all caught hold of her, and pulled her till she sat down on a stone, and climbed into her lap, and clung round her neck, and caught hold of her hands; and then they all put their thumbs into their mouths, and began cuddling and purring like so many kittens, as they ought to have done. While those who could get nowhere else sat down on the sand, and cuddled her feet—for no one, you know, wears shoes in the water, except horrid old bathing-women, who are afraid of the water-babies pinching their horny toes. And Tom stood staring at them; for he could not understand what it was all about.

"And who are you, you little darling?" she said.

"Oh, that is the new baby!" they all cried, pulling their thumbs out of their mouths; "and he never had any mother," and they all put their thumbs back again, for they did not wish to lose any time.

"Then I will be his mother, and he shall have the very best place; so get out all of you, this moment."

And she took up two great armfuls of babies—nine hundred under one arm, and thirteen hundred under the other—and threw them away, right and left, into the water. But they minded it no more than the naughty boys in Struwwelpeter minded when St. Nicholas dipped them in his inkstand; and did not even take their thumbs out of their mouths, but came paddling and wriggling back to her like so many tadpoles, till you could see nothing of her from head to foot for the swarm of little babies.

But she took Tom in her arms and laid him in the softest place of all, and kissed him, and patted him, and talked to him, tenderly and low, such things as he had never heard before in his life; and Tom looked up into her eyes, and loved her, and loved, till he fell fast asleep from pure love.

And when he woke she was telling the children a story. And what story did she tell them? One story she told them, which begins every Christmas Eve, and yet never ends at all for ever and ever; and, as she went on, the children took their thumbs out of their mouths, and listened quite seriously; but not sadly at all: for she never told them anything sad; and Tom listened too, and never grew tired of listening. And he listened so long that he fell fast asleep again, and when he woke the lady was nursing him still.

"Don't go away," said little Tom. "This is so nice. I never had anyone to cuddle me before."

"Don't go away," said all the children; "you have not sung us one song."

"Well, I have time for only one. So what shall it be?"

"The doll you lost! The doll you lost!" cried all the babies at once.

So the strange fairy sang:—

> I *once had a sweet little doll, dears,*
> *The prettiest doll in the world;*
> *Her cheeks were so red and so white, dears,*
> *And her hair was so charmingly curled.*
>
> But I *lost my poor little doll, dears,*
> *As I played in the heath one day;*
> *And I cried for her more than a week, dears;*
> *But I never could find where she lay.*
>
> I *found my poor little doll, dears,*
> *As I played in the heath one day:*
> *Folks say she is terribly changed, dears,*
> *For her paint is all washed away,*
>
> *And her arm trodden off by the cows, dears,*
> *And her hair not the least bit curled:*
> *Yet for old sakes' sake she is still, dears,*
> *The prettiest doll in the world.*

What a silly song for a fairy to sing!

And what silly water-babies to be quite delighted at it!

Well, but you see they have not the advantage of Aunt Agitate's Arguments in the sea-land down below.

"Now," said the fairy to Tom, "will you be a good boy for my sake, and torment no more sea-beasts, till I come back?"

"And you will cuddle me again?" said poor little Tom.

"Of course I will, you little duck. I should like to take you with me, and cuddle you all the way, only I must not;" and away she went.

So Tom really tried to be a good boy, and tormented no sea-beasts after that, as long as he lived; and he is quite alive, I assure you, still.

Oh, how good little boys ought to be, who have kind cuddly mammas to cuddle them and tell them stories; and how afraid they ought to be of growing naughty, and bringing tears into their mammas' pretty eyes.

Chapter VI

"Thou little child, yet glorious in the might
Of heaven-born freedom on thy Being's height,
Why with such earnest pains dost thou provoke
The years to bring the inevitable yoke —
Thus blindly with thy blessedness at strife?
Full soon thy soul shall have her earthly freight,
And custom lie upon thee with a weight
Heavy as frost, and deep almost as life."

WORDSWORTH.

Chapter VI

ERE I come to the very saddest part of all my story. I know some people will only laugh at it, and call it much ado about nothing. But I know one man who would not; and he was an officer with a pair of grey moustaches as long as your arm, who said once in company, that two of the most heartrending sights in the world, which moved him most to tears, which he would do anything to prevent or remedy, were a child over a broken toy and a child stealing sweets.

The company did not laugh at him; his moustaches were

too long and too grey for that: but after he was gone, they called him sentimental, and so forth, all but one dear little old quaker lady with a soul as white as her cap, who was not, of course, generally partial to soldiers; and she said very quietly, like a quaker:

"Friends, it is borne upon my mind that that is a truly brave man."

Now you may fancy that Tom was quite good, when he had everything that he could want or wish: but you would be very much mistaken. Being quite comfortable is a very good thing; but it does not make people good. Indeed, it sometimes makes them naughty, as it has made the people in America; and as it made the people in the Bible, who waxed fat and kicked, like horses overfed and underworked. And I am very sorry to say that this happened to little Tom. For he grew so fond of the sea-bull'seyes and sea-lollipops, that his foolish little head could think of nothing else: and he was always longing for more, and wondering when the strange lady would come again and give him some, and what she would give him, and how much, and whether she would give him more than the others. And he thought of nothing but lollipops by day, and dreamt of nothing else by night—and what happened then?

That he began to watch the lady to see where she kept the sweet things; and began hiding and sneaking and following her about, and pretending to be looking the other way, or going after something else, till he found out that she kept them in a beautiful mother-of-pearl cabinet, away in a deep crack of the rocks. And he longed to go to the cabinet, and yet he was afraid; and then he longed again, and was less afraid; and at last, by continual thinking about it, he longed so violently that he was not afraid at all. And one night, when all the other children were asleep, and he could not sleep for thinking of lollipops, he crept away among the rocks, and got to the cabinet, and behold! it was open.

But, when he saw all the nice things inside, instead of being delighted, he was quite frightened, and wished he had never come there. And then he would only touch them, and he did; and then he would only taste one, and he did; and then he would only eat one, and he did; and then he would only eat two, and then three, and so on; and then he was terrified lest

she should come and catch him, and began gobbling them down so fast that he did not taste them, or have any pleasure in them: and then he felt sick, and would have only one more; and then only one more again; and so on till he had eaten them all up.

And all the while, close behind him, stood Mrs. Bedoneby-asyoudid.

Some people may say, But why did she not keep her cupboard locked? Well, I know. It may seem a very strange thing, but she never does keep her cupboard locked; everyone may go and taste for themselves, and fare accordingly. It is very odd, but so it is; and I am quite sure that she knows best. Perhaps she wishes people to keep their fingers out of the fire by having them burnt. She took off her spectacles, because she did not like to see too much; and in her pity she arched up her eyebrows into her very hair, and her eyes grew so wide that they would have taken in all the sorrows of the world, and filled with great big tears, as they too often do.

But all she said was:

"Ah, you poor little dear! you are just like all the rest."

But she said it to herself, and Tom neither heard nor saw her. Now, you must not fancy that she was sentimental at all. If you do, and think that she is going to let off you, or me, or any human being when we do wrong because she is too tender-hearted to punish us, then you will find yourself very much mistaken, as many a man does every year and every day.

But what did the strange fairy do when she saw all her lollipops eaten?

Did she fly at Tom, catch him by the scruff of the neck, hold him, howk him, hump him, hurry him, hit him, poke him, pull him, pinch him, pound him, put him in the corner, shake him, slap him, set him on a cold stone to reconsider himself, and so forth?

Not a bit. You may watch her at work, if you know where to find her. But you will never see her do that. For, if she had, she knew quite well, Tom would have fought, and kicked, and bit, and said bad words, and turned again that moment into a naughty little heathen chimney-sweep, with his hand, like Ishmael's of old, against every man, and every man's hand against him.

Did she question him, hurry him, frighten him, threaten him,

And there he was the last of the Gairfowl, standing
up on the All-alone-stone, all alone.

to make him confess? Not a bit. You may see her, as I said, at her work often enough, if you know where to look for her: but you will never see her do that. For if she had, she would have tempted him to tell lies in his fright; and that would have been worse for him, if possible, than even becoming a heathen chimney-sweep again.

No. She leaves that for anxious parents and teachers (lazy ones, some call them), who, instead of giving children a fair trial, such as they would expect and demand for themselves, force them by fright to confess their own faults—which is so cruel and unfair, that no judge on the bench dare do it to the wickedest thief or murderer, for the good British law forbids it—ay, and even punish them to make them confess, which is so detestable a crime, that it is never committed now, save by Inquisitors, and Kings of Naples, and a few other wretched people of whom the world is weary. And then they say, "We have trained up the child in the way he should go, and when he grew up he has departed from it. Why then did Solomon say that he would not depart from it?" But perhaps the way of beating, and hurrying, and frightening, and questioning, was not the way that the child should go; for it is not even the way in which a colt should go, if you want to break it in, and make it a quiet, serviceable horse.

Some folks may say, "Ah! but the Fairy does not need to do that, if she knows everything already." True. But if she did not know, she would not surely behave worse than a British judge and jury; and no more should parents and teachers either.

So she just said nothing at all about the matter, not even when Tom came next day with the rest for sweet things. He was horribly afraid of coming: but he was still more afraid of staying away, lest anyone should suspect him. He was dreadfully afraid, too, lest there should be no sweets—as was to be expected, he having eaten them all—and lest then the fairy should inquire who had taken them. But, behold! she pulled out just as many as ever, which astonished Tom, and frightened him still more.

And, when the fairy looked him full in the face, he shook from head to foot: however, she gave him his share like the rest, and he thought within himself that she could not have found him out.

But, when he put the sweets into his mouth, he hated the taste of them; and they made him so sick, that he had to get away as fast as he could; and terribly sick he was, and very cross and unhappy, all the week after.

Then, when next week came, he had his share again; and again the fairy looked him full in the face; but more sadly than she had ever looked. And he could not bear the sweets, but took them again in spite of himself.

And, when Mrs. Doasyouwouldbedoneby came, he wanted to be cuddled like the rest; but she said very seriously:

"I should like to cuddle you; but I cannot, you are so horny and prickly."

And Tom looked at himself: and he was all over prickles, just like a sea-egg.

Which was quite natural; for you must know and believe that people's souls make their bodies, just as a snail makes its shell (I am not joking, my little man; I am in serious, solemn, earnest). And, therefore, when Tom's soul grew all prickly with naughty tempers, his body could not help growing prickly too, so that nobody would cuddle him, or play with him, or even like to look at him.

What could Tom do now, but go away and hide in a corner, and cry? For nobody would play with him, and he knew full well why.

And he was so miserable all that week that, when the ugly fairy came, and looked at him once more full in the face, more seriously and sadly than ever, he could stand it no longer, and thrust the sweetmeats away, saying, "No, I don't want any; I can't bear them now," and then burst out crying, poor little man, and told Mrs. Bedonebyasyoudid every word as it happened.

He was horribly frightened when he had done so; for he expected her to punish him very severely. But, instead, she only took him up and kissed him, which was not quite pleasant, for her chin was very bristly indeed; but he was so lonely-hearted, he thought that rough kissing was better than none.

"I will forgive you, little man," she said. "I always forgive everyone the moment they tell me the truth of their own accord."

"Then you will take away all these nasty prickles?"

"That is a very different matter. You put them there yourself, and only you can take them away."

"But how can I do that?" asked Tom, crying afresh.

"Well, I think it is time for you to go to school; so I shall fetch you a school-mistress, who will teach you how to get rid of your prickles." And so she

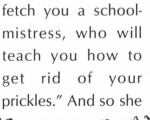

went away.

Tom was frightened at the notion of a schoolmistress; for he thought she would certainly come with a birch rod or a cane; but he comforted himself, at last, that she might be something like the old woman in Vendale—which she was not in the least; for, when the fairy brought her, she was the most beautiful little girl that ever was seen, with long curls floating behind her like a golden cloud, and long robes floating all round her like a silver one.

"There he is," said the fairy; "and you must teach him to be good, whether you like or not."

"I know," said the little girl; but she did not seem quite to like, for she put her finger in her mouth, and looked at Tom under her brows; and Tom put his finger in his mouth, and looked at her under his brows, for he was horribly ashamed of himself.

The little girl seemed hardly to know how to begin; and perhaps she would never have begun at all, if poor Tom had not burst out crying, and begged her to teach him to be good, and help him to cure his prickles; and at that she grew so tender-hearted, that she began teaching him as prettily as ever child was taught in the world.

And what did the little girl teach Tom? She taught him, first, what you have been taught ever since you said your first prayers at your mother's knees; but she taught him much more simply.

For the lessons in that world, my child, have no such hard words in them as the lessons in this, and therefore the water-babies like them better than you like your lessons, and long to learn them more and more; and grown men cannot puzzle nor quarrel over their meaning, as they do here on land; for those lessons all rise clear and pure, like the Test out of Overton Pool, out of the everlasting ground of all life and truth.

So she taught Tom every day in the week; only on Sundays she always went away home, and the kind fairy took her place. And, before she had taught Tom many Sundays, his prickles had vanished quite away, and his skin was smooth and clean again.

"Dear me!" said the little girl; "why, I know you now. You are the very same little chimney-sweep who came into my bedroom."

"Dear me!" cried Tom. "And I know you, too, now. You are the very little white lady whom I saw in bed." And he jumped at her, and longed to hug and kiss her; but did not, remembering that she was a lady born; so he only jumped round and round her, till he was quite tired.

And then they began telling each other all their story—how he had got into the water, and she had fallen over the rock; and how he had swam down to the sea, and how she had flown out of the window; and how this, that, and the other, till it was all talked out: and then they both began over again, and I can't say which of the two talked fastest.

And then they set to work at their lessons again, and both liked them so well, that they went on well till seven full years were past and gone.

You may fancy that Tom was quite content and happy all those seven years; but the truth is, he was not. He had always one thing on his mind, and that was—where little Ellie went, when she went home on Sundays.

To a very beautiful place, she said.

But what was the beautiful place like, and where was it?

Ah! that is just what she could not say. And it is strange, but true, that no one can say; and that those who have been oftenest in it, or even nearest to it, can say least about it, and make people understand least what it is like. There are a good many folks about the Other-end-of-Nowhere (where Tom went afterwards), who pretend to know it from north to south as well as if they had been penny postmen there; but, as they are safe at the Other-end-of-Nowhere, nine hundred and ninety-nine million miles away, what they say cannot concern us.

But the dear, sweet, loving, wise, good, self-sacrificing people, who really go there, can never tell you anything about it, save that it is the most beautiful place in all the world; and, if you ask them more, they grow modest, and hold their peace, for fear of being laughed at; and quite right they are.

So all that good little Ellie could say was, that it was worth all the rest of the world put together. And of course that only made Tom the more anxious to go likewise.

"Miss Ellie," he said, at last, "I will know why I cannot go with you when you go home, on Sundays, or I shall have no peace, and give you none either."

"You must ask the fairies that."

So when the fairy, Mrs. Bedonebyasyoudid, came next, Tom asked her.

"Little boys who are only fit to play with sea-beasts cannot go there," she said. "Those who go there must go first where they do not like, and do what they do not like, and help somebody they do not like."

"Why, did Ellie do that?"

"Ask her."

And Ellie blushed, and said, "Yes, Tom; I did not like coming here at first; I was so much happier at home, where it is always Sunday. And I was afraid of you, Tom, at first, because—because—"

"Because I was all over prickles? But I am not prickly now, am I, Miss Ellie?"

"No," said Ellie. "I like you very much now; and I like coming here, too."

"And perhaps," said the fairy, "you will learn to like going where you don't like, and helping someone that you don't like, as Ellie has."

But Tom put his finger in his mouth, and hung his head down; for he did not see that at all.

So when Mrs. Doasyouwouldbedoneby came, Tom asked her; for he thought in his little head, "She is not so strict as her sister, and perhaps she may let me off more easily."

Ah, Tom, Tom, silly fellow! and yet I don't know why I should blame you, while so many grown people have got the very same notion in their heads.

But, when they try it, they get just the same answer as Tom did. For, when he asked the second fairy, she told him just what the first did, and in the very same words.

Tom was very unhappy at that. And, when Ellie went home on Sunday, he fretted and cried all day, and did not care to listen to the fairy's stories about good children, though they were prettier than ever. Indeed, the more he overheard of them, the less he liked to listen, because they were all about children who did what they did not like, and took trouble for other people, and worked to feed their little brothers and sisters, instead of caring only for their play. And, when she began to tell a story about a holy child in old times, who was martyred by the heathen because it would not worship idols, Tom could bear no more, and ran away and hid among the rocks.

And, when Ellie came back, he was shy with her, because he fancied she looked down on him, and thought him a coward. And then he grew quite cross with her, because she was superior to him, and did what he could not do. And poor Ellie was quite surprised and sad; and at last Tom burst out crying; but he would not tell her what was really in his mind.

And all the while he was eaten up with curiosity to know where Ellie went to; so that he began not to care for his playmates, or for the sea-palace, or anything else. But perhaps that made matters all the easier for him; for he grew so discontented with everything round him, that he did not care to stay, and did not care where he went.

"Well," he said, at last, "I am so miserable here, I'll go; if only you will go with me."

"Ah!" said Ellie, "I wish I might; but the worst of it is, that the fairy says, that you must go alone, if you go at all. Now don't poke that poor crab about, Tom" (for he was feeling very naughty and mischievous), "or the fairy will have to punish you."

Tom was very nearly saying, "I don't care if she does;" but he stopped himself in time.

"I know what she wants me to do," he said, whining most dolefully. "She wants me to go after that horrid old Grimes. I don't like him, that's certain. And if I find him, he will turn me into a chimney-sweep again, I know. That's what I have been afraid of all along."

"No, he won't—I know as much as that. Nobody can turn water-babies into sweeps, or hurt them at all, as long as they

are good."

"Ah," said naughty Tom, "I see what you want; you are persuading me all along to go, because you are tired of me, and want to get rid of me."

Little Ellie opened her eyes very wide at that, and they were all brimming over with tears.

"Oh, Tom, Tom!" she said, very mournfully—and then she cried, "Oh, Tom! where are you?"

And Tom cried, "Oh, Ellie, where are you?"

For neither of them could see each other—not the least. Little Ellie vanished quite away, and Tom heard her voice calling him, and growing smaller and smaller, and fainter and fainter, till all was silent.

Who was frightened then but Tom? He swam up and down among the rocks, into all the halls and chambers, faster than ever he swam before, but could not find her. He shouted after her, but she did not answer; he asked all the other children, but they had not seen her; and at last he went up to the top of the water and began crying and screaming for Mrs. Doasyouwouldbedoneby, but she did not come. Then he began crying and screaming for Mrs. Bedonebyasyoudid—which perhaps was the best thing to do—for she came in a moment.

"Oh!" said Tom. "Oh dear, oh dear! I have been naughty to Ellie, and I have killed her—I know I have killed her."

"Not quite that," said the fairy; "but I have sent her away home, and she will not come back again for I do not know how long."

And at that Tom cried so bitterly, that the salt sea was swelled with his tears, and the tide was 0.3,954,620,819 of an inch

higher than it had been the day before: but perhaps that was owing to the waxing of the moon. It may have been so; but it is considered right in the new philosophy, you know, to give spiritual causes for physical phenomena—especially in parlour tables; and, of course, physical causes for spiritual ones, like thinking, and praying, and knowing right from wrong. And so they odds it till it comes even, as folks say down in Berkshire.

"How cruel of you to send Ellie away!" sobbed Tom. "However, I will find her again, if I go to the world's end to look for her."

The fairy did not slap Tom, and tell him to hold his tongue: but she took him on her lap very kindly, just as her sister would have done; and put him in mind how it was not her fault, because she was wound up inside, like watches, and could not help doing things whether she liked or not. And then she told him how he had been in the nursery long enough, and must go out now and see the world, if he intended ever to be a man; and how he must go all alone by himself, as everyone else that ever was born has to go, and see with his own eyes, and smell with his own nose, and make his own bed and lie on it, and burn his own fingers if he put them into the fire. And then she told him how many fine things there were to be seen in the world, and what an odd, curious, pleasant, orderly, respectable, well-managed, and, on the whole, successful (as, indeed, might have been expected) sort of a place it was, if people would only be tolerably brave and honest and good in it; and then she told him not to be afraid of anything he met, for nothing would harm him if he remembered all his lessons, and did what he knew was right. And at last she comforted poor little Tom so much, that he was quite eager to go, and wanted to set out that minute. "Only," he said, "if I might see Ellie once before I went!"

"Why do you want that?"

"Because—because I should be so much happier if I thought

she had forgiven me."

And in the twinkling of an eye there stood Ellie, smiling, and looking so happy that Tom longed to kiss her; but was still afraid it would not be respectful, because she was a lady born.

"I am going, Ellie!" said Tom. "I am going, if it is to the world's end. But I don't like going at all, and that's the truth."

"Pooh! pooh! pooh!" said the fairy. "You will like it very well indeed, you little rogue, and you know that at the bottom of your heart. But if you don't, I will make you like it. Come here, and see what happens to people who do only what is pleasant."

And she took out of one of her cupboards (she had all sorts of mysterious cupboards in the cracks of the rocks) the most wonderful waterproof book, full of such photographs as never were seen. For she had found out photography (and this is a fact) more than 13,598,000 years before anybody was born; and, what is more, her photographs did not merely represent light and shade, as ours do, but colour also, and all colours, as you may see if you look at a black cock's tail, or a butterfly's wing, or, indeed, most things that are or can be, so to speak. And, therefore, her photographs were very curious and famous, and the children looked with great delight for the opening of the book.

And on the title-page was written, *The History of the great and famous nation of the Doasyoulikes, who came away from the country of Hardwork, because they wanted to play on the Jews' harp all day long.*

In the first picture they saw these Doasyoulikes living in the land of Readymade, at the foot of the Happy-go-lucky Mountains, where flapdoodle grows wild; and if you want to know what that is, you must read Peter Simple.

They lived very much such a life as those jolly old Greeks in Sicily, whom you may see painted on the ancient vases, and really there seemed to be great excuses for them, for they had no need to work.

Instead of houses, they lived in the beautiful caves of tufa, and bathed in the warm springs three times a day; and, as for clothes, it was so warm there that the gentlemen walked about in little beside a cocked hat and a pair of straps, or some light summer tackle of that kind; and the ladies all gathered gossamer in autumn (when they were not too lazy) to make their winter dresses.

They were very fond of music, but it was too much trouble to learn the piano or the violin; and, as for dancing, that would have been too great an exertion. So they sat on ant-hills all day long, and played on the Jews' harp; and, if the ants bit them, why they just got up and went to the next ant-hill, till they were bitten there likewise.

And they sat under the flapdoodle-trees, and let the flapdoodle drop into their mouths; and under the vines, and squeezed the grape-juice down their throats; and if any little pigs ran about ready roasted, crying, "Come and eat me," as was their fashion in that country, they waited till the pigs ran against their mouths, and then took a bite, and were content, just as so many oysters would have been.

They needed no weapons, for no enemies ever came near their land; and no tools, for everything was ready-made to their hand; and the stern old fairy Necessity never came near them to hunt them up, and make them use their wits, or die.

And so on, and so on, and so on, till there were never such comfortable, easy-going, happy-go-lucky people in the world.

"Well, that is a jolly life," said Tom.

"You think so?" said the fairy. "Do you see that great peaked mountain there behind," said the fairy, "with smoke coming out of its top?"

"Yes."

"And do you see all those ashes, and slag, and cinders, lying about?"

"Yes."

"Then turn over the next five hundred years, and you will see what happens next."

And behold the mountain had blown up like a barrel of gunpowder, and then boiled over like a kettle, whereby one-third of the Doasyoulikes were blown into the air, and another third were smothered in ashes; so that there was only one-third left.

"You see," said the fairy, "what comes of living on a burning mountain."

"Oh, why did you not warn them?" said little Ellie.

"I did warn them all that I could. I let the smoke come out of the mountain; and wherever there is smoke there is fire. And I laid the ashes and cinders all about; and wherever there are cinders, cinders may be again. But they did not like to face facts, my dears, as very few people do; and so they invented a cock-and-bull story, which, I am sure, I never told them, that the smoke was the breath of a giant, whom some gods or other had buried under the mountain; and that the cinders were what the dwarfs roasted the little pigs whole with; and other nonsense of that kind. And, when folks are in that humour, I cannot teach them save by the good old birch rod."

And then she turned over the next five hundred years: and

there were the remnant of the Doasyoulikes, doing as they liked, as before. They were too lazy to move away from the mountain; so they said, if it has blown up once, that is all the more reason that it should not blow up again. And they were few in number: but they only said, The more the merrier, but the fewer the better fare. However, that was not quite true; for all the flapdoodle-trees were killed by the volcano, and they

had eaten all the roast pigs, who, of course, could not be expected to have little ones. So they had to live very hard, on nuts and roots which they scratched out of the ground with sticks. Some of them talked of sowing corn, as their ancestors used to do, before they came into the land of Readymade; but they had forgotten how to make ploughs (they had forgotten even how to make Jews' harps by this time), and had eaten all the seed-corn which they brought out of the land of Hardwork years since; and of course it was too much trouble to go away and find more. So they lived miserably on roots and nuts, and all the weakly little children had great stomachs, and then died.

"Why," said Tom, "they are growing no better than savages!"

"And look how ugly they are all getting!" said Ellie.

"Yes; when people live on poor vegetables instead of roast beef and plum pudding, their jaws grow large, and their lips grow coarse, like the poor Paddies who eat potatoes."

And she turned over the next five hundred years. And there they were all living up in trees, and making nests to keep off the rain. And underneath the trees lions were prowling about.

"Why," said Ellie, "the lions seem to have eaten a good many of them, for there are very few left now."

"Yes," said the fairy; "you see, it was only the strongest and most active ones who could climb the trees and so escape."

"But what great, hulking, broad-shouldered chaps they are," said Tom; "they are a rough lot as ever I saw."

"Yes, they are getting very strong now; for the ladies will not marry any but the very strongest and fiercest gentlemen, who can help them up the trees out of the lions' way."

And she turned over the next five hundred years. And in that they were fewer still, and stronger, and fiercer; but their feet had changed shape very oddly, for they laid hold of the branches with their great toes, as if they had been thumbs, just as a Hindoo tailor uses his toes to thread his needle.

The children were very much surprised, and asked the fairy whether that was her doing.

"Yes and no," she said, smiling. "It was only those who could use their feet as well as their hands who could get a good living: or, indeed, get married; so that they got the best of everything, and starved out all the rest; and those who are left keep up a regular breed of toe-thumb-men, as a breed of shorthorns, or Skye terriers, or fancy pigeons is kept up."

"But there is a hairy one among them," said Ellie.

"Ah!" said the fairy, "that will be a great man in his time, and chief of all the tribe."

And, when she turned over the next five hundred years, it was true.

For this hairy chief had had hairy children, and they hairier children still; and everyone wished to marry hairy husbands, and have hairy children too; for the climate was growing so damp that none but the hairy ones could live: all the rest coughed and sneezed, and had sore throats, and went into consumptions, before they could grow up to be men and women.

Then the fairy turned over the next five hundred years. And

they were fewer still.

"Why, there is one on the ground picking up roots," said Ellie, "and he cannot walk upright!"

No more he could; for in the same way that the shape of their feet had altered, the shape of their backs had altered also.

"Why," cried Tom, "I declare they are all apes."

"Something fearfully like it, poor foolish creatures," said the fairy. "They are grown so stupid now, that they can hardly think; for none of them have used their wits for many hundred years. They have almost forgotten, too, how to talk. For each stupid child forgot some of the words it heard from its stupid parents, and had not wits enough to make fresh words for itself. Beside, they are grown so fierce and suspicious and brutal, that they keep out of each other's way, and mope and sulk in the dark forests, never hearing each other's voice, till they have forgotten almost what speech is like. I am afraid they will all be apes very soon, and all by doing only what they liked."

And in the next five hundred years they were all dead and gone, by bad food and wild beasts and hunters; all except one tremendous old fellow with jaws like a jack, who stood full seven feet high; and M. Du Chaillu came up to him, and shot him, as he stood roaring and thumping his breast. And he remembered that his ancestors had once been men, and tried to say, "Am I not a man and a brother?" but had forgotten how to use his tongue; and then he had tried to call for a doctor, but he had forgotten the word for one. So all he said was, "Ubboboo!" and died.

And that was the end of the great and jolly nation of the Doasyoulikes. And when Tom and Ellie came to the end of the book they looked very sad and solemn; and they had good reason so to do, for they really fancied that the men were apes, and never thought, in their simplicity, of asking whether the creatures had hippopotamus majors in their brains or not: in which case, as you have been told already, they could not possibly have been apes, though they were more apish than the apes of all aperies.

"But could you not have saved them from becoming apes?" said little Ellie at last.

"At first, my dear; if only they would have behaved like men, and set to work to do what they did not like. But the longer they waited, and behaved like the dumb beasts, who only do what they like, the stupider and clumsier they grew; till at last they were past all cure, for they had thrown their own wits away. It is such things as this that help to make me so ugly, that I know not when I shall grow fair."

"And where are they all now?" asked Ellie.

"Exactly where they ought to be, my dear."

"Yes," said the fairy solemnly, half to herself, as she closed the wonderful book. "Folks say now that I can make beasts into men, by circumstance, and selection, and competition, and so forth. Well, perhaps they are right; and perhaps, again, they are wrong. That is one of the seven things which I am forbidden to tell till the coming of the Cocqcigrues; and, at all events, it is no concern of theirs. Whatever their ancestors were, men they are; and I advise them to behave as such, and act accordingly. But let them recollect this, that there are two sides to every question, and a downhill as well as an uphill road; and if I can turn beasts into men, I can, by the same laws of circumstance, and selection, and competition, turn men into beasts. You were very near being turned into a beast once or twice, little Tom. Indeed, if you had not made up your mind to go on this journey and see the world, like an Englishman, I am not sure but that you would have ended as an eft in a pond."

"Oh, dear me!" said Tom; "sooner than that, and be all over slime. I'll go this minute, if it is to the world's end."

Chapter VII

"And Nature, the old Nurse, took
The child upon her knee,
Saying 'Here is a story book
Thy father hath written for thee.

'Come wander with me,' she said,
'Into regions yet untrod,
And read what is still unread
In the Manuscripts of God. '

And he wandered away and away
With Nature, the dear old Nurse,
Who sang to him night and day
The rhymes of the universe."

LONGFELLOW.

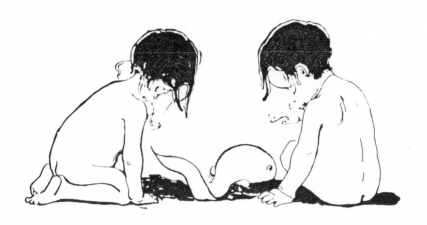

Chapter VII

 ow," said Tom, "I am ready to be off, if it's to the world's end."

"Ah!" said the fairy, "that is a brave, good boy. But you must go farther than the world's end, if you want to find Mr. Grimes; for he is at the Other-end-of-Nowhere. You must go to Shiny Wall, and through the white gate that never was opened; and then you will come to Peacepool, and Mother Carey's Haven, where the good whales go when they die. And there Mother Carey will tell you the way to the Other-end-of-Nowhere, and there you will find Mr. Grimes."

"Oh, dear!" said Tom. "But I do not know my way to Shiny Wall, or where it is at all."

"Little boys must take the trouble to find out things for themselves, or they will never grow to be men; so that you must ask all the beasts in the sea and the birds in the air, and if you have been good to them, some of them will tell you the way to Shiny Wall."

"Well," said Tom, "it will be a long journey, so I had better start at once. Good-bye, Miss Ellie; you know I am getting a big boy, and I must go out and see the world."

"I know you must," said Ellie; "but you will not forget me, Tom? I shall wait here till you come."

And she shook hands with him, and bade him good-bye. Tom longed very much again to kiss her; but he thought it would not be respectful, considering she was a lady born; so he promised not to forget her; but his little whirl-about of a head was so full of the notion of going out to see the world, that it forgot her in five minutes; however, though his head forgot her, I am glad to say his heart did not.

So he asked all the beasts in the sea, and all the birds in the air, but none of them knew the way to Shiny Wall. For why? He was still too far down south.

Then he met a ship, far larger than he had ever seen a gallant ocean steamer, with a long cloud of smoke trailing behind; and he wondered how she went on without sails, and swam up to her to see. A school of dolphins were running races round and round her, going three feet for her one, and Tom asked them the way to Shiny Wall; but they did not know. Then he tried to find out how she moved, and at last he saw her screw, and was so delighted with it that he played under her quarter all day, till he nearly had his nose knocked off by the fans, and thought it time to move. Then he watched the sailors upon deck, and the ladies, with their bonnets and parasols; but none of them could see him, because their eyes were not opened—as, indeed, most people's eyes are not.

At last there came out into the quarter-gallery a very pretty lady, in deep black widow's weeds, and in her arms a baby. She leaned over the quarter-gallery, and looked back and back to-ward England far away; and as she looked she sang:

I

"Soft, soft wind, from out the sweet south sliding,
Waft thy silver cloud-webs athwart the summer sea;
Thin, thin threads of mist on dewy fingers twining,
Weave a veil of dappled gauze to shade my babe and me.

II

"Deep, deep Love, within thine own abyss abiding,
Pour Thyself abroad, O Lord, on earth and air and sea;
Worn weary hearts within Thy holy temple hiding,
Shield from sorrow, sin, and shame my helpless babe and me."

Her voice was so soft and low, and the music of the air so sweet, that Tom could have listened to it all day. But as she held the baby over the gallery-rail, to show it the dolphins leaping and the water gurgling in the ship's wake, lo! and behold, the baby saw Tom.

He was quite sure of that; for when their eyes met, the baby smiled and held out its hands; and Tom smiled and held out his hands too; and the baby kicked and leaped, as if it wanted to jump overboard to him.

"What do you see, my darling?" said the lady; and her eyes followed the baby's till she too caught sight of Tom, swimming about among the foam-beads below.

She gave a little shriek and start; and then she said, quite quietly, "Babies in the sea? Well, perhaps it is the happiest place for them," and waved her hand to Tom, and cried, "Wait a little, darling, only a little; and perhaps we shall go with you and be at rest."

And at that an old nurse, all in black, came out and talked to her, and drew her in. And Tom turned away northward, sad and wondering; and watched the great steamer slide away into the dusk, and the lights on board peep out one by one, and die out again, and the long bar of smoke fade away into the evening mist, till all was out of sight.

And he swam northward again, day after day, till at last he met the King of the Herrings, with a curry-comb growing out of his nose, and a sprat in his mouth for a cigar, and asked him the way to Shiny Wall; so he bolted his sprat head foremost, and said:

"If I were you, young gentleman, I should go to the Allalonestone, and ask the last of the Gairfowl. She is of a very ancient clan, very nearly as ancient as my own; and knows a good deal which these modern upstarts don't, as ladies of old houses are likely to do."

Tom asked his way to her, and the King of the Herrings told him very kindly; for he was a courteous old gentleman of the old school, though he was horribly ugly, and strangely bedizened too, like the old dandies who lounge in the clubhouse windows.

But just as Tom had thanked him and set off, he called after him: "Hi! I say, can you fly?"

"I never tried," says Tom. "Why?"

"Because, if you can, I should advise you to say nothing to the old lady about it. There; take a hint. Good-bye."

And away Tom went for seven days and seven nights due north-west, till he came to a great codbank, the like of which he never saw before. The great cod lay below in tens of thousands, and gobbled shellfish all day long; and the blue

sharks roved above in hundreds, and gobbled them when they came up. So they ate, and ate, and ate each other, as they had done since the making of the world; for no man had come here yet to catch them, and find out how rich old Mother Carey is.

And there he saw the last of the Gairfowl, standing up on the Allalonestone, all alone. And a very grand old lady she was, full three feet high, and bolt upright, like some old Highland chieftainess. She had on a black velvet gown, and a white pinner and apron, and a very high bridge to her nose (which is a sure mark of high breeding), and a large pair of white spectacles on it, which made her look rather odd: but it was the ancient fashion of her house.

And instead of wings, she had two little feathery arms with which she fanned herself, and complained of the dreadful heat; and she kept on crooning an old song to herself, which she learned when she was a little baby-bird, long ago—

> *"Two little birds, they sat on a stone,*
> *One swam away, and then there was one;*
> *With a fal-lal-la-lady.*
>
> *The other swam after, and then there was none,*
> *And so the poor stone was left all alone;*
> *With a fal-lal-la-lady."*

It was "flew" away, properly, and not "swam" away: but as she could not fly, she had a right to alter it. However, it was a very fit song for her to sing, because she was a lady herself.

Tom came up to her very humbly, and made his bow: and the first thing she said was:

"Have you wings? Can you fly?"

"Oh dear, no, ma'am; I should not think of such a thing," said cunning little Tom.

"Then I shall have great pleasure in talking to you, my dear. It is quite refreshing nowadays to see anything without wings. They must all have wings, forsooth, now, every new upstart sort of bird, and fly. What can they want with flying, and raising themselves above their proper station in life? In the days of my ancestors no birds ever thought of having wings, and did very well without; and now they all laugh at me because I keep to the good old fashion. Why, the very marrocks and dovekies have got wings, the vulgar creatures, and poor little ones enough they are; and my own cousins too, the razor-bills, who are gentlefolk born, and ought to know better than to ape their inferiors."

And so she was running on, while Tom tried to get in a word edgeways; and at last he did, when the old lady got out of breath, and began fanning herself again; and then he asked if she knew the way to Shiny Wall.

"Shiny Wall? Who should know better than I? We all came from Shiny Wall, thousands of years ago, when it was decently cold, and the climate was fit for gentlefolk; but now, what with the heat, and what with these vulgar-winged things who fly up and down and eat everything, so that gentle-people's hunting is all spoilt, and one really cannot get one's living, or hardly venture off the rock for fear of being flown against by some creature that would not have dared to come within a mile of one a thousand years ago—what was I saying? Why, we have quite gone down in the world, my dear, and have nothing left but our honour. And I am the last of my family. A friend of mine and I came and settled on this rock when we were young, to be out of the way of low people. Once we were a great nation, and spread over all the Northern Isles. But men shot us so, and knocked us on the head, and took our eggs—why, if you will believe it, they say that on the coast of Labrador the sailors used to lay a plank from the rock on board the thing they call their ship, and drive us along the plank by hundreds, till we tumbled down into the ship's waist in heaps; and then, I suppose, they ate us, the nasty fellows! Well—but—what was I saying? At last there were none of us left, except on the old

Gairfowlskerry, just off the Iceland coast, up which no man could climb. Even there we had no peace; for one day, when I was quite a young girl, the land rocked, and the sea boiled, and the sky grew dark, and all the air was filled with smoke and dust, and down tumbled the old Gairfowlskerry into the sea. The dovekies and marrocks, of course, all flew away; but we were too proud to do that. Some of us were dashed to pieces, and some drowned; and those who were left got away to Eldey, and the dovekies tell me they are all dead now, and that another Gairfowlskerry has risen out of the sea close to the old one, but that it is such a poor flat place that it is not safe to live on; and so here I am left alone."

This was the Gairfowl's story, and, strange as it may seem, it is every word of it true.

"If you only had had wings!" said Tom; "then you might all have flown away too."

"Yes, young gentleman; and if people are not gentlemen and ladies, and forget that noblesse oblige, they will find it as easy to get on in the world as other people who don't care what they do. Why, if I had not recollected that noblesse oblige, I should not have been all alone now." And the poor old lady sighed.

"How was that, ma'am?"

"Why, my dear, a gentleman came hither with me, and after we had been here some time, he wanted to marry—in fact, he actually proposed to me. Well, I can't blame him; I was young, and very handsome then, I don't deny; but you see, I could not hear of such a thing, because he was my deceased sister's husband, you see?"

"Of course not, ma'am," said Tom; though, of course, he

knew nothing about it. "She was very much diseased, I suppose?"

"You do not understand me, my dear. I mean, that being a lady, and with right and honourable feelings, as our house always has had, I felt it my duty to snub him, and howk him, and peck him continually, to keep him at his proper distance; and, to tell the truth, I once pecked him a little too hard, poor fellow, and he tumbled backwards off the rock, and—really, it was very unfortunate, but it was not my fault—a shark coming by saw him flapping, and snapped him up. And since then I

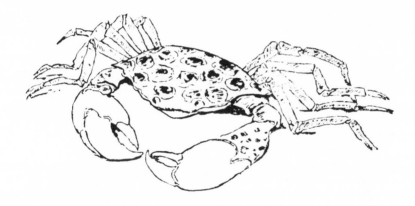

have lived all alone—

With a fal-lal-la-lady.

And soon I shall be gone, my little dear, and nobody will miss me; and then the poor stone will be left all alone."

"But, please, which is the way to Shiny Wall?" said Tom.

"Oh, you must go, my little dear—you must go. Let me see—I am sure—that is—really, my poor old brains are getting quite puzzled. Do you know, my little dear, I am afraid, if you want to know, you must ask some of these vulgar birds about, for

I have quite forgotten."

And the poor old Gairfowl began to cry tears of pure oil; and Tom was quite sorry for her; and for himself too, for he was at his wits' end whom to ask.

But by there came a flock of petrels, who are Mother Carey's own chickens; and Tom thought them much prettier than Lady Gairfowl, and so perhaps they were; for Mother Carey had had a great deal of fresh experience between the time that she invented the Gairfowl and the time that she invented them. They flitted along like a flock of black swallows, and hopped and skipped from wave to wave, lifting up their little feet behind them so daintily, and whistling to each other so tenderly, that Tom fell in love with them at once, and called them to know the way to Shiny Wall.

"Shiny Wall? Do you want Shiny Wall? Then come with us and we will show you. We are Mother Carey's own chickens, and she sends us out over all the seas, to show the good birds the way home."

Tom was delighted, and swam off to them, after he had made his bow to the Gairfowl. But she would not return his bow: but held herself bolt upright, and wept tears of oil as she sang:

"And so the poor stone was left all alone;

With a fal-lal-la-lady."

But she was wrong there; for the stone was not left all alone: and the next time that Tom goes by it, he will see a sight worth seeing.

The old Gairfowl is gone already: but there are better things come in her place; and when Tom comes he will see the fishing-

It took the form of the grandest old lady
he had ever seen.

smacks anchored there in hundreds, from Scotland, and from Ireland, and from the Orkneys, and the Shetlands, and from all the Northern ports, full of the children of the old Norse Vikings, the masters of the sea. And the men will be hauling in the great cod by thousands, till their hands are sore from the lines; and they will be making cod-liver oil and guano, and salting down the fish; and there will be a man-of-war steamer there to protect them, and a lighthouse to show them the way; and you and I, perhaps, shall go some day to the Allalonestone to the great summer sea-fair, and dredge strange creatures such as man never saw before; and we shall hear the sailors boast that it is not the worst jewel in Queen Victoria's crown, for there are eighty miles of cod bank, and food for all the poor folk in the land. That is what Tom will see, and perhaps you and I shall see it too. And then we shall not be sorry because we cannot get a gairfowl to stuff, much less find gairfowl enough to drive them into stone pens and slaughter them, as the old Norsemen did, or drive them on board along a plank till the ship was victualled with them, as the old English and French rovers used to do, of whom dear old Hakluyt tells—but we shall remember what Mr. Tennyson says, how

"The old order changeth, giving place to the new,
And God fulfils Himself in many ways."

And now Tom was all agog to start for Shiny Wall; but the petrels said no. They must go first to Allfowlsness, and wait there for the great gathering of all the seabirds, before they start for their summer breeding-places far away in the Northern isles; and there they would be sure to find some birds which were going to Shiny Wall; but where Allfowlsness was, he must promise never to tell, lest men should go there and shoot the birds, and stuff them, and put them into stupid museums, instead of leaving them to play and breed and work in Mother Carey's water garden, where they ought to be.

So where Allfowlsness is nobody must know; and all that is to be said about it is, that Tom waited there many days, and as he waited he saw a very curious sight. On the rabbit burrows on the shore there gathered hundreds and hundreds of hoodiecrows, such as you see in Cambridgeshire. And they made such a noise that Tom came on shore and went up to see what was the matter.

And there he found them holding their great caucus, which they hold every year in the North; and all their stump orators were speechifying; and for a tribune, the speaker stood on an old sheep's skull.

And they cawed and cawed, and boasted of all the clever things they had done; how many lambs' eyes they had picked out, and how many dead bullocks they had eaten, and how many young grouse they had swallowed whole, and how many grouse eggs they had flown away with, stuck on the point of their bills, which is the hoodiecrow's particularly clever feat, of which he is as proud as a gipsy is of doing the hokany-baro; and what that is, I won't tell you.

And at last they brought out the prettiest, neatest young lady crow that ever was seen, and set her in the middle, and all began abusing and vilifying, and rating, and bullyragging her, because she had stolen no grouse eggs, and had actually dared to say that she would not steal any. So she was to be tried publicly by their laws (for the hoodies always try some offenders in their great yearly parliament). And there she stood in the middle, in her black gown and grey hood, looking as meek and as neat as a quakeress, and they all bawled at her at once—

And it was in vain that she pleaded

That she did not like grouse eggs;

That she could get her living very well without them;

That she was afraid to eat them, for fear of the gamekeepers;

That she had not the heart to eat them, because the grouse were such pretty, kind, jolly birds,

And a dozen reasons more.

For all the other scaul-crows set upon her, and pecked her to death there and then, before Tom could come to help her; and then flew away, very proud of what they had done.

Now, was not this a scandalous transaction?

But they are true republicans, these hoodies, who do every one just what he likes, and make other people do so too; so that for any freedom of speech, thought, or action, which is allowed among them, they might as well be American citizens of the new school.

But the fairies took the good crow, and gave her nine new sets of feathers running, and turned her at last into the most beautiful bird of paradise with a green velvet suit and a long tail, and sent her to eat fruit in the Spice Islands, where cloves and nutmegs grow.

And Mrs. Bedonebyasyoudid settled her account with the wicked hoodies. For as they flew away, what should they find

but a nasty dead dog?—on which they all set to work, pecking and gobbling and cawing and quarrelling to their hearts' content. But the moment afterwards, they all threw up their bills into the air, and gave one screech; and then turned head over heels backward, and fell down dead, one hundred and twenty-three of them at once. For why? The fairy had told the gamekeeper in a dream to fill the dead dog full of strychnine; and so he did.

And after a while the birds began to gather at Allfowlsness, in thousands and tens of thousands, blackening all the air, swans and brant geese, harlequins and eiders, harelds and garganeys, smews and goosanders, divers and loons, grebes and dovekies, auks and razor-bills, gannets and petrels, skuas and terns, with gulls beyond all naming or numbering; and they paddled and washed and splashed and combed and brushed themselves on the sand, till the shore was white with feathers; and they quacked and clucked and gabbled and chattered and screamed and whooped as they talked over matters with their friends, and settled where they were to go and breed that summer, till you might have heard them ten miles off; and lucky it was for them that there was no one to hear them but the old keeper, who lived all alone upon the Ness, in a turf hut thatched with heather and fringed round with great stones slung across the roof by bent ropes, lest the winter gales should blow the hut right away. But he never minded the birds nor hurt them, because they were not in season; indeed, he minded but two things in the whole world, and those were, his Bible and his grouse; for he was as good an old Scotchman as ever knit stockings on a winter's night—only, when all the birds were going, he toddled out, and took off his cap to them, and wished them a merry journey and a safe return; and then gathered up all the feathers which they had left, and cleaned them to sell down south, and make featherbeds for stuffy people to lie on.

Then the petrels asked this bird and that whether they would take Tom to Shiny Wall; but one set was going to Sutherland, and one to the Shetlands, and one to Norway, and one to Spitzbergen, and one to Iceland, and one to Greenland; but none would go to Shiny Wall. So the good-natured petrels said that they would show him part of the way themselves, but they were only going as far as Jan Mayen's land; and after that he must shift for himself.

And then all the birds rose up, and streamed away in long black lines, north, and north-east, and north-west, across the bright blue summer sky; and their cry was like ten thousand packs of hounds, and ten thousand peals of bells. Only the puffins stayed behind, and killed the young rabbits, and laid their eggs in the rabbit-burrows; which was rough practice, certainly; but a man must see to his own family.

And, as Tom and the petrels went north-eastward, it began to blow right hard; for the old gentleman in the grey greatcoat, who looks after the big copper boiler in the Gulf of Mexico, had got behindhand with his work; so Mother Carey had sent an electric message to him for more steam; and now the steam was coming, as much in an hour as ought to have come in a week, puffing and roaring and swishing and swirling, till you could not see where the sky ended and the sea began. But Tom and the petrels never cared, for the gale was right abaft, and away they went over the crests of the billows, as merry as so many flying-fish.

And at last they saw an ugly sight—the black side of a great ship, waterlogged in the trough of the sea. Her funnel and her masts were overboard, and swayed and surged under her lee; her decks were swept as clean as a barn floor, and there was no living soul on board.

The petrels flew up to her, and wailed round her; for they were very sorry indeed, and also they expected to find some salt pork; and Tom scrambled on board of her and looked round, frightened and sad.

And there, in a little cot, lashed tight under the bulwark, lay a baby fast asleep; the very same baby, Tom saw at once, which he had seen in the singing lady's arms.

He went up to it, and wanted to wake it; but behold, from under the cot out jumped a little black and tan terrier dog, and began barking and snapping at Tom, and would not let him touch the cot.

Tom knew the dog's teeth could not touch him; but at least it could shove him away, and did; and he and the dog fought and struggled, for he wanted to help the baby, and did not want to throw the poor dog overboard; but, as they were struggling, there came a tall green sea, and walked in over the weather side of the ship, and swept them all into the waves.

"Oh, the baby, the baby!" screamed Tom; but the next moment he did not scream at all; for he saw the cot settling down through the green water, with the baby smiling in it, fast asleep; and he saw the fairies come up from below, and carry baby and cradle gently down in their soft arms; and then he knew it was all right, and that there would be a new water-baby in St. Brandan's Isle.

And the poor little dog?

Why, after he had kicked and coughed a little, he sneezed

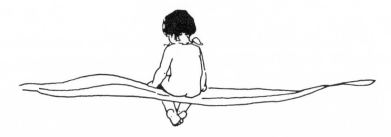

so hard, that he sneezed himself clean out of his skin, and turned into a water-dog, and jumped and danced round Tom, and ran over the crests of the waves, and snapped at the jelly-fish and the mackerel, and followed Tom the whole way to the Other-end-of-Nowhere.

Then they went on again, till they began to see the peak of Jan Mayen's Land, standing up like a white sugar-loaf, two miles above the clouds.

And there they fell in with a whole flock of mollymocks, who were feeding on a dead whale.

"These are the fellows to show you the way," said Mother Carey's chickens; "we cannot help you farther north. We don't like to get among the ice pack, for fear it should nip our toes; but the mollys dare anywhere."

So the petrels called to the mollys; but they were so busy and greedy, gobbling and pecking and spluttering and fighting over the blubber, that they did not take the least notice.

"Come, come," said the petrels, "you lazy greedy lubbers, this young gentleman is going to Mother Carey, and if you don't attend on him, you won't earn your discharge from her, you know."

"Greedy we are," says a great fat old molly, "But lazy we ain't; and, as for lubbers, we're no more lubbers than you. Let's have a look at the lad."

And he flapped right into Tom's face, and stared at him in the most impudent way (for the mollys are audacious fellows, as all whalers know), and then asked him where he hailed from, and what land sighted last.

And, when Tom told him, he seemed pleased, and said he was a good plucked one to have got so far.

"Come along, lads," he said to the rest, "and give this little chap a cast over the pack, for Mother Carey's sake. We've eaten blubber enough for to-day, we'll e'en work out a bit of our time by helping the lad."

So the mollys took Tom up on their backs, and flew off with him, laughing and joking—and oh, how they did smell of train oil!

"Who are you, you jolly birds?" asked Tom.

"We are the spirits of the old Greenland skippers" (as every sailor knows), "who hunted here, right whales and horse-whales, full hundreds of years agone. But, because we were saucy and greedy, we were all turned into mollys, to eat whale's blubber all our days. But lubbers we are none, and could sail a ship now against any man in the North Seas, though we don't hold with this new-fangled steam. And it's a shame of those black imps of petrels to call us so; but because they're her grace's pets, they think they may say anything they like."

"And who are you?" asked Tom of him, for he saw that he was the king of all the birds.

"My name is Hendrick Hudson, and a right good skipper was I; and my name will last to the world's end, in spite of all the wrong I did. For I discovered Hudson River, and I named Hudson's Bay; and many have come in my wake that dared not have shown me the way. But I was a hard man in my time, that's truth, and stole the poor Indians off the coast of Maine, and sold them for slaves down in Virginia; and at last I was so cruel to my sailors, here in these very seas, that they set me adrift in an open boat, and I never was heard of more. So now I'm the king of all the mollys, till I've worked out my time."

And now they came to the edge of the pack, and beyond it they could see Shiny Wall looming, through mist, and snow, and storm. But the pack rolled horribly upon the swell, and the ice giants fought and roared, and leapt upon each other's backs, and ground each other to powder, so that Tom was afraid to venture among them, lest he should be ground to powder too. And he was the more afraid, when he saw lying among the ice pack the wrecks of many a gallant ship; some with masts and yards all standing, some with the seamen frozen fast on board. Alas, alas, for them! They were all true English hearts; and they came to their end like good knights-errant, in searching for the white gate that never was opened yet.

But the good mollys took Tom and his dog up and flew with them safe over the pack and the roaring ice giants, and set them down at the foot of Shiny Wall.

"And where is the gate?" asked Tom.

"There is no gate," said the mollys.

"No gate?" cried Tom aghast.

"None; never a crack of one, and that's the whole of the secret, as better fellows, lad, than you have found to their cost; and if there had been, they'd have killed by now every right whale that swims the sea."

"What am I to do, then?"

"Dive under the floe, to be sure, if you have pluck."

"I've not come so far to turn now," said Tom; "so here goes

for a header."

"A lucky voyage to you, lad," said the mollys; "we knew you were one of the right sort. So good-bye."

"Why don't you come too?" asked Tom.

But the mollys only wailed sadly "We can't go yet, we can't go yet," and flew away over the pack.

So Tom dived under the great white gate which never was opened yet, and went on in black darkness, at the bottom of the sea, for seven days and seven nights. And yet he was not a bit frightened. Why should he be? He was a brave English lad, whose business is to go out and see all the world.

And at last he saw the light, and clear clear water overhead; and up he came a thousand fathoms, among clouds of sea-moths, which fluttered round his head. There were moths with pink heads and wings and opal bodies, that flapped about slowly; moths with brown wings that flapped about quickly; yellow shrimps that hopped and skipped most quickly of all; and jellies of all the colours in the world, that neither hopped nor skipped, but only dawdled and yawned, and would not get out of his way. The dog snapped at them till his jaws were tired; but Tom hardly minded them at all, he was so eager to get to the top of the water, and see the pool where the good whales go.

And a very large pool it was, miles and miles across, though the air was so clear that the ice cliffs on the opposite side looked as if they were close at hand. All round it the ice cliffs rose, in walls and spires and battlements, and caves and bridges, and stories and galleries, in which the ice-fairies live, and drive away the storms and clouds, that Mother Carey's pool may lie calm from year's end to year's end. And the sun acted policeman, and walked round outside every day, peeping just over the top of the ice wall, to see that all went right; and now and then he played conjuring tricks, or had an exhibition of fireworks, to amuse the ice-fairies. For he would make himself into four or five suns at once, or paint the sky with rings and crosses and crescents of white fire, and stick himself in the middle of them, and wink at the fairies; and I dare say they were very much amused, for anything's fun in the country.

And there the good whales lay, the happy sleepy beasts, upon the still oily sea. They were all right whales, you must know, and finners, and razor-backs, and bottle-noses, and spotted sea-unicorns with long ivory horns. But the sperm whales are such raging ramping, roaring, rumbustious fellows, that. if Mother Carey let them in, there would be no more peace in Peacepool. So she packs them away in a great pond by themselves at the South Pole, two hundred and sixty-three miles south-south-east of Mount Erebus, the great volcano in the ice; and there they butt each other with their ugly noses, day and night from year's end to year's end. And if they think that sport—why, so do their American cousins.

But here there were only good quiet beasts, lying about like the black hulls of sloops, and blowing every now and then jets of white steam, or sculling round with their huge mouths open, for the sea-moths to swim down their throats. There were no threshers there to thresh their poor old backs, or sword-fish to stab their stomachs, or saw-fish to rip them up, or ice-sharks to bite lumps out of their sides, or whalers to harpoon and lance them. They were quite safe and happy there; and all they had to do was to wait quietly in Peacepool, till Mother Carey sent for them to make them out of old beasts into new.

Tom swam up to the nearest whale, and asked the way to Mother Carey.

"There she sits in the middle," said the whale.

Tom looked; but he could see nothing in the middle of the pool, but one peaked iceberg; and he said so.

"That's Mother Carey," said the whale, "as you will find when you get to her. There she sits making old beasts into new all the year round."

"How does she do that?"

"That's her concern, not mine," said the old whale; and yawned so wide (for he was large) that there swam into his mouth 943 sea-moths, 13,846 jelly-fish no bigger than pins' heads, a string of salpae nine yards long, and forty-three little ice-crabs, who gave each other a parting pinch all round, tucked their legs under their stomachs, and determined to die decently, like Julius Caesar.

"I suppose," said Tom, "she cuts up a great whale like you into a whole shoal of porpoises?"

At which the old whale laughed so violently that he coughed

up all the creatures; who swam away again very thankful at having escaped out of that terrible whalebone net of his, from which bourne no traveller returns; and Tom went on to the iceberg, wondering.

And, when he came near it, it took the form of the grandest old lady he had ever seen—a white marble lady, sitting on a white marble throne. And from the foot of the throne there swum away, out and out into the sea, millions of new-born creatures, of more shapes and colours than man ever dreamed. And they were Mother Carey's children, whom she makes out of the sea-water all day long.

He expected, of course like some grown people who ought to know better—to find her snipping, piecing, fitting, stitching, cobbling, basting, filing, planing, hammering, turning, polishing, moulding, measuring, chiselling, clipping, and so forth, as men do when they go to work to make anything.

But, instead of that, she sat quite still with her chin upon her hand, looking down into the sea with two great grand blue eyes, as blue as the sea itself. Her hair was as white as the snow—for she was very very old—in fact, as old as anything which you are likely to come across, except the difference between right and wrong.

And, when she saw Tom, she looked at him very kindly.

"What do you want, my little man? It is long since I have seen a water-baby here."

Tom told her his errand, and asked the way to the Other-end-of-Nowhere.

"You ought to know yourself, for you have been there already."

"Have I, ma'am? I'm sure I forget all about it."

"Then look at me."

And, as Tom looked into her great blue eyes, he recollected the way perfectly.

Now, was not that strange?

"Thank you, ma'am," said Tom. "Then I won't trouble your ladyship any more; I hear you are very busy."

"I am never more busy than I am now," she said, without stirring a finger.

"I heard, ma'am, that you were always making new beasts out of old."

"So people fancy. But I am not going to trouble myself to make things, my little dear. I sit here and make them make themselves."

"You are a clever fairy, indeed," thought Tom. And he was quite right.

That is a grand trick of good old Mother Carey's, and a grand answer, which she has had occasion to make several times to impertinent people.

There was once, for instance, a fairy who was so clever that she found out how to make butterflies. I don't mean sham ones; no, but real live ones, which would fly, and eat, and lay eggs, and do everything that they ought; and she was so proud of her skill that she went flying straight off to the North Pole, to boast to Mother Carey how she could make butterflies.

But Mother Carey laughed.

"Know, silly child," she said, "that anyone can make things, if they will take time and trouble enough; but it is not everyone who, like me, can make things make themselves."

But people do not yet believe that Mother Carey is as clever as all that comes to; and they will not till they, too, go the Journey to the Other-end-of-Nowhere.

"And now, my pretty little man," said Mother Carey, "you are sure you know the way to the Other-end-of-Nowhere?"

Tom thought; and behold, he had forgotten it utterly.

"That is because you took your eyes off me."

Tom looked at her again and recollected, and then looked away, and forgot in an instant.

"But what am I to do, madam? For I can't keep looking at you when I am somewhere else."

"You must do without me, as most people have to do, for nine hundred and ninety-nine thousandths of their lives; and look at the dog instead; for he knows the way well enough, and will not forget it. Besides, you may meet some very queer-tempered people there, who will not let you pass without this passport of mine, which you must hang round your neck and take care of; and, of course, as the dog will always go behind you, you must go the whole way backward."

"Backward!" cried Tom. "Then I shall not be able to see my way."

"On the contrary, if you look forward, you will not see a step before you, and be certain to go wrong; but, you look behind you, and watch carefully whatever you have passed, and especially keep your eye on the dog who goes by instinct, and therefore can't go wrong, you will know what is coming next as plainly as you saw it in a looking-glass."

Tom was very much astonished: but he obeyed her, for he had learnt always to believe what the fairies told him.

"So it is, my dear child," said Mother Carey; "and I will tell you a story, which will show you that I am perfectly right, as it is my custom to be."

"Once on a time, there were two brothers. One was called Prometheus, because he always looked before him, and boasted that he was wise beforehand. The other was called Epimetheus, because he always looked behind him, and did not boast at all; but said humbly, like the Irishman, that he had sooner prophesy after the event.

"Well, Prometheus was a very clever fellow, of course, and invented all sorts of wonderful things. But, unfortunately, when they were set to work, to work was just what they would not do; wherefore very little has come of them, and very little is left of them; and now nobody knows what they were, save a few archaeological old gentlemen who scratch in queer corners, and find little there save Ptinum Furem, Blaptem Mortisagam, Acarum, Horridum, and Tineam Laciniarum.

"But Epimetheus was a very slow fellow, certainly, and went among men for a clod, and a muff, and a milksop, and a slowcoach, and a bloke, and a boodle, and so forth. And very little he did, for many years; but what he did, he never had to do over again."

"And what happened at last? There came to the two brothers the most beautiful creature that ever was seen, Pandora by name; which means, All the gifts of the Gods. But because she had a strange box in her hand, this fanciful, forecasting, suspicious, prudential, theoretical, deductive, prophesying Prometheus, who was always settling what was going to happen, would have nothing to do with pretty Pandora and her box.

"But Epimetheus took her and it, as he took everything that came; and married her for better for worse as every man ought whenever he has even the chance of a good wife. And they opened the box between them, of course, to see what was inside; for, else, of what possible use could it have been to them?

"And out flew all the ills which flesh is heir to; all the children of the four great bogies, Self-will, Ignorance, Fear, and Dirt—for instance:

Measles,	*Quacks,*
Scarlatina,	*Unpaid Bills,*
Idols,	*Tight stays,*
Hooping-coughs,	*Potatoes,*
Wars,	*Bad Wine,*
Peacemongers,	*Despots,*
Famines,	*Demagogues,*

and, worst of all, Naughty Boys and Girls:

but one thing remained at the bottom of the box, and that was, Hope.

"So Epimetheus got a great deal of trouble, as most men do

in this world; but he got the three best things in the world into the bargain—a good wife, and experience, and hope; while Prometheus had just as much trouble, and a great deal more (as you will hear), of his own making; with nothing beside, save fancies spun out of his own brain, as a spider spins her web out of her stomach.

"And Prometheus kept on looking before him so far ahead, that as he was running about with a box of lucifers (which were the only useful things he ever invented, and do as much harm as good), he trod on his own nose, and tumbled down

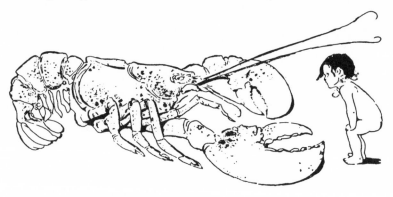

(as most deductive philosophers do), whereby he set the Thames on fire; and they have hardly put it out again yet. So he had to be chained to the top of a mountain, with a vulture by him to give him a peck whenever he stirred, lest he should turn the whole world upside down with his prophecies and his theories.

"But stupid old Epimetheus went working and grubbing on, with the help of his wife Pandora, always looking behind him to see what had happened, till he really learnt to know now and then what would happen next; and understood so well which side his bread was buttered, and which way the cat jumped, that he began to make things which would work, and go on working, too; to till and drain the ground, and to make looms, and ships, and railroads, and steam ploughs, and electric telegraphs, and all the things which you see in the Great Exhibition; and to foretell famine, and bad weather, and the price of stocks, and the end of President Lincoln's policy; till at last he grew as rich as a Jew, and as fat as a farmer; and people thought twice before they meddled with him, but only once before they asked him to help them; for, because he earned his money well, he could afford to spend it well likewise.

"And his children are the men of science, who get good lasting work done in the world, but the children of Prometheus are the fanatics, and the theorists, and the bigots, and the bores, and the noisy windy people, who go telling silly folk what will happen, instead of looking to see what has happened already."

Now, was not Mother Carey's a wonderful story? And, I am happy to say, Tom believed it every word.

For so it happened to Tom likewise. He was very sorely tried; for though. by keeping the dog to heels (or rather to toes, for he had to walk backward), he could see pretty well which way the dog was hunting, yet it was much slower work to go backwards than to go forwards. But, what was more trying still, no sooner had he got out of Peacepool, than there came running to him all the conjurors, fortune-tellers, astrologers, prophesiers, projectors, prestigiators, as many as were in those parts (and there are too many of them everywhere), Old Mother Shipton on her broomstick, with Merlin, Thomas the Rhymer, Gerbertus, Rabanus Maurus, Nostradamus, Zadkiel, Raphael Moore, Old Nixon, and a good many in black coats and white ties who might have known better, considering in what century they were born, all bawling and screaming at him, "Look ahead, only look ahead; and we will show you what man never saw before, and right away to the end of the world!"

But I am proud to say that, though Tom had not been at Cambridge—for, if he had, he would have certainly been senior wrangler—he was such a little dogged, hard, gnarly, foursquare brick of an English boy, that he never turned his head round once all the way from Peacepool to the Other-end-of-Nowhere: but kept his eye on the dog, and let him pick out the scent, hot or cold, straight or crooked, wet or dry, up hill or down dale; by which means he never made a single mistake, and saw all the wonderful and hitherto by-no-mortal-man-imagined things, which it is my duty to relate to you in the next chapter.

Chapter VIII

"Come to me, O ye children!
For I hear you at your play;
And the questions that perplexed me
Have vanished quite away.

"Ye open the Eastern windows,
That look towards the sun,
Where thoughts are singing swallows,
And the brooks of morning run.

"For what are all our contrivings
And the wisdom of our books,
When compared with your caresses,
And the gladness of your looks?

"Ye are better than all the ballads
That ever eere sung or said;
For ye are living poems,
And all the rest are dead."

LONGFELLOW.

Chapter VIII and Last

ERE begins the never-to-be-too-much-studied account of the nine-hundred-and-ninety-ninth part of the wonderful things which Tom saw on his journey to the Other-end-of-Nowhere; which all good little children are requested to read; that, if ever they get to the Other-end-of-Nowhere, as they may very probably do, they may not burst out laughing, or try to run away, or do any other silly, vulgar thing which may offend Mrs. Bedonebyasyoudid.

Now, as soon as Tom had left Peacepool, he came to the white lap of the great sea-mother, ten thousand fathoms deep;

where she makes world-pap all day long, for the steam-giants to knead, and the fire-giants to bake, till it has risen and hardened into mountain-loaves and island-cakes.

And there Tom was very near being kneaded up in the world-pap, and turned into a fossil water-baby; which would have astonished the Geological Society of New Zealand some hundreds of thousands of years hence.

For, as he walked along in the silence of the sea twilight, on the soft white ocean floor, he was aware of a hissing, and a roaring, and a thumping, and a pumping, as of all the steam-engines in the world at once. And, when he came near, the water grew boiling hot; not that that hurt him in the least; but it also grew as foul as gruel; and every moment he stumbled over dead shells, and fish, and sharks, and seals, and whales, which had been killed by the hot water.

And at last he came to the great sea-serpent himself, lying dead at the bottom; and, as he was too thick to scramble over, Tom had to walk round him three-quarters of a mile and more, which put him out of his path sadly; and, when he had got round, he came to the place called Stop. And there he stopped, and just in time.

For he was on the edge of a vast hole in the bottom of the sea, up which was rushing and roaring clear steam enough to work all the engines in the world at once; so clear, indeed, that it was quite light at moments; and Tom could see almost up to the top of the water above, and down below into the pit for nobody knows how far.

But, as soon as he bent his head over the edge, he got such a rap on the nose from pebbles, that he jumped back again; for the steam, as it rushed up, rasped away the sides of the hole, and hurled it up into the sea in a shower of mud and gravel and ashes; and then it spread all around, and sank again, and covered in the dead fish so fast, that before Tom had stood there five minutes he was buried in silt up to his ankles, and began to be afraid that he should have been buried alive.

And perhaps he would have been, but that while he was thinking, the whole piece of ground on which he stood was torn off and blown upwards, and away flew Tom a mile up through the sea, wondering what was coming next.

At last he stopped—thump! and found himself tight in the legs of the most wonderful bogey which he had ever seen.

It had I don't know how many wings, as big as the sails of a windmill, and spread out in a ring like them; and with them it hovered over the steam which rushed up, as a bali hovers over the top of a fountain. And for every wing above it had a leg below, with a claw like a comb at the tip, and a nostril at the root; and in the middle it had no stomach and one eye; and as for its mouth, that was all on one side, as the madreporiform tubercle in a star-fish is. Well, it was a very strange beast; but no stranger than some dozens which you may see.

"What do you want here," it cried quite peevishly, "getting in my way?" and it tried to drop Tom: but he held on tight to its claws, thinking himself safer where he was.

So Tom told him who he was, and what his errand was. And the thing winked its one eye, and sneered—

"I am too old to be taken in in that way. You have come after gold—I know you have."

"Gold! What is gold?" And really Tom did not know; but the suspicious old bogey would not believe him.

But after a while Tom began to understand a little. For, as the vapours came up out of the hole, the bogey smelt them with his nostrils, and combed them and sorted them with his combs; and then, when they steamed up through them against his wings, they were changed into showers and streams of metal. From one wing fell gold dust, and from another silver, and from another copper, and from another tin, and from another lead, and so on, and sank into the soft mud, into veins and cracks, and hardened there. Whereby it comes to pass that the rocks are full of metal.

But, all of a sudden, somebody shut off the steam below, and the hole was left empty in an instant; and then down rushed the water into the hole in such a whirlpool that the bogey man spun round and round as fast as a tee-totum. But that was all in his day's work like a fair fall with the hounds; so all he did was to say to Tom—

"Now is your time, youngster to get down, if you are in earnest, which I don't believe."

"You'll soon see," said Tom; and away he went as bold as Baron Munchausen, and shot down the rushing cataract like a salmon at Ballisodare.

And, when he got to the bottom, he swam till he was washed on shore safe upon the Other-end-of-Nowhere: and he found it, to his surprise, as most other people do, much more like This-end-of-Somewhere than he had been in the habit of expecting.

And first he went through Waste-paper-land, where all the stupid books lie in heaps, up hill and down dale, like leaves in a winter wood; and there he saw people digging and grubbing among them, to make worse books out of bad ones, and thrashing chaff to save the dust of it; and a very good trade they drove thereby, especially among children.

Then he went by the sea of slops, to the mountain of messes, and the territory of tuck, where the ground was very sticky, for it was all made of bad toffee (not Everton toffee, of course), and full of deep cracks and holes choked with wind-fallen fruit, and green gooseberries, and sloest and crabs, and whinberries, and hips and haws, and all the nasty things which little children will eat if they can get them. But the fairies hide them out of the way in that country as fast as they can, and very hard work

they have, and of very little use it is. For as fast as they hide away the old trash, foolish and wicked people make fresh trash full of lime and poisonous paints, and actually go and steal receipts out of old Madame Science's big book to invent poisons for little children, and sell them at wakes and fairs and tuckshops. Very well. Let them go on. Dr. Letheby and Dr. Hassall cannot catch them, though they are setting traps for them all day long. But the Fairy with the birch-rod will catch them all in time, and make them begin at one corner of their shops, and eat their way out at the other; by which time they will have got such stomach-aches as will cure them of poisoning little children.

Next he saw all the little people in the world, writing all the little books in the world, about all the other little people in the world; probably because they had no great people to write about; and if the names of the books were not Squeeky, nor the Pumplighter, nor the Narrow Narrow World, nor the Hills of the Chattermuch, nor the Children's Twaddeday, why then they were something else. And all the rest of the little people in the world read the books, and thought themselves each as good as the President; and perhaps they were right, for everyone knows his own business best. But Tom thought he would sooner have a jolly good fairy tale, about Jack the Giant-killer or Beauty and the Beast, which taught him something that he didn't know already.

And next he came to the centre of Creation (the hub, they call it there), which lies in latitude 42.21 South, and longitude 108.56 East.

And there he found all the wise people instructing mankind in the science of spirit-rapping, while their house was burning over their heads; and when Tom told them of the fire, they held an indignation meeting forthwith, and unanimously determined to hang Tom's dog for coming into their country with gunpowder in his mouth. Tom couldn't help saying that though they did fancy they had carried all the wit away with them out of Lincolnshire two hundred years ago, yet if they had had one such Lincolnshire nobleman among them as good old Lord Yarborough, he would have called for the fire-engines before he hanged other people's dogs. But it was of no use, and the dog was hanged; and Tom couldn't even have his carcase; for they had abolished the have-his-carcase act in that country, for fear lest when rogues fell out, honest men should come by their own. And so they would have succeeded perfectly, as they always do, only that (as they also always do) they failed in one little particular, viz., that the dog would not die, being a water-dog, but bit their fingers so abominably that they were forced to let him go, and Tom likewise, as British subjects. Whereon they recommenced rapping for the spirits of their fathers; and very much astonished the poor old spirits were when they came, and saw how, according to the laws of Mrs. Bedonebyasyoudid, their descendants had weakened their constitution by hard living.

Then came Tom to the Island of Polupragmosyne, which some call Rogues' Harbour (but they are wrong; for that is in the middle of Bramshill Bushest and the county police have cleared it out long ago). There everyone knows his neighbour's business better than his own; and a very noisy place it is, as might be expected, considering that all the inhabitants are ex-officio on the wrong side of the house in the "Parliament of Man, and the Federation of the World"; and are always making wry mouths, and crying that the fairies' grapes were sour.

There Tom saw ploughs drawing horses, nails driving hammers, birds' nests taking boys, books making authors, bulls keeping china-shops, monkeys shaving cats, dead dogs dril-ling live lions, blind brigadiers shelfed as principals of col-leges, play-actors

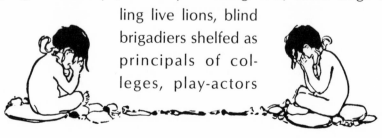

not in the least shelfed as popular preachers; and, in short, every one set to do something which he had not learnt, because in what he had learnt, or pretended to learn, he had failed.

There stands the Pantheon of the Great Unsuccessful, from the builders of the Tower of Babel to those of the Trafalgar Fountains; in which politicians lecture on the constitutions which ought to have marched, conspirators on the revolutions which ought to have succeeded, economists on the schemes which ought to have made everyone's fortune, projectors on the discoveries which ought to have set the Thames on fire; and (in due time) presidents on the union which ought to have re-united, and secretaries of state on the green-backs which ought to have done just as well as hard money. There cobblers lecture on orthopedy (whatsoever that may be) because they cannot sell their shoes; and poets on Aesthetics (whatsoever that may be) because they cannot sell their poetry. There philosophers demonstrate that England would be the freest and richest country in the world, if she would only turn Papist again; penny-a-liners abuse *The Times*, because they have not wit enough to get on its staff; and young ladies walk about with lockets of Charles the First's hair (or of somebody else's, when the Jews' genuine stock is used up), inscribed with the neat and appropriate legend—which indeed is popular through all that land, and which, I hope, you will learn to translate in due time, and to perpend likewise:—

"Victrix causa diis placuit, sed victa puellis."

When he got into the middle of the town, they all set on him at once, to show him his way; or rather, to show him that he did not know his way; for as for asking him what way he wanted to go, no one ever thought of that.

But one pulled him hither, and another poked him thither, and a third cried—

"You mustn't go west, I tell you; it is destruction to go west."

"But I am not going west, as you may see," said Tom.

And another, "The east lies here, my dear; I assure you this is the east."

"But I don't want to go east," said Tom.

"Well then at all events, whichever way you are going, you are going wrong," cried they all with one voice—which was the only thing which they ever agreed about; and all pointed at once to all the thirty-and-two points of the compass, till Tom thought all the signposts in England had got together, and fallen fighting.

And whether he would have ever escaped out of the town, it is hard to say, if the dog had not taken it into his head that they were going to pull his master in pieces, and tackled them so sharply about the gastrocnemius muscle, that he gave them some business of their own to think of at last; and while they were rubbing their bitten calves, Tom and the dog got safe away.

On the borders of that island he found Gotham, where the wise men live; the same who dragged the pond because the moon had fallen into it, and planted a hedge round the cuckoo, to keep spring all the year. And he found them bricking up the town gate, because it was so wide that little folks could not get through. And, when he asked why, they told him they were expanding their liturgy. So he went on; for it was no business

of his; only he could not help saying that in his country, if the
kitten could not get in at the same hole as the cat, she might
stay outside and mew.

But he saw the end of such fellows, when he came to the
island of the Golden Asses, where nothing but thistles grow.
For there they were all turned into mokes with ears a yard
long, for meddling with matters which they do not understand,
as Lucius did in the story. And like him, mokes they must
remain, till, by the laws of development, the thistles develop
into roses. Till then, they must comfort themselves with the
thought, that the longer their ears are, the thicker their hides;
and so a good beating don't hurt them.

Then came Tom to the great land of Hearsay, in which are
no less than thirty and odd kings, beside half a dozen Republics,
and perhaps more by next mail.

And there he fell in with a deep, dark, deadly, and destructive
war, waged by the princes and potentates of those parts, both
spiritual and temporal, against what do you think? One thing
I am sure of. That unless I told you you would never know;
nor how they waged that war either; for all their strategy and
art military consisted in the safe and easy process of stopping
their ears and screaming, "Oh, don't tell us!" and then running
away.

So when Tom came into the land, he found them all high
and low, man, woman, and child, running for their lives day
and night continually, and entreating not to be told they didn't
know what; only the land being an island, and they having a
dislike to the water (being a musty lot for the most part) they
ran round and round the shore for ever, which (as the island
was exactly of the same circumference as the planet on which

"You are our dear Mrs. Do-as-you-would-be-done-by."

we have the honour of living) was hard work, especially to those who had business to look after. But before them, as bandmaster and fugleman, ran a gentleman shearing a pig; the melodious strains of which animal led them for ever, if not to conquest, still to flight; and kept up their spirits mightily with the thought that they would at least have the pig's wool for their pains.

And running after them, day and night, came such a poor, lean, seedy, hard-worked old giant, as ought to have been

cockered up, and had a good dinner given him, and a good wife found him, and been set to play with little children; and then he would have been a very presentable old fellow after all; for he had a heart, though it was considerably overgrown with brains.

He was made up principally of fish bones and parchment, put together with wire and Canada balsam; and smelt strongly of spirits, though he never drank anything but water; but spirits he used somehow, there was no denying. He had a great pair of spectacles on his nose, and a butterfly net in one hand, and a geological hammer in the other; and was hung all over with pockets full of collecting boxes, bottle, microscopes, telescopes, barometers, ordnance maps, scalpels, forcepts, photographic apparatus, and all other tackle for finding out everything about everything, and a little more too. And, most strange of all, he was running not forwards but backwards, as fast as he could.

Away all the good folks ran from him, except Tom, who stood his ground and dodged between his legs; and the giant, when he had passed him, looked down, and cried, as if he was quite pleased and comforted—

"What? Who are you? And you actually don't run away, like all the rest?" But he had to take his spectacles off, Tom remarked, in order to see him plainly.

Tom told him who he was; and the giant pulled out a bottle and a cork instantly, to collect him with.

But Tom was too sharp for that, and dodged between his legs and in front of him; and then the giant could not see him at all.

"No, no, no!" said Tom, "I've not been round the world, and through the world, and up to Mother Carey's haven, beside being caught in a net and called a Holothurian and a Cephalopod, to be bottled up by any old giant like you."

And when the giant understood what a great traveller Tom had been, he made a truce with him at once, and would have kept him there to this day to pick his brain, so delighted was he at finding anyone to tell him what he did not know before.

"Ah, you lucky little dog!" said he at last, quite simply—for he was the simplest, pleasantest, kindliest old Doinie Sampson of a giant that ever turned the world upside down without intending—"Ah, you lucky little dog! If I had only been where you have been, to see what you have seen!"

"Well," said Tom, "if you want to do that you had best put your head under water for a few hours, as I did; and turn into a water-baby, or some other baby, and then you might have a chance."

"Turn into a baby, eh? If I could do that, and know what was happening to me for but one hour, I should know everything then, and be at rest. But I can't; I can't be a little child again; and I suppose if I could, it would be no use, because then I should know nothing about what was happening to me. Ah, you lucky little dog!" said the poor old giant.

"But why do you run after all these poor people?" said Tom, who liked the giant very much.

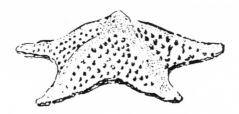

"My dear, it's they that have been running after me, father and son, for hundreds and hundreds of years, throwing stones at me till they have knocked my spectacles fifty times, and calling me a malignant and a turbaned Turk, who beat a Venetian and traduced the state—goodness only knows what they mean, for I never read poetry—and hunting me round and round—though catch me they can't, for every time I go over the same ground, I go the faster, and grow the bigger.

While all I want is to be friends with them, and to tell them something to their advantage, like Mr. Joseph Ady; only somehow they are so strangely afraid of hearing it. But, I suppose I am not a man of the world, and have no tact."

"But why don't you turn round and tell them so?"

"Because I can't. You see, I am one of the sons of Epimetheus, and must go backwards, if I am to go at all."

"But why don't you stop, and let them come up to you?"

"Why, my dear, only think. If I did, all the butterflies and cockyolybirds would fly past me, and then I could catch no more new species, and should grow rusty and mouldy, and die. And I don't intend to do that, my dear; for I have a destiny before me, they say; though what it is I don't know, and don't care."

"Don't care?" said Tom.

"No. Do the duty which lies nearest you, and catch the first beetle you come across, is my motto; and I have thriven by it for some hundred years. Now, I must go on. Dear me while I have been talking to you, at least nine new species have escaped me."

And on went the giant, behind before like a bull in a china shop, till he ran into the steeple of the great idol temple (for they are all idolaters in those parts, of course, else they would never be afraid of giants), and knocked the upper half clean off, hurting himself horribly about the small of the back.

But little he cared; for as soon as the ruins of the steeple were well between his legs, he poked and peered among the falling stones, and shifted his spectacles, and pulled out his pocket-magnifier, and cried—

"An entirely new Oniscus, and three obscure Podurelae! Beside a moth which M. le Roi des Papillons (though he, like all Frenchmen, is given to hasty inductions) says is confined to the limits of the Glacial Drift. This is most important!"

And down he sat on the nave of the temple (not being a man of the world) to examine his Podurellae. Whereon (as was to be expected) the roof caved in bodily smashing the idols, and sending the priests flying out of doors and windows, like rabbits out of a burrow when a ferret goes in.

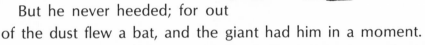

But he never heeded; for out of the dust flew a bat, and the giant had him in a moment.

"Dear me!" This is even more important! Here is a cognate species to that which Macgilliwaukie Brown insists is confined to the Buddhist Temples of Little Thibet; and now when I look at it, it may be only a variety produced by difference of climate!"

And having bagged his bat, up he got, and on he went; while all the people ran, being in none the better humour for having their temple smashed for the sake of three obscure species of Podurella, and a Buddhist bat.

"Well?" thought Tom; "this is a very pretty quarrel, with a good deal to be said on both sides. But it is no business of mine."

And no more it was; because he was a water-baby, and had the original sow by the right ear; which you will never have, unless you be a baby, whether of the water, the land, or the air, matters not, provided you can only keep on continually being a baby.

So the giant ran round after the people, and the people ran round after the giant, and they are running unto this day for aught I know, or do not know; and will run till either he, or they, or both, turn into little children. And then, as Shakespeare says (and therefore it must be true)—

"Jack shall have Gill
Nought shall go ill
The man shall have his mare again, and all go well."

Then Tom came to a very famous island, which was called, in the days of the great traveller Captain Gulliver, the Isle of Laputa. But Mrs. Bedonebyasyoudid has named it over again, the Isle of Tomtoddies, all heads and no bodies.

And when Tom came near it, he heard such a grumbling and grunting and growling and wailing and weeping and whining that he thought people must be ringing little pigs, or cropping puppies' ears, or drowning kittens; but when he came nearer still, he began to hear words among the noise; which was the Tomtoddies' song which they sing morning and evening, and all night too, to their great idol Examination—

"I can 't learn my lesson: the examiner's coming!"

And that was the only song which they knew.

And when Tom got on shore the first thing he saw was a great pillar, on one side of which was inscribed, "Playthings not allowed here;" at which he was so shocked that he would not stay to see what was written on the other side. Then he looked round for the people of the island; but instead of men, women, and children, he found nothing but turnips and radishes, beet and mangold wurzel, without a single green leaf among them, and half of them burst and decayed, with toadstools growing out of them. Those which were left began crying to Tom, in half a dozen different languages at once, and all of them badly spoken, "I can't learn my lesson; do come and help me!" And one cried, "Can you show me how to extract this square root?"

And another, "Can you tell me the distance between a Lyrce and, B Camelopardalis?"

And another, "What is the latitude and longitude of Snooksville, in Noman's County, Oregon, U.S.?"

And another, "What was the name of Mutius Scaevola's thirteenth cousin's grandmother's maid's cat?"

And another, "How long would it take a school inspector of average activity to tumble head over heels from London to York?"

And another, "Can you tell me the name of a place that nobody ever heard of, where nothing ever happened, in a country which has not been discovered yet?"

And another, "Can you show me how to correct this hopelessly corrupt passage of Graidiocolosyrtus Tabenniticus, on the cause why crocodiles have no tongues?"

And so on, and so on, and so on, till one would have thought they were all trying for tide-waiters' places, or cornetcies in the heavy dragoons.

"And what good on earth

will it do you if I did tell you?" quoth Tom.

Well, they didn't know that; all they knew was the examiner was coming.

Then Tom stumbled on the hugest and softest nimble-comequick turnip you ever saw filling a hole in a crop of swedes, and it cried to him, "Can you tell me anything at all about anything you like?"

"About what?" says Tom.

"About anything you like; for as fast as I learn things I forget them again. So my mamma says that my intellect is not adapted for methodic science, and says that I must go in for general information."

Tom told him that he did not know general information, nor any officers in the army; only he had a friend once that went for a drummer—but he could tell him a great many strange things which he had seen in his travels.

So he told him prettily enough, while the poor turnip listened very carefully; and the more he listened, the more he forgot, and the more water ran out of him.

Tom thought he was crying; but it was only his poor brains

running away, from being worked so hard; and as Tom talked, the unhappy turnip streamed down all over with juice, and split and shrank till nothing was left of him but rind and water; whereat Tom ran away in a fright, for he thought he might be taken up for killing the turnip.

But, on the contrary, the turnip's parents were highly delighted, and considered him a saint and a martyr, and put up a long inscription over his tomb about his wonderful talents, early development, and unparalleled precocity. Were they not a foolish couple? But there was a still more foolish couple next to them, who were beating a wretched little radish, no bigger than my thumb, for sullenness and obstinacy and willful stupidity, and never knew that the reason why it couldn't learn or hardly even speak was, that there was a great worm inside it eating out all its brains. But even they are no foolisher than some hundred score of papas and mammas, who fetch the rod when they ought to fetch a new toy, and send to the dark cupboard instead of to the doctor.

Tom was so puzzled and frightened with all he saw that he was longing to ask the meaning of it; and at last he stumbled over a respectable old stick lying half covered with earth. But a very stout and worthy stick it was, for it belonged to good Roger Ascham in old time, and had carved on its head King Edward the Sixth, with the Bible in his hand.

"You see," said the stick, "there were as pretty little children once as you could wish to see, and might have been so still if they had been only left to grow up like human beings, and then handed over to me; but their foolish fathers and mothers, instead of letting them pick flowers, and make dirt-pies, and get birds' nests, and dance round the gooseberry bush, as little children should, kept them always at lessons, working, working, working, learning weekday lesson all weekdays, and Sunday lessons all Sunday, and weekly examinations every Saturday, and monthly examinations every month, and yearly examinations every year, everything seven times over, as if once was not enough, and enough as good as a feast—till their brains grew big, and their bodies grew small, and they were all changed into turnips, with little but water inside; and still their foolish parents actually pick the leaves off them as fast as they grow, lest they should have anything green about them."

"Ah!" said Tom, "if dear Mrs. Doasyouwouldbedoneby knew of it she would send them a lot of tops, and balls, and marbles, and ninepins, and make them all as jolly as sand-boys."

"It would be no use," said the stick. "They can't play now, if they tried. Don't you see how their legs have turned to roots and grown into the ground, by never taking any exercise, but sapping and moping always in the same place? But here comes the Examiner-of-all-Examiners. So you had better get away, I warn you, or he will examine you and your dog into the bargain, and set him to examine all the other dogs, and you to examine all the other water-babies. There is no escaping out of his hands, for his nose is nine thousand miles long, and can go down chimneys and through keyholes, upstairs, downstairs, in my lady's chamber, examining all little boys, and the little boys' tutors likewise. But when he is thrashed—so Mrs. Bedone-byasyoudid has promised me—I shall have the thrashing of him: and if I don't lay it on with a will it's a pity."

Tom went off: but rather slowly and surly; for he was somewhat minded to face this same Examiner-of-all-Examiners, who came striding among the poor turnips, binding heavy burdens and grievous to be borne, and laying them on little children's shoulders, like the Scribes and Pharisees of old, and not touching the same with one of his fingers; for he had plenty of money, and a fine house to live in, and so forth, which was more than the poor little turnips had.

But when he got near, he looked so big and burly and dictatorial, and shouted so loud to Tom to come and be examined, that Tom ran for his life, and the dog too. And really it was time; for the poor turnips, in their hurry and fright, crammed themselves so fast to be ready for the Examiner, that they burst and popped by dozens all round him, till the place

sounded like Aldershot on a field-day, and Tom thought he should be blown into the air, dog and all.

As he went down to the shore he passed the poor turnip's new tomb. But Mrs. Bedonebyasyoudid had taken away the epitaph about talents and precocity and development, and put up one of her own instead which Tom thought much more sensible:

> "Instruction sore long time I bore,
> And cramming was in vain;
> Till Heaven did please my woes to ease,
> By water on the brain."

So Tom jumped into the sea, and swam on his way, singing:

> "Farewell, Tomtoddies all; I thank my stars
> That nought I know save those three royal r's:
> Reading and riting sure, with rithmetick,
> Will help a lad of sense through thin and thick."

Whereby you may see that Tom was no poet; but no more was John Bunyan, though he was as wise a man as you will meet in a month of Sundays.

And next he came to Oldwivesfabledom, where the folks were all heathens, and worshipped a howling ape.

And there he found a little boy sitting in the middle of the road, and crying bitterly.

"What are you crying for?" said Tom.

"Because I am not as frightened as I could wish to be."

"Not frightened? You are a queer little chap; but, if you want to be frightened, here goes—Boo!"

"Ah," said the little boy, "that is very kind of you; but I don't feel that it has made any impression."

Tom offered to upset him, punch him, stamp on him, fettle him over the head with a brick, or anything else whatsoever which would give him the slightest comfort.

But he only thanked Tom very civilly, in fine long words

which he had heard other folk use, and which, therefore, he thought were fit and proper to use himself; and cried on till his papa and mamma came, and sent off for the Powwow man immediately. And a very goodnatured gentleman and lady they were, though they were heathens; and talked quite pleasantly to Tom about his travels, till the Powwow man arrived, with his thunderbox under his arm.

And a well-fed, ill-favoured gentleman he was, as ever served her Majesty at Portland. Tom was a little frightened at first, for he thought it was Grimes. But he soon saw his mistake; for Grimes always looked a man in the face; and this fellow never did. And when he spoke, it was fire and smoke; and when he sneezed, it was squibs and crackers; and when he cried (which he did whenever it paid him), it was boiling pitch; and some of it was sure to stick.

"Here we are again!" cried he, like the clown in a pantomime. "So you can't feel frightened, my little dear—eh? I'll do that for you. I'll make an impression on you! Yah! Boo! Whirroo! Hullabaloo!"

And he rattled, thumped, brandished his thunderbox, yelled, shouted, raved, roared, stamped, and danced corroboree like any black fellow; and then he touched a spring in the thunderbox, and out popped turnip-ghosts and magic-lanterns and pasteboard bogeys and spring-heeled Jacks and syllabalas, with such a horrid din, clatter, clank, roll, rattle, and roar, that the little boy turned up the whites of his eyes, and fainted right away.

And at that his poor heathen papa and mamma were as much delighted as if they had found a gold mine; and fell down upon their knees before the Powwow man, and gave him a

palanquin with a pole of solid silver and curtains of cloth of
gold; and carried him about in it on their own backs; but as
soon as they had taken him up, the pole stuck to their shoulders,
and they could not set him down any more, but carried him
on willy-nilly, as Sindbad carried the old man of the sea; which
was a pitiable sight to see; for the father was a very brave
officer, and wore two swords and a blue button; and the mother
was as pretty a lady as ever had pinched feet like a Chinese.
But, you see, they had chosen to do a foolish thing just once
too often; so, by the laws of Mrs. Bedonebyasyoudid, they had
to go on doing it whether they chose or not, till the coming of
the Coqcigrues.

Ah! don't you wish that someone would go and convert
those poor heathens, and teach them not to frighten their little
children into fits?

"Now, then," said the Powwow man to Tom, "wouldn't you
like to be frightened, my little dear? For I can see plainly that
you are a very wicked, naughty, graceless, reprobate boy."

"You're another," quoth Tom, very sturdily. And when the
man ran at him and cried "Boo!" Tom ran at him in return and
cried "Boo!" likewise, right in his face, and set the little dog
upon him; and at his legs the dog went.

At which, if you will believe it, the fellow turned tail,
thunderbox and all, with a "Woof!" like an old sow on the
common; and ran for his life, screaming, "Help! thieves! murder!

fire! He is going to kill me! I am a ruined man! He will murder me; and break, burn, and destroy my precious and invaluable thunderbox; and then you will have no more thunder showers in the land. Help! help! help!"

At which the papa and mamma and all the people of Oldwivesfabledom flew at Tom, shouting, "Oh, the wicked, impudent, hard-hearted, graceless boy! Beat him, kick him, shoot him, drown him, hang him, burn him!" and so forth; but luckily they had nothing to shoot, hang, or burn him with, for the fairies had hid all the killing-tackle out of the way a little while before; so they could only pelt him with stones; and some of he stones went clean through him and came out the other side. But he did not mind that a bit; for the holes closed up again as fast as they were made, because he was a water-baby. However, he was very glad when he was safe out of the country, for the noise there made him all but deaf.

Then he came to a very quiet place, called Leaveheavenalone. And there the sun was drawing water out of the sea to make steam-threads, and the wind was twisting them up to make cloud-patterns, till they had worked between them the loveliest wedding veil of Chantilly lace and hung it up in their own Crystal Palace for anyone to buy who could afford it; while the good old sea never grudged, for she knew they would pay her back honestly. So the sun span, and the wind wove and all went well with the great steam-loom; as is likely, considering— and considering—and considering—

And at last after innumerable adventures each more wonderful than the last, he saw before him a huge building, much bigger, and—what is most surprising—a little uglier than a certain new lunatic asylum, but not quite built of the same materials. None of it, at least—or, indeed, for aught that I ever saw any part of any other building whatsoever—is cased with nine-inch brick inside and out, and filled up with rubble between the walls, in order that any gentleman who has been confined during her Majesty's pleasure may be unconfined during his own pleasure, and take a walk in the neighbouring park to improve his spirits, after an hour's light and wholesome labour with his dinner-fork or one of the legs of his iron bedstead. No. The walls of this building were built on an entirely different principle, which need not be described, as it has not yet been discovered.

Tom walked towards this great building, wondering what it was, and having a strange fancy that he might find Mr. Grimes inside it, till he saw running toward him, and shouting "Stop!" three or four people, who, when they came nearer, were nothing else than policemen's truncheons, running along without legs or arms.

Tom was not astonished. He was long past that. Besides, he had seen the naviculae in the water move nobody knows how, a hundred times, without arms, or legs, or anything to stand in their stead. Neither was he frightened; for he had been doing no harm.

So he stopped; and, when the foremost truncheon came up and asked his business, he showed Mother Carey's pass; and the truncheon looked at it in the oddest fashion; for he had one eye in the middle of his upper end, so that when he looked at anything, being quite stiff he had to slope himself, and poke himself, till it was a wonder why he did not tumble over; but, being quite full of the spirit of justice (as all policemen, and their truncheons, ought to be), he was always in a position of stable equilibrium, whichever way he put himself.

"All right—pass on," said he at last. And then he added: "I had better go with you, young man." And Tom had no objection, for such company was both respectable and safe; so the truncheon coiled its thong neatly round its handle, to prevent tripping itself up, for the thong had got loose in running—and marched on by Tom's side.

"Why have you no policemen to carry you?" asked Tom, after a while.

"Because we are not like those clumsy-made truncheons in the land-world, which cannot go without having a whole man to carry them about. We do our own work for ourselves; and do it very well, though I say it who should not."

"Then why have you a thong to your handle?" asked Tom.

"To hang ourselves up by, of course, when we are off duty."

Tom had got his answer, and had no more to say till they came up to the great iron door of the prison.

And there the truncheon knocked twice with its own head.

A wicket in the door opened, and out looked a tremendous old brass blunderbuss charged up to the muzzle with slugs, who was the porter; and Tom started back a little at the sight of him.

"What case is this?" he asked in a deep voice, out of his broad bell-mouth.

"If you please, sir, it is no case; only a young gentleman from her ladyship, who wants to see Grimes the master-sweep."

"Grimes?" said the blunderbuss. And he pulled in his muzzle, perhaps to look over his prison-lists.

"Grimes is up chimney No. 345," he said from inside. "So the young gentleman had better go on to the roof."

Tom looked up at the enormous wall, which seemed at least ninety miles high, and wondered how he should ever get up; but, when he hinted that to the truncheon, it settled the matter in a moment. For it whisked round, and gave him such a shove behind as sent him up to the roof in no time, with his little dog under his arm.

And there he walked along the leads till he met another truncheon, and told him his errand

"Very good," it said. "Come along; but it will be of no use. He is the most unremorseful hard-hearted, foul-mouthed fellow I have in charge; and thinks about nothing but beer and pipes, which are not allowed here, of course."

So they walked along over the leads and very sooty they were, and Tom thought the chimneys must want sweeping very much. But he was surprised to see that the soot did not stick to his feet, or dirty them in the least. Neither did the live coals, which were lying about in plenty, burn him; for, being a water-baby, his radical humours were of a moist and cold nature, as you may read at large in Lemnius, Cardan, Van Helmont, and other gentlemen, who knew much as they could, and no man can know more.

And at last they came to chimney No. 345. Out of the top

of it, his head and shoulders just showing, stuck poor Mr. Grimes; so sooty, and bleared, and ugly, that Tom could hardly bear to look at him. And in his mouth was a pipe; but it was not alight, though he was pulling at it with all his might.

"Attention. Mr. Grimes," said the truncheon; "here is a gentleman come to see you."

But Mr. Grimes only said bad words; and kept grumbling, "My pipe won't draw. My pipe won't draw."

"Keep a civil tongue, and attend!" said the truncheon; and popped up just like Punch, hitting Grimes such a crack over the head with itself, that his brains rattled inside like a dried walnut in its shell. He tried to get his hands out and rub the place, but he could not, for they were stuck fast in the chimney.

Now he was forced to attend.

"Hey!" he said, "why, it's Tom! I suppose you have come here to laugh at me, you spiteful little atomy?"

Tom assured him he had not, but only wanted to help him.

"I don't want anything except beer, and that I can't get; and a light to this bothering pipe, and that I can't get either."

"I'll get you one," said Tom; and he took up a live coal (there were plenty lying about) and put it to Grimes's pipe; but it went out instantly.

"It's no use," said the truncheon, leaning itself up against the chimney and looking on. "I tell you, it is no use. His heart is so cold that it freezes everything that comes near him. You will see that presently, plain enough."

"Oh, of course, it's my fault. Everything's always my fault," said Grimes. "Nows don't go to hit me again" (for the truncheon started upright, and looked very wicked); "you know, if my arms were only free, you daren't hit me then."

The truncheon leant back against the chimney, and took no notice of the personal insult, like a well-trained policeman as it was, though he was ready enough to avenge any transgression against morality or order.

"But can't I help you in any other way? Can't I help you to get out of this chimney?" said Tom.

"No," interposed the truncheon; "he has come to the place where everybody must help themselves, and he will find it out, I hope, before he is done with me."

"Oh, yes," said Grimes, "of course it's me. Did I ask to be brought here into the prison? Did I ask to be set to sweep your foul chimneys? Did I ask to have lighted straw put under me to make me go up? Did I ask to stick fast in the very first chimney of all, because it was so shamefully clogged up with soot? Did I ask to stay here—I don't know how long—a hundred years, I do believe, and never get my pipe, nor my beer, nor nothing fit for a beast let alone a man?"

"No," answered a solemn voice behind. "No more did Tom, when you behaved to him in the very same way."

It was Mrs. Bedonebyasyoudid. And when the truncheon saw her it started bolt upright—Attention!—and made such a low bow, that if it had not been full of the spirit of justice, it must have tumbled on its end, and probably hurt its one eye. And Tom made his bow too.

"Oh, ma'am," he said, "don't think about me; that's all past and gone, and good times and bad times and all times pass over. But may not I help poor Mr. Grimes? Mayn't I try and get some of these bricks away that he may move his arms?"

"You may try, of course," she said.

So Tom pulled and tugged at the bricks; but he could not

move one. And then he tried to wipe
Mr. Grimes's face: but the soot would not
come off.

"Oh, dear!" he said, "I have come all this
way, through all these terrible places, to help
you, and now I am of no use after all."

"You had best leave me alone," said
Grimes; "you are a goodnatured, forgiving
little chap, and that's truth; but you'd best
be off. The hail's coming on soon, and it will
beat the eyes out of your little head."

"What hail?"

"Why, hail that falls every evening here;
and, till it comes close to me, it's like so much
warm rain, but then it turns to hail over my
head, and knocks me about like small shot."

"That hail will never come any more," said
the strange lady. "I have told you before what
it was. It was your mother's tears, those which
she shed when she prayed for you by her
bedside, but your cold heart froze it into hail.
But she is gone to heaven now, and will weep
no more for her graceless son."

Then Grimes was silent a while, and then
he looked very sad.

"So my old mother's gone, and I never
there to speak to her! Ah! A good woman
she was, and might have been a happy one,
in her little school there in Vendale, if it hadn't
been for me and my bad ways."

"Did she keep the school in Vendale?" asked Tom. And then he told Grimes all the story of his going to her house, and how she could not abide the sight of a chimney-sweep, and then how kind she was, and how he turned into a water-baby.

"Ah!" said Grimes, "good reason she had to hate the sight of a chimney-sweep. I ran away from her and took up with the sweeps, and never let her know where I was, nor sent her a penny to help her, and now it's too late—too late!" said Mr. Grimes.

And he began crying and blubbering like a great baby, till his pipe dropped out of his mouth, and broke all to bits.

"Oh dear, if I was but a little chap in Vendale again, to see the clear beck, and the apple-orchard, and the yew-hedge, how different I would go on! But it's too late now. So you go along, you kind little chap, and don't stand to look at a man crying that's old enough to be your father, and never feared the face of man, nor of worse neither. But I'm beat now, and beat I must be. I've made my bed, and I must lie on it. Foul I would be, and foul I am, as an Irishwoman said to me once; and little I heeded her. It's all my own fault: but it's too late," and he cried so bitterly that Tom began crying too.

"Never too late," said the fairy, in such a strange, soft, new voice that Tom looked up at her, and she was so beautiful for the moment, that Tom half fancied she was her sister.

No more was it too late. For, as poor Grimes cried and blubbered on, his own tears did what his mother's could not do, and Tom's could not do, and nobody's on earth could do for him; for they washed the soot off his face and off his clothes, and then they washed the mortar away from between the bricks, and the chimney crumbled down, and Grimes began to get out of it.

Up jumped the truncheon, and was going to hit him on the crown a tremendous thump, and drive him down again like a cork into a bottle. But the strange lady put it aside.

"Will you obey me if I give you a chance?"

"As you please, ma'am. You're stronger than me, that I know too well, and wiser than me, I know too well also. And, as for being my own master, I've fared ill enough with that as yet. So whatever your ladyship pleases to order me; for I'm beat, and that's the truth."

"Be it so then—you may come out. But remember, disobey me again, and into a worse place still you go."

"I beg pardon, ma'am, but I never disobeyed you that I know of. I never had the honour of setting eyes upon you till I came to these ugly quarters."

"Never saw me? Who said to you, Those that will be foul, foul they will be?"

Grimes looked up; and Tom looked up too; for the voice was that of the Irishwoman who met them the day that they went out together to Harthover. "I gave you your warning then; but you gave it yourself a thousand times before and since. Every bad word that you said—every cruel and mean thing that you did every time that you got tipsy—every day that you went dirty— you were disobeying me, whether you knew it or not."

"If I'd only known, ma'am. "

"You knew well enough that you were disobeying something, though you did not know it was me. But come out and take your chance. Perhaps it may be your last."

So Grimes stept out of the chimney, and, really, if it had not been for the scars on his face, he looked as clean and respectable as a master-sweep need look. "Take him away," said she to the truncheon. "and give him his ticket-of-leave."

"And what is he to do, ma'am?"

"Get him to sweep out the crater of Etna; he will find some very steady men working out their time there, who will teach him his business; but mind, if that crater gets choked again, and there is an earthquake in consequence, bring them all to me, and I shall investigate the case very severely."

So the truncheon marched off Mr. Grimes, looking as meek as a drowned worm.

And for aught I know, or do not know, he is sweeping the crater of Etna to this very day.

"And now," said the fairy to Tom, "your work here is done. You may as well go back again."

"I should be glad enough to go," said Tom "but how am I to get up that great hole again, now the steam has stopped blowing?"

"I will take you up the backstairs: but I must bandage your eyes first; for I never allow anybody to see those backstairs of mine."

"I am sure I shall not tell anybody about them, ma'am, if you bid me not."

"Aha! So you think, my little man. But you would soon forget your promise if you got back into the land-world. For if people only once found out that you had been up my backstairs, you would have all the fine ladies kneeling to you, and the rich men emptying their purses before you, and statesmen offering you place and power; and young and old, rich and poor, crying to you, 'Only tell us the great backstairs secret and we will be your slaves; we will make you lord, king, emperor, bishop, archbishop, pope, if you like—only tell us the secret of the backstairs. For thousands of years we have been paying, and petting, and obeying, and worshipping quacks who told us they had the key of the backstairs, and could smuggle us up them; and in spite of all our disappointments, we will honour, and glorify, and adore, and beatify, and translate, and apotheotize you likewise, on the chance of your knowing something about the backstairs, that we may all go on pilgrimage to it, and, even if we cannot get up it; lie at the foot of it, and cry—

'Oh backstairs,
precious backstairs,
invaluable backstairs,
requisite backstairs,
necessary backstairs,
good-natured backstairs,
cosmopolitan backstairs,
comprehensive backstairs,
accommodating backstairs,
well-bred backstairs,
comfortable backstairs,
humane backstairs,
reasonable backstairs,
long-sought backstairs,
coveted backstairs,
aristocratic backstairs,
respectable backstairs,
gentlemanlike backstairs,
ladylike backstairs,
commercial backstairs,
economical backstairs,
practical backstairs,
logical backstairs,
deductive backstairs,
orthodox backstairs,
probable backstairs,
credible backstairs,
demonstrable backstairs,
irrefragable backstairs,
potent backstairs,
all-but-omnipotent backstairs,
etc.

Save us from the consequences of our own actions, and from the cruel fairy, Mrs. Bedonebyasyoudid!' Do not you think that you would be a little tempted then to tell what you know, laddie?"

Tom thought so certainly. "But why do they want so to know all about the backstairs?" asked he, being a little frightened at the long words, and not understanding them the least, as, indeed, he was not meant to do, or you either.

"That I shall not tell you. I never put things into little folks' heads which are but too likely to come there of themselves. So come—now I must bandage your eyes." So she tied the bandage on his eyes with one hand, and with the other she took it off.

"Now," she said, "you are safe up the stairs." Tom opened his eyes very wide, and his mouth too; for he had not, as he thought, moved a single step. But, when he looked round him, there could be no doubt that he was safe up the backstairs, whatsoever they may be which no man is going to tell you, for the plain reason that no man knows.

The first thing which Tom saw was the black cedars, high and sharp against the rosy dawn; and St. Brandan's Isle reflected double in the still broad silver sea. The wind sang softly in the cedars, and the water sang among the caves; the sea-birds sang as they streamed out into the ocean, and the land-birds as they built among the boughs; and the air was so full of song that it stirred St. Brandan and his hermits, as they slumbered in the shade, and they moved their good old lips, and sang their morning hymn amid their dreams. But among all the songs one came across the water more sweet and clear than all; for it was the song of a young girl's voice.

And what was the song which she sang? Ah, my little man, I am too old to sing that song, and you too young to understand it. But have patience, and keep your eye single, and your hands clean, and you will learn some day to sing it yourself, without needing any man to teach you.

And as Tom neared the island, there sat upon a rock the most graceful creature that ever was seen, looking down, with her chin upon her hand, and paddling with her feet in the water. And when they came to her she looked up, and behold it was Ellie.

"Oh, Miss Ellie," said he, "how you are grown!"

"Oh! Tom," said she, "how you are grown, too!"

And no wonder; they were both quite grown up—he into a tall man, and she into a beautiful woman.

"Perhaps I may be grown," she said, "I have had time enough, for I have been sitting here waiting for you many a hundred years, till I thought you were never coming."

"Many a hundred years?" thought Tom; but he had seen so much in his travels that he had quite given up being astonished; and, indeed, he could think of nothing but Ellie. So he stood and looked at Ellie, and Ellie looked at him; and they liked the employment so much that they stood and looked for seven years more, and neither spoke nor stirred.

At last they heard the fairy say, "Attention, children! Are you never going to look at me again?"

"We have been looking at you all this while," they said. And so they thought they had been.

"Then look at me once more," said she.

They looked—and both of them cried out at once, "Oh, who are you, after all?"

"You are our dear Mrs. Doasyouwouldbedoneby."

"No, you are good Mrs. Bedonebyasyoudid; but you are grown quite beautiful now!"

"To you," said the fairy. "But look again."

"You are Mother Carey," said Tom, in a very low, solemn voice; for he had found out something which made him very happy, and yet frightened him more than all that he had ever seen.

But you are grown quite young again.

"To you," said the fairy. "Look again!"

"You are the Irishwoman who met me the day I went to Harthover!"

And when they looked she was neither of them, and yet all of them at once.

"My name is written in my eyes, if you have eyes to see it there."

And they looked into her great, deep, soft eyes, and they changed again and again into every hue, as the light changes in a diamond.

"Now read my name," said she, at last.

And her eyes flashed, for one moment, clear, white, blazing light: but the children could not read her name; for they were dazzled, and hid their faces in their hands.

"Not yet, young things, not yet," said she, smiling; and then she turned to Ellie.

"You may take him home with you now on Sundays, Ellie. He has won his spurs in the great battle, and become fit to go with you, and be a man; because he has done the thing he did not like."

So Tom went home with Ellie on Sundays, and sometimes

on weekdays, too; and he is now a great man of science, and can plan railroads, and steam engines, and electric telegraphs, and rifled guns, and so forth; and knows everything about everything, except why a hen's egg don't turn into a crocodile, and two or three other little things which no one will know till the coming of the Cocqcigrues. And all this from what he learnt when he was a water-baby, underneath the sea.

"And of course Tom married Ellie!"

My dear child, what a silly notion! Don't you know that no one ever marries in a fairy tale, under the rank of a prince or a princess?

"And Tom's dog?"

Oh, you may see him any clear night in July; for the old dog-star was so worn out by the last three hot summers that there have been no dog-days since; so that they had to take him down and put Tom's dog up in his place. Therefore, as new brooms sweep clean, we may hope for some warm weather this year. And this is the end of my story.

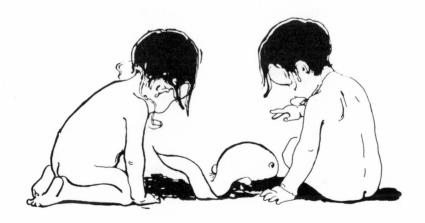

Moral

AND now, my dear little man, what should we learn from this parable?

We should learn thirty-seven or thirty-nine things, I am not exactly sure which; but one thing, at least, we may learn, and that is this—when we see efts in the ponds, never to throw stones at them, or catch them with crooked pins, or put them into vivariums with sticklebacks, that the sticklebacks may prick them in their poor little stomachs, and make them jump out of the glass into somebody's workbox, and so come to a bad end. For these efts are nothing else but the water-babies who are stupid and dirty, and will not learn their lessons and keep themselves clean; and, therefore (as comparative anatomists will tell you fifty years hence, though they are not learned enough to tell you now), their skulls grow flat, their jaws grow out, and their brains grow small, and their tails grow long, and they lose all their ribs (which I am sure you would not like to do), and their skins grow dirty and spotted, and they never get into the clear rivers, much less into the great wide sea, but hang about in dirty ponds, and live in the mud, and eat worms, as they deserve to do.

But that is no reason why you should ill-use them; but only

why you should pity them, and be kind to them, and hope that some day they will wake up, and be ashamed of their nasty, dirty, lazy, stupid life, and try to amend, and become something better once more. For, perhaps, if they do so, then after 379,423 years, nine months, thirteen days, two hours, and twenty-one minutes (for aught that appears to the contrary), if they work very hard and wash very hard all that time, their brains may grow bigger, and their jaws grow smaller, and their ribs come back, and their tails wither off, and they will turn into waterbabies again, and, perhaps, after that into land-babies; and after that, perhaps, into grown men.

You know they won't? Very well, I dare say you know best. But, you see, some folks have a great liking for those poor efts. They never did anybody harm, or could if they tried; and their only fault is, that they do no good—any more than some thousands of their betters. But what with ducks, and what with pike, and what with sticklebacks, and what with waterbeetles, and what with naughty boys, they are "sae sair haddened doun", as the Scotsmen say, that it is wonder how they live; and some folks can't help hoping with good Bishop Butler, that they may have another chance to make things fair and even, somewhere, somewhen, somehow.

Meanwhile, do you learn your lessons, and thank God that you have plenty of cold water to wash in; and wash in it too, like a true English man. And then, if my story is not true, something better is; and if I am not quite right, still you will be, as long as you stick to hard work and cold water.

But remember always, as I told you at first, that this is all a fairy tale, and only fun and pretence; and, therefore, you are not to believe a word of it, even if it is true.

If you enjoyed this Longmeadow Press Edition you may want to add the following titles to your collection:

ITEM No.	TITLE	PRICE
0-681-00649-8	White Fang	2.95
0-681-00695-1	Call of the Wild	2.95
0-681-00644-7	Alice's Adventures in Wonderland	10.95
0-681-00586-6	Black Beauty	10.95

Ordering is easy and convenient.
Order by phone with Visa, MasterCard, American Express or Discover:
☎ **1-800-322-2000,** Dept. 706
or send your order to:
Longmeadow Press, Order/Dept. 706,
P.O. Box 305188, Nashville, TN 37230-5188

Name _____

Address _____

City _____ State _____ Zip _____

Item No.	Title	Qty	Total

Check or Money Order enclosed Payable to Longmeadow Press	Subtotal	
Charge: ❑ MasterCard ❑ VISA ❑ American Express ❑ Discover	Tax	
Account Number	Shipping	2.95
☐☐☐☐ ☐☐☐☐ ☐☐☐☐ ☐☐☐☐	Total	

Card Expires

☐☐☐☐   Signaure _____ Date _____

Please add your applicable sales tax: AK, DE, MT, OR, 0.0%—CO, 3.8%—AL, HI, LA, MI, WY, 4.0%—VA. 4.5%—GA, IA, ID, IN, MA, MD, ME, OH, SC, SD, VT, WI, 5.0%—AR, AZ, 5.5%—MO, 5.725%—KS, 5.9%—CT, DC, FL, KY, NC, ND, NE, NJ, PA, WV, 6.0%—IL, MN, UT, 6.25%—MN, 6.5%—MS, NV, NY, RI, 7.0%—CA, TX, 7.25%—OK, 7.5%—WA. 7.8%—TN, 8.25%

14

•

"You're a church mouse," Martin the priest says to five-year-old Christina, referring to the increasing delight with which she visits Mass, organ concerts, baptisms, communions, and all the other Catholic rites which have always confused her Protestant mother so.

Her mother is uncertain as to how to react to Christina's predilection. She well understands her childish enjoyment of the sensual, theatrical elements of the Catholic Church and doesn't attempt to influence her one way or the other; at this very moment, especially, she couldn't, even if she were inclined to, for she has been discharged from the Salzburg clinic only one and a half hours ago and can hardly move her body from the waist up. Her left arm lies stiff in its sling, and it feels as if the ribs on her left side, where they performed the mastectomy, are broken.

She arrives at Martin's village on the brightest of all August days, holding on desperately to her daughter with her right arm and trying in vain to stop the sobs that are racking her body. "There's no need to cry," Christina says gently. "Martin and I prayed for you every day and always lit a candle." Martin grins sheepishly, expecting, perhaps, Protestant indignation to rain down on his head; nothing of the kind is forthcoming, for she feels nothing but implicit gratitude and knows for certain that every good thought, addressed to whichever God in whichever church, is of vital importance to help her through the coming nights and days.

To begin with, conversation is difficult, even the most banal topics become weighty, so we resort to watching television. Leaving no doubt as to her and her parents' background, Christina asks Martin, "Don't you have a show tonight?" Martin says No and has clearly earned a black mark in Christina's book, being relegated to the realms of open-air theaters that only deign to perform in fair weather. She sulks until a slapstick comedy comes on and custard pies begin to fly. The pictures on the screen pass her mother by blankly, she feels as though she were a guest on another planet; far removed from humor, news, and commentaries, she sits there welded to her verdict. She sees no way of prying herself loose, sees herself condemned to just pretending to live in future, to playing her part in daily life and happenings like an actor in a long run of a play that doesn't absorb him. Whether sitting down, lying, standing, walking, she is completely possessed by her vile, uncontested verdict, her baffling exile, and begins to look for the reason why, as she's been programmed to do. For the moment, she would still like to crush indifference and raise her protesting voice so loud that it echoes around the universe—but hadn't the wise men told her the way to do it? Hadn't they said, "Don't get excited, only do the things you want to do, the things you enjoy, the things that give you pleasure"? What is pleasure? as the prisoner asked in the jail-yard, then tripped over a straw on his quest for the sun. When Mother died, her doctor said, "If we only knew what cancer is, if we had the slightest notion, we could congratulate ourselves. Some of my colleagues heave a sigh of relief when a lung-cancer patient admits to being a smoker."

Later, they brought me up to bed. Martin has given us his bedroom; it's bigger than either of the two guest rooms, and he's put in a small bed for Christina. The room is rustic and simple, with a baroque, red-brown cupboard, a square table, and a painting of the Virgin Mary in a carved, flaking gold frame. "You comforter of the lowly," I read, again trapped in my cell of fear. It's a simple, not especially monastic, modern room with large windows. There's a wide road at the end of the small garden, and the passing trucks cause Mary, the cupboard, and the table to rattle. Opposite, there's a church. Martin's church.

I lie on my back and am unable to move. I spend a long sleepless night because I am without pain killers. I lie there and curse the tyrants and go-betweens I had grown so attached to, the U-boat commander and Red Fluff, even the nurses; I swear and blaspheme and can't forgive them for turning me over to pain again, the pain that glows throughout the night and clamors at each quarter hour the church clock softly chimes. It hisses at each gentle breath my daughter takes, snorts each time my husband snores. I see the picture of the helpless turtle lying on its back in the midday sun, then see the first sweet-corn-colored rays of a new hot August day stream up around Martin's church steeple.

Life in the presbytery starts out at surprisingly high tempo and volume; people come and go, the door slams continuously. They want to arrange a baptism, a burial, want to get married, need money, advice, or comfort. Martin is the community psychiatrist, soul therapist, village manager, and marriage counselor. Kathi, his housekeeper, shows them in and out with a firmly fixed smile and a dachshund barking at her heels, makes the beds, dusts the furniture, cleans the ashtrays, cooks, and answers the constantly ringing telephone with, "This is the Catholic presbytery." Kathi comes from a large Lower Bavarian family and has been with Martin for thirteen years. Kathi's somewhat sidelong glances seem to indicate a sly and fractious character at first sight, but on closer acquaintanceship she proves to be much the opposite: forthright, straight up and down; her prickly, cryptic humor is always ready to hand and sponsors many a laugh throughout the day, showing no particular respect for her employer's profession either. She brings up our breakfast, helps Christina wash herself, helps her stiff-armed mother to struggle into her clothes, saying only, "It certainly is a beastly illness," as she sees the tape, and leaves it at that.

Martin yells, "It's a madhouse here until midday, then it gets quieter." Mother and child go for a walk.

She puts on a billowing poncho that hides her sling and the

stiff arm, dons a pair of big dark glasses, takes her daughter by the hand, and sets off down the tidy village main street. She's about to do something for the first time which other women do as part of the daily routine: go shopping with her child. Even this she approaches as though it were part of the role she's been assigned, but she manages to underplay; hesitantly, glumly trying to keep her distance and not be fooled by the feeling of freedom, she begins the outing. Reflected in the shop windows, she sees a thin, long-haired woman holding a slender delicate-looking child by the hand as they advance slowly, stop in front of the village toy shop, and mount the three steps. They climb them very carefully, in keeping with the woman's weak condition and the child's handicapped legs. They speak quietly and behave discreetly, knowing that they're conspicuous enough in this village community to begin with, hoping that no one will notice their wounds. Only once does the mother catch herself starting to fume as she sees a chubby child streaking along the street followed by a nonchalantly trotting grandmother. Apart from timidly asking, "Are you in pain, Mama?" her beautiful ash-blonde daughter is loving the aimless wandering, the undisturbed togetherness.

The road and the sidewalk are of asphalt, and geometrically straight; behind the closely built row of houses there's a strip of firm sandy ground in front of the fields, which are beginning to steam in the August morning sun. The mother tries to imagine what it must be like to have lived all one's life in this street, to have grown more and more incensed as the number of trucks and cars and motorcycles increased from year to year, to have enjoyed the stillness of Saturday-Sunday, to have gone to Martin's church with the same regularity as one went about one's work, to have heard his lovingly prepared sermons often play around one's ears like the splashing of a fountain, to have noticed the war only through the bombers flying over, and the ration cards, the odd tank passing through followed by straggling refugees—excepting, of course, those whose sons and husbands had been killed, their names now chiseled into the granite memorial under the bizarre word "fallen."

The apothecary is the most cosmopolitan-looking shop in the village. It has wide glass doors and a glass counter, adaptable Swedish shelves, and dozens of stand-up cardboard advertisements selling health by way of grinning octogenarians and pumpkin-sized babies. "Sickness" seems to have been outlawed, thanks to the apothecary and its up-to-date marketing methods. Next door there's a sad Old World store that has yesterday's cosmetics, unattractive health-food packages, and shriveled organic apples full of wormholes. The stationer's shop, on the other hand, offers an overwhelming number of magazines and housewife pamphlets, their front pages adorned exclusively with exiled kings and queens, discarded empresses, the occasional reigning sovereign. In the farthest, darkest corner there's a revolving stand half full of dusty paperbacks: two Kleists, three Ludwig Thomas, four Goethes, one Schiller, and lots of thrillers with bloodthirsty jackets, but even they don't appear to attract too much patronage. Seven women are inspecting this week's offer of offset-colored monarchs. Beside the magazines there are pencils trussed up in rubber bands like bunches of asparagus, school books, lighters, erasers, and a dozen ugly imitation-leather briefcases stuck up high on the topmost shelf with outside chances of being sold. Next door again, an optician's as big as a dollhouse. The tiny window is divided by an embroidered curtain drawn across the lower half; above it one can see the eyes, forehead, and hair of a very old lady; below her and in front of the curtain, there's a single three-dimensional picture of a curly-headed girl with glasses that's illuminated from time to time by a revolving red light.

I wanted so much to grow old, the mother thinks as she looks at the eyes of the old woman, who is staring down at them vacantly. I'd always looked forward to it, hoping to find a magic in old age that's inaccessible to youth. Her thoughts are scattered by the dangerous, unforgivable "Why me?"

The old lady's lifeless stare is beginning to unsettle Christina. "Let's go on, Mama," she says, fidgeting, and keeps looking back until she can see the eyes no longer. A little farther on there's a needlecraft store, a drab boutique in the recess of a courtyard, a butcher shop, a hotel with a restaurant, and, at the end of the street, a plant nursery with a shop in front displaying fat dahlias, early asters, pots full of snapdragons, cornflowers, delphiniums, and lupines.

On the other side of the street is the bakery. Baking seems to have a cheering effect on people; bakers and their wives are invariably jolly, patient, and considerate. Maybe it's because they get up before the sun, even in summer, or perhaps it's the smell, or the symbolic value of bread, the guarantee golden loaves give against starvation. Whatever the reason, the proprietors here run true to form. They are round and hearty, with unlined pink faces and whitish, floury hands. With endless patience they explain the Bavarian names of their cakes and pastries, compare them to the Berlin expressions, throw up their hands in delight when they hear that their "Moor's head" is called a "Nigger kiss" up there. They poke each other in the ribs and clouds of flour rise from their aprons; then they present Christina with a string of candy, a marzipan piglet, and a red and white toadstool, pack the pastries we've bought with infinite care, and seem reluctant to part with them, like a painter with a cherished picture.

I've never been a great one for shopping and this morning's no exception. I stand around covertly, trying to fit in with the village atmosphere, dig uncertainly in my purse, and don't notice that a wanton urge to buy is taking hold of me until I'm in the thick of it and pointing at all manner of things we don't need at all; I buy sweaters that are neither particularly attractive nor particularly cheap, buy coats for Christina, several umbrellas, jackets, head scarves, buy shamelessly, orgiastically; suddenly the thought of dying people's hands jolts me—the way they grab at things. I buy a big linen tablecloth, twenty skeins of wool, and needles, planning to embroider it, knowing full well that I'll never finish it, my patience will never go the distance; the thought that perhaps other circumstances might prevent me from finishing it has me scurrying to the nearest piece of wood and tapping it three times, but I stay in the role of the housewife who's blowing several pay envelopes and the holiday money all at once, and turn up at Martin's house with my right hand loaded with shopping bags and my body bathed in perspiration.

Kathi helps me in with the swag, Christina tugs at the yapping dachshund and yelps as it nips her leg, Martin tumbles down the stairs, pale with anxiety. In the afternoon we all sit at the broad living-room table under the blue and white lampshade and wolf the pastries, relaxed now. Suddenly I am filled with the feeling of belonging, of being at home. How light I feel too, I think to myself, light and self-confident, I am beginning to live from hour to hour instead of minute to minute, I'm eating cake and laughing at Martin's jokes, I'm taking part, not just pretending any more; I look at my child, who's got a dab of cream on her nose, and start to cry and haven't the foggiest idea why. Martin rests his hand on my neck and tells Christina, "Those are tears of joy, Mama is so happy to be with you again."

Later we drive out to the Bichlhof meadow in Martin's jalopy. We lie in the grass and gaze at the sky through the long grass, watch it grow paler and mistier, autumnal almost. Behind us there's a mountain that's shaped like a sugar loaf, before us there are apple trees and rolling fields. Christina is pummeling Martin like a piece of dough, kneading and knocking on him. He starts to say, "The decrees of the Church would be more understand-able for the ordinary—" but the rest gets battered out of him. We drive home in the spattering rain, the *"belle aujourd'hui"* sputters out like a dying firework. Martin changes gear with a grinding noise that sets the teeth on edge and yells, "Come to Mass tonight, and come up front with the others at the end. Kathi'll tell you when."

We eat at six, at half-past Martin crosses the street and dis-appears into his vestry, at seven the bells begin to peal; Kathi, Christina, and I pull on our raincoats. I walk through the small cemetery and feel like a coward running for shelter. It will be the first time that I've seen Martin in his church.

It's a country church, not too bombastic, almost homely in fact. The interior has been kept as it always was, I imagine, early baroque, there's a Gothic cross on the altar, and niches are at the side with smaller altars, carved figures of the Virgin and St. Anthony. We take our seats in the middle of the fourth row, the great table is right in front of us. Kathi's presence is reassuring as regards the choreography, she'll tell us when to stand up and when to kneel; even so I don't feel too comfortable, a feeling of treachery creeps up. The vestry bell rings and a remarkably well-played organ swells to life, awakening childhood memories, tightening my throat with flabby sentimentality, removing fear. Martin comes through the narrow door. He's wearing white alb and chasuble, and approaches the altar with loping, almost hasty steps, kneels down with his hands together. Even in these strange garments he remains friend Martin, there is no barrier between the altar and the fourth row. I suddenly realize that Martin is an emanator too: I can read his thoughts quite clearly, they spring at me across the pews.

The church is three quarters full although it's a weekday. The people get up awkwardly, an umbrella clatters to the floor, Martin turns around and looks directly into the faces of his congregation, not two or three feet above them, or up to the stained-glass windows. I note this with a feeling of relief, as though an old friend had proved himself once more. And without any warning I envy Martin, envy him his health and strength, hate my own never-ending stream of anxiety. And without noticing it I discover that I've gripped Christina's hand and want to tell her that she daren't leave me alone, that she must stay with me; without her I don't have the strength to continue.

She looks at me in surprise and whispers, "You're hurting me," wakens me from my egomaniac nightmare. I see Martin's face, and it has grown ashen, almost as pale as his chasuble. He looks at me and the pause seems to expand like a balloon. I fear that people must notice that something's different today, but no, no head turns in my direction. Martin says, "We begin our divine service in the name of the Father, and of the Son, and of the Holy Ghost, amen." His voice is not at all unctuous, it sounds exactly as it does in his living room—and comes over the microphone splendidly, the singer notes.

"First, allow me to say a few words in explanation of our

lesson for today," he says simply; once again his eyes return to my face, searchingly, restlessly, but the paleness has disappeared. A woman in front of me is fiddling with her hair, another searching in her handbag, the rest listen intently. ("I'm not so much interested in dogma as in the condition of suffering," he once said to me, "and in doing my best to understand it." Another time: "Some people are more lonely than others; you belong to the very lonely, although you fight it and devour people the moment you sense a scrap of affinity, as a release from the loneliness. You spend most of your waking hours trying to explain yourself.")

Standing in front of the altar, Martin says, "And Jesus cried out with a loud voice: My God, my God, why hast Thou forsaken me? . . . And Jesus cried out with a loud voice, and gave up the ghost—" I don't hear the rest; that Jesus "cried out" makes him accessible, there's suddenly a path leading up to the fortress that had appeared impenetrable till now— He beckons me to ascend. His cry makes mine excusable. Why don't we cry out any more? Why has crying out been outlawed in our woebegone Sparta of overkill and boutiques and trends? Why? To ignore death and suffering, to resort to brutality to make them laughable, must surely be a declaration of cowardice. He cried out. How immense must our dread be that we make death laughable.

A young man comes forward and reads the parish announcements with a scratchy childish voice. The liturgy is simple, severe almost. Martin knocks all my arguments on the head and seems to say, It doesn't have to be bombastic. No pomp and ceremony, just quiet and straightforward, as you Protestants will have it. Martin, you're a fox when it comes to your religion, you're a cunning old fox. No—I think—basically he's a Parsifal, he'll walk across the waters, the sharks may bite his legs off but he'll still be smiling when his torso reaches the other side. And he's refused to allow himself to slide into the smooth stretches of cynical sanctimony.

Four attendants bring in a hand-tooled golden chalice. On the base, in enamel, there's a pelican ripping its breast open to feed its young. They ripped me open to save me for you, I think to myself—stop it, you're parading your self-pity again, the self-centeredness of the sick and condemned, you make me sick.

Martin says, "This is my body, this is my blood . . ." Christina is getting restless, she's fidgeting with Kathi's umbrella, but looks up as the Lord's Prayer begins and listens reverently, folding her hands. I wonder when I heard it last, I can't even remember the text: OurFatherwhichartinheavenhallowedbeThyname . . . it was in an air-raid shelter thirty years ago, at Ostkreuz railway station. I'd been traveling back from Berlin-Babelsberg alone when the raid began and we all ran down to the cellars; they panicked as the roof caved in and the phosphorus wriggled its way through the grating and down the walls like a nest of serpents. Not long after this I'd prayed again; on the march to the prison camp they'd locked us into a church for the night and sat outside shooting out the stained-glass windows; the man with dysentery who was squashed by the tank two days later lay beside me moaning and the wounded screamed like toads, the men who were dying gasped and their breath rattled dryly in their throats, the church stank of vomit and excrement and I lay under a pew that had a nail in it; it stuck into my shoulder as I lay there wedged in between the pew and the groaning man and clenched my fists as I tried to remember the rest of the prayer, started from the beginning again, and always got stuck at the same place: giveusthisdayyourdailybread . . .

Martin's voice seeps into my memories, as though he were coming closer: ". . . who taught us how to live and how to die, how to be happy and how to be sad, who had been acclaimed and deserted, admired and betrayed, and had attained the highest degree of human evolution . . ."

The people stand up and walk forward, surround Martin and the great table. For a moment the sight of them all crowding together looks farcical, incongruous, thoughts of summer clearance sales and bargain hunters plow through my sense of belonging. Kathi nudges me and bends down to Christina. "Mama will be back right away," she says. Christina seems very impressed that I'm allowed to join the crowd, that we're not just plain outsiders. Carefully I walk up to the table and wait in the background. Martin places the bread in each pair of outstretched hands, he doesn't put it into their mouths, doesn't feed them, only distributes. They stand in the aisles and chew quite naturally, which strikes me as being very odd; "Communion is the link from God to man, and from man to man." Martin looks at me. His thoughtful smile becomes almost playful, like a boy who's decided on a prank. The bread is lying in my hand, I raise it and look at it, then begin to chew, and feel the flush creeping up my neck—I'm blushing, and can't do a thing about it, it rushes up to my cheeks and forehead. "Thank you," I say, my mouth still half full, "thank you for accepting me." Confused and mixing up the rows, I find my way back to my seat. They are singing a hymn but I know neither the text nor the melody. Martin raises his hands in prayer and says, "May the Almighty God bless us and keep us, in the name of the Father, and of the Son, and of the Holy Ghost, amen." The organ plays a toccata and he goes back to the vestry exactly as he'd entered, the door closing noiselessly behind him. Christina tugs at my hand, looks up at me excitedly, then becomes uncertain as she asks, "Do you feel different?" I say Yes. "In what way, different?" "I feel surprised, pleased, as though Martin had given me a present."

The church is empty except for an elderly lady who's switching around the contents of three bags. Martin appears behind me and says, "Shall we go?"

On the way back he asks, "What was the matter? Right at the beginning it looked as if you'd take to your heels."

"You're right."

The church, the cemetery, and the main street seem to have been spring-cleaned by the warm fine rain.

"D'you know what? I can't even remember the Lord's Prayer any more," I tell him. "There were nights in the hospital when I desperately tried to pray. I wasn't able to say anything; the only word I could think of was 'help.'"

"You're in good company," Martin answers. "Theresa of Avila struggled for fifteen years to find a way to speak to God.

She knew of the speechlessness, of the absurdity when prayer becomes idle prattle. She wanted nothing less than intimate discourse with the mystery we call God." He pauses and then says, "Your deep belief in the infinity of Jesus made me do something today which is most unusual, although you are a baptized Christian."

"What do you say when a child dies? What do you say to the parents?"

"A five-year-old died three weeks ago. 'I'd like to tell you why I'm a Christian,' I said to them. 'The world is a very gossipy place, very loud and presumptuous until somebody dies, then it grows quiet. Everyone gets embarrassed and nobody knows what to say. There, where the world loses its tongue, the Church offers a message.' I love the Church because of this message, I love it because, in the middle of the world's laughter, it tells us that man has a goal, and it opens its mouth just as the others are shrugging their shoulders."

"It's high time the taboo was removed from death."

"There are a great many instances where man complains to his God, it's not all praise by any means. In the songs of Jeremiah and Job, for example, and, above all, in Jesus's cry on the cross."

"Sometimes it seems to me that there's not very much that has been left us except isolation and possessions. And even in resisting possessions, we're admitting that covetousness is in us and, in the end, we shall become that which we sought to resist. And it's harder to fight when you've got nothing than when you've got a little, funnily enough. In this case I know what I'm talking about, I've been through the mill of rags and riches. We Germans have been programmed to look for the main chance, the first thought is always a clear 'What's in it for me?' And every straight question must have a straight answer, which is the surest way of creating misunderstandings."

"Seneca says, 'One must determine what is more important: to give up one's offices, or to give up oneself.' "

While Martin and Kathi are looking for the door key, I say, "What does democracy mean in a country where authoritarianism begins at home? Where a blow is only a 'smack' and people terrorize their children in order 'to make a man' out of them? England and France are no different in this respect, and their doctors don't stand any nonsense either. I'll never forget the professor in Paris who came to my hotel and lanced the abscess on my eyelid with a safety pin he'd borrowed from the chambermaid. And in England a famous Harley Street specialist looked at my throat and forbade me to speak for six months; when I asked him how on earth I could possibly manage it, he said, 'Buy yourself a pad and pencil,' and slammed the door behind me. Thank God, it turned out that the state of my vocal cords had to do with the fact that I'd become pregnant, and two weeks later I made a record in Germany and was no hoarser than I am normally anyway. Speechlessness set in when I received his bill, however."

Kathi remembers that she put the key under the mat. She stoops to get it as I ask, "Why didn't St. Martin part with his whole coat?"

"He had to keep something of his uniform, otherwise he'd never have got a replacement."

"I might have known you'd have an excuse for your namesake."

After a second night "outside," another night of uninhibited pain, the morning is overcast with clouds heavy as udders. It's Martin's day off and we'd planned to drive to the Fraueninsel, an island on Lake Chiemsee. Full of matinal murkiness, I go down with Christina to the living room, where the big table is laid for breakfast. Martin creeps in and, wondrous to relate, even Kathi turns out to be no great morning person: she munches silently and is a far cry from the bright lady on the telephone who says, "This is the Catholic presbytery." The dachshund, whom we've named the Murderer since he nipped Christina's leg, is still sleeping.

We peer gloomily into the rain and absentmindedly stir our cups of tea. Christina's been chewing the same mouthful for the last quarter of an hour. Living with Martin under the same roof is extraordinarily easy and harmonious considering he's no family man and has had no experience whatever with small children; it occurs to me that the explanation might lie in reincarnation, that we've known each other before. While we munch and wait for the morning ether to lift, I remember the first time he came to see me do a concert. He sat in the front row and at first I felt that we were standing opposite each other on a busy city street clothed only in unbecoming bathing suits. I felt ashamed of my brazen emanations; wedded as they were here to bawdy jazz, they seemed cheap in his presence, and my rape act more than wanton. But Martin was ecstatic. "You come over like a panther—where do you get the energy from for two and a half hours? There were moments when your thoughts came ringing through like a bell."

I make the first step toward resuming sane relationships. "I'd like to start painting again," I say, with some effort, to which Martin raises his bleary eyes and murmurs, "Rouault said that one starts to paint as the result of humiliation—it's a good thought." There's a ring at the door followed by violent knocking. The Murderer wakes up with a barrage of yaps, Kathi goes out indignantly and comes back, looking distorted by shock; she stands stiffly in the middle of the room and stutters something to Martin in Bavarian dialect. Martin knocks over the sugar bowl and hurries out. I hear voices, then a door closing, then it's quiet. Kathi comes awkwardly back to the table, sits down stiffly, and says, "Goodness, goodness. A little boy of seven. He was playing by the river at the back there with his sister, they slipped off the sandbank, the sister managed to get to the bank but when they pulled him out he was dead. I saw him only yesterday." Martin comes quickly to the door with his hat on and calls out, "I'll go over and see."

Two hours later he comes back, stands in the hall sipping a cup of tea, then we drive to the Chiemsee in silence. A few frayed-looking grubby swans are floating disconsolately in the water, bobbing up and down on the little waves and bumping into the poles of the jetty. Only one of them is pitting its strength against the wind and the waves. It strains forward with its neck craned and its breast swollen, and there's no way of telling whether it's been rejected by the others or whether it's just not feeling sociable today, looking like a lone revolutionary as it sails out of sight into the mist and the rain.

In the stern of the small boat there's a tarpaulin shelter, and Christina and I sit there hugging each other like chimpanzees. My left arm gives a warning, stinging pain. As we are halfway over to the island I say to Martin, "Don't throw me overboard but I must tell you something that is strange to your creed and which is confusing me; I've been trying to find an explanation for it for months now, but I'm convinced that there isn't one. Please listen. About nine months ago a woman wrote to me from Idaho in the States. She told me that my father, who died six months after I was born, would like to send me a message on my birthday, the twenty-eighth of December. There's nothing very strange in that, I often get fan mail from crackpots who've read up on my background. So far so good, but then she went on to say—in very well-written English—that my father would like to do away with any doubts on my part by describing a photo he'd once given me and which I'd lost during the air raids in Berlin. The photo had had a dark stripe across the top left corner and showed my father leaning against a loose net on a tennis court; he'd been wearing a V-neck sweater and long white pants, and had his racquet under his arm. It must have been midday, for the sun was very high and his deep-set eyes were dark shadows. His ears had stuck out prominently. Apart from my mother and I, nobody knew of the existence of this photo, and my mother died more than ten years ago—even she didn't know that I'd lost the picture. The woman from Idaho wrote that there was an enclosed note on which my father had guided her hand to write down the message. I opened the piece of paper, and written in old German script, in my father's handwriting, was the message: 'I can give you so little. May your life ripen in love and joy nonetheless, that we may all be united in God. I am always with you, your Father.' There's no explanation for the exact description of the photo, nor for the odd message, made more odd by the fact that it reached me shortly before this last series of operations and the verdict. Oddest of all is that my father was a rebel and an atheist as well, he died while he was trying to strangle the priest who'd insisted on giving him the last rites in the hospital."

Martin looks away into the irregularly dripping rain, wipes his wet face, and answers, "I can't allow myself to accept it. I sense that something like telepathy does exist, but I can no more explain to myself how it comes about than I can explain or understand electricity—still, this message of your father's seems to me to be monstrous."

"Well, you're not a solipsist, anything but, so just accept that you don't understand it. We talk about astrology, although the astrologers are self-taught and therefore not acceptable to the scientists. We talk about parapsychology and 'half sciences' in the same woolly manner, although we don't give them a seat at the universities and so rob them of all chance of ever becoming a science. I've never understood why ignorance and the delight in staying that way should be the basis for belief and the continuing uncontested existence of accepted sciences."

We get out and slither along the wet jetty. Martin says, "You must have a look at the gate house, it's the oldest building on Bavarian soil, from the time of Tassilo." It's icy cold in the ancient house but all discomfort is forgotten at the sight of the massive walls with their noble red-chalk drawings; the angels seem to have been sketched in casually, playfully, look as though they might leave again at any minute. Martin looks up at the semicircular Romanesque window facing the east and says, "It was the symbol of light, the symbol of Christ, Lux Oriente. Even the Magyars, who knocked down everything they could lay their hands on, even they couldn't destroy its beauty."

We walk over to the Gothic minster opposite the gate house. The original walls are Romanesque also, but the interior has been renovated at a later date and appears clumsy, fawning almost, in comparison with the dignity of the pure Romanesque basilica.

In the evening Martin writes his sermon, sermon for a drowned boy. I hear his typewriter clattering until midnight. The morning begins with the usual presbytery busyness, at midday Martin comes in looking gray and worn. "People take a lot of strength," he says. "Only Wolfgang Amadeus can help now," and plays the E-flat Symphony on his tinny mono record player; he lights a cigarette awkwardly and puffs like a beginner, enjoying it but looking a little uncertain too.

"We feel at home in your home," I write in the guest book he'd placed on top of our suitcases, begging me to forgive him being such a nuisance. "I shall miss you both," Martin says. "I thought I'd got used to my bachelor existence. Right at the beginning celibacy and being alone was often almost unbearable, but then one settles down to the rhythm. I even enjoy it, but now, after these weeks with you both, I feel . . ." He grins and scratches his balding head, rubs his short youthful nose, and says, "Well, you know what I mean." We clamber into his VW jalopy, Christina and I hold each other's hand comfortingly as we leave the safety of his presbytery and rattle down the now-familiar main street, look back and see Kathi and the Murderer, the steaming fields, and Martin's church growing smaller in the distance.

15

•

To be perfectly honest, the suckling pigs almost ruined the festivities for me; I couldn't bear to see them revolving on the spits over the glowing coals, their bodies soft pink and then all charred, rain dripping into their slit bellies. And it was, after all, my first own house, and we were celebrating the completion of the roof truss, in time-honored, mid-European tradition.

Everything between heaven and earth was dripping with rain, and the small orderly stream that runs along the side of our former millhouse was threatening to jump its cemented bed. The inner courtyard was filled to bursting with our admirably steadfast guests, all huddled together under a tangle of umbrellas. The guests included a brass band, two mayors, one lawyer, our neighbors, the building contractor, his foreman, carpenters, painters, plumbers, electricians, and a host of laborers.

We've moved in already and have installed ourselves in the one wing where the roof is completely finished; there, right under the finished roof on the top floor, we've set up house in two rooms. Three or four windows are still missing, and the doors don't shut properly as yet, and one can only gain access to the rooms by way of a ladder that resembles the ones chickens use to get up to their roost, but there's a table there, with three chairs, and a double and a single bed. In one corner there's even an electric piano on which the team, Hansi Hammerschmid and the singer–lyric writer, are trying to compose songs for the next record. They've never tried writing on a building site before, and they're having to admit that two cement mixers, a bulldozer, a crane, lots of pneumatic drills and power saws are powerful competition for an electric piano. She writes her lyrics with earplugs on; Hansi has carefully noted the times of the beer and coffee breaks and uses these to good advantage. Until the new windows arrive, whatever the team gets down on paper has a tendency to waft away the minute they've written it.

The landscape still appears to her to have posed for the illustrations to her favorite book of fairy tales; it has bottle-green meadows, brown-black plowed fields, dwarf fruit trees with wide crowns, linden trees, oaks, silver birches, shaggy larches, bristly gooseberry and black-currant bushes, white scrubbed-looking houses with fenceless gardens and windows decked out with lush petunias, begonias, and geraniums, and there, at the foot of everything, the chameleon lake. With a ruffle of its surface, it changes from glacier turquoise to mother-of-pearl, ripples through shades of green to blue to asphalt gray. In the middle of the lake on the east side, rising straight up out of it, leaving no space for a path or a bank, are the mountains, capped on the north by the Traunstein, a proud and knotty block of stone with a Nefertiti profile looking to the sky. Beside it, running to the south to join the great Alps, its smaller sisters, among them the "Sleeping Greek," with its retroussé nose.

The west side, our side, rises gently from the lakeside, spreads into a plain for some two or three miles, rising then into softly formed, thickly wooded hills. It seems as though every possible variation of beauty has been thought of and applied, the mountains are indeed majestic, but not overpowering, and the lake, the rich valley, and the wooded hills allow people to settle there and breathe. A leisured landscape, populated by leisurely folk.

Running through the valley, about a mile back from the lake, there's a single railway track, and in places there are still manually operated level crossings, with little houses for the signalmen. Three minutes before a train's due, the man cranks down the barrier, a bell ringing automatically as he does so. A little way behind one of these crossings, within earshot of the bell, in the midst of this perfect leisured landscape, shielded by trees and hidden away in a natural hollow, is the mill. "Why in a hollow?" some people ask when they hear of our choice. "Why not on top of a hill?" Why not the magnificent view, the sweeping panorama, why not see it all at one glance, have it at your elbow along with the TV and the Scotch, up there with the elite? Why not murder your fantasy, leave nothing whatsoever to the imagination? They sit on their hilltops like champagne corks, sit crouched over their beauty like eagles over prey, stripping it systematically to the bone. Grab a piece before it's all gone, there ain't too much left.

Easy to guess: the mill has no view. It's very large, but molded into the landscape, disrupting no one's vista, and is flanked by farmhouses. It forces its owners and their guests to climb to the top of its four stories if they want to see the lake, and on leaving it too, the mill offers a variety of revelations as regards outlook. Otherwise it's buttoned up tight and lives introspectively around the atrium of its courtyard, with its fountain and spreading walnut tree. Lying in the natural hollow, the mill is protected from the winds and the hail, which in these climes can get malevolent to the point of blowing in the windows and smashing tiles on the roof. The hallways are asymmetrical, and one of the walls slants to accommodate the preconceived passage of the stream outside; in fact, it has everything it takes to drive a modern, black-and-white purist architect out of his tiny mind, and for this reason David took the job of adapting the mill to our needs more and more into his own hands. With the help of the local builder and his troops, he withstood all cut-and-dried arguments brought forth by the architect he'd initially employed and set about faithfully preserving the mill's asymmetry and slanting-wall character.

All is well on this festive rainy day as the guests stand grouped around the fountain and the walnut tree under their shiny umbrellas, some of them already a little pink from the locally distilled apple-and-pear schnapps. They listen to the blare of the brass, then to the speech delivered by the foreman and his chief carpenter. The two clamber up to the newly completed truss, hoist a beribboned fir tree, and launch into the speech; the carpenter begins, but soon needs a prompt from the foreman, who's standing behind him with the text in his hands. The prompts become more and more necessary until finally the carpenter gives up, raises his glass to a chorus of bravos from below, and leaves the rest to the foreman. After this David makes a short speech of welcome and leads the way into the far-from-finished kitchen, bidding them to warm their toes at the open fireplace and set about the sausage, ham, and sauerkraut, the wine, the beer, and the schnapps. The warmth of the fire and the schnapps soon makes itself felt, the band sets feet tapping and couples spinning in a waltz.

All is well; the previous owner's tax debts have been removed from the registry book with the help of the local lawyer, the mill is on its way to becoming habitable, and the hostess's left arm is beginning to show signs of life and mobility again. Only the suckling pigs, revolving in the rain and smoke, disturb her. David and Hansi take turns basting and desperately pumping the bellows, but must soon admit that the pigs have laid down their lives for nothing, the charred pink meat is inedible. The hostess stands holding a green glass filled with mineral water—in deference to her hepatitis—toasts her guests, and feigns a little festive tipsiness. "This is where I wish to stay, here I wish to live," she murmurs to herself—or so she thinks. "Live!" cries Jozsi, a sixty-year-old Hungarian bricklayer, and falls down in the courtyard mud. He sits up, triumphantly brandishing an intact bottle of schnapps. "Right you are!" he laughs uproariously, "we must live!" He raises the bottle to his lips, then rolls over in the mud and falls asleep.

On this auspicious day she stands there in "her" courtyard and "her" mud, feeling more and more bloated with the pride of possession, optimistic in spite of suckling pigs and verdicts. Admittedly, she has hepatitis, a stone-filled gall bladder, and increasingly aggravating adhesions in her belly, is by and large not a good insurance risk, nor can she rightfully lay claim to the luxury of optimism. Moreover, her intestine keeps knotting itself up, unraveling only with the aid of stringent drugs which do nothing to improve her general state of health. The diet she's been put on to counteract the effects of the cobalt rays falls afoul of her finicky hepatitis: what's good for the one is murder for the other. She still has to face six sessions with the one-eyed cobalt monster, and although she hasn't the slightest desire ever to see a hospital again, the thought that she will soon be able to dispense with the services of her many doctors and professors leaves her feeling rejected, abandoned, dumped.

Her child will speak Austrian dialect and start school in the nearby village in a few months' time—but this is still too far ahead, she immediately puts a stop to all thought about it. Her present thoughts are about the fact that she's had the marvelous audacity to plump for a "home," and that she's no longer interested in impressing anyone. She won't sit on the edge of her seat any more, won't paw the ground in her eagerness to get up and go, she'll outlaw her volatile temper and kick ambition in the seat of the pants. She'll lean back in a comfortable seat in the orchestra and watch the others work up a lather. At this point the flea of reality gives her a fearful bite, making her spill a little of the mineral water she's passing off as vodka. "Don't kid yourself," the flea says, "your habits are cemented in foundations as solid as the ones they made for the new steel girders here in the mill. Your dreams of pastoral seclusion are going to run aground on the coral reefs where your subconscious has its headquarters and does nothing but sit and hatch its murky plots. The verdict will make a tiny bit of difference, sure, but basically you won't change a scrap." Let's hope not, she thinks to herself, feeling guilty the moment she thinks it. She raises her glass first to the stone figure of Catherine, the patron saint of mills, standing on her granite column behind the fountain, then to the Lourdes Madonna nestling in her niche high up on the wall; she's been there for many a year, braving the elements beneath a rusty little green tin roof, but she's not looking too wet at the moment as she gazes out at the familiar rain.

Jozsi, the old Hungarian, awakens from his nap in the mud, stretches himself, and gets to his feet, flings back his head to take a heavenly shower, and raises the bottle of schnapps to his chapped lips from time to time as he pursues the theme of "living." Between slugs he thoughtfully and exploringly mutters, "Live, yes, that's it," over and over again in many shades of volume and intonation, as though unsure of his ground, wanting to reassure himself.

The hostess tries to squeeze back into the crowded kitchen; she bumps into the local lawyer, who says, "If you want to feel at home and happy here, take heed of the advice everyone will offer you," whereupon he and the hostess twinkle at each other as though they were sharing an exclusive and enviable secret, then lift their glasses and drain them. Werner raises his stentorian voice and sings "The Pearl of Tyrol," a song new to the hostess. She's none the wiser ten minutes later, when Werner belts out the final bars, for the song is in Austrian dialect. Werner looks greatly encouraged by the swell of applause, lifts a bottle of red wine to the ceiling, and starts the song from the beginning again. Werner is very tall and very thin, with a very lined, very yellow face, and is obsessed with the mill. At the end of the day he remains behind and works on his beams and balconies, carving and planing with dark, imperturbable dedication, trotting home alone in the dusk. While singing, he rests his gnarled hand on Franz's shoulder. Franz, the foreman, is equally industrious and can be described in one word: fat. All attempts to soften this description by alluding to him as "stocky," or "well-built," or even "plump," dry on one's lips as one takes a good, honest look at him: he's fat. He's fat all over, but most especially around the midriff; the ripe bulge of his belly disregards such paltry encumbrances as shirt buttons and looms large and naked and pink over the top of his trousers as he stands there lending his gentle baritone harmonies to Werner's tenor lead, his soaring descants often rudely cut off by a rush of mortar and dust rising from his stirred-up lungs, his fat bloodshot eyes swiveling as though on stalks as they flit gleefully from the sausage to the sauerkraut to the great mug of beer in his hand.

David rams flaming torches into the mud and sticks fresh candles into the swimming remains of spent ones, while Hansi still refuses to admit defeat in his struggle with the sickening suckling pigs. Nobody watches the clock, nobody seems to be in a hurry; after months of constant noise, the neighbors, the laborers, and the hollow dwellers sit peacefully together. The shabby mill, still a gutted gaping shell among the other pert houses of the hamlet, appears to straighten up and resolve that it, too, will soon be neat, white, and decorative, no more a neighborhood eyesore.

The brass-band leader approaches the hostess, takes her in his arms, and sweeps her across the uneven floorboards, spins her around until she's close to fainting, lets go of her uneasily, and helps her to a chair in a dark corner. There she sits, listening to the music and the laughter. One thing is certain: she feels better since the operation in Salzburg. Although the academicians flatly refuse to acknowledge it, mutter "scientifically not proven," and ascribe her feelings to psychosomatic wishful thinking, she sticks to her guns: she feels better. An abscess as big as a pin's head between the roots of one crummy tooth can cause heart trouble, rheumatism, kidney colics, laryngitis, and circulatory collapse and pave the way to many another dire physical up-heaval—but that "cherry-size" item is supposed to have had no influence on the rest of the works? Was a mere trifle, so to speak? There's a wire crossed and smoldering somewhere, a whiff of mumbo-jumbo in the air, and once more she mistrusts the "three doctors, three opinions" science, its disconnected passage from surgeon to gynecologist to internal specialist. "A couple of cells always manage to evade us and slip away . . ." Where to? Where do the serene little cellules hole up under the glazed eye of research as it waits forlornly at the end of the line for public funds? Where are they, the recalcitrant scuttling bugs known as cancer?

Werner and Franz go floundering by on the wave of song and schnapps, and the hostess bangs the door shut on her morbid dungeon. She sees her child linking hands with the neighbors' children and skipping through the legs of the adult guests, and feels a long-forgotten warm sensation rising within herself, a warmth she'd known some three decades ago, at the beginning of her acting career, a time when she'd been in love with everything and everybody, had believed everything and everybody to be good and right and proper, without exception, and had had a fund of suitable excuses ready to hand for anything that seemed inexplicable or hostile. In this manner she had defended the newly won blinkers that enabled her to believe in the implicit good in human beings and urged her to live up to the noble standards set by the classics that formed the basis of her daily studies. No war, no bombs, no prison camp could do anything to dislodge her blinkers. Behind them, she painted herself a pleasant picture of life in which horror and terror were summarily dismissed as exceptions to the rule; the paranoiac mania and diabolical perversion she was currently experiencing would, when it reached the end of its course, however terrible that end might be, quietly disappear forever and leave the stage clear for the normal, intended state of goodness and optimism. Astonishingly, and with a minimum of effort, she did manage to develop a point of view from which she was able to see people in a light that reflected them as benevolently as only an immensely naïve god could have hoped to create them. Particularly at the end of the war, she went panting up to each new acquaintance with the trust and enthusiasm of a mollycoddled, friendly puppy, was taken for many a painful and expensive ride as a consequence, but nevertheless hung on for dear life to her blinkers. She braved emigration and endless brickbats of resentment against "the Germans," survived dozens of doctors and hospitals, defamation and libel in the press too, until finally, after many years, during which time her blinkers (optimism-with-a-purpose is the trendy German phrase for it) were put to many a sore trial, she arrived at the widely acclaimed and generally aspired-to state of common sense, or open mistrust. Generally speaking, that is to say, for she still persisted in relapsing into her featherbed of pleasant artlessness, and even to the present day she doesn't care for the cynical curve that twists lips out of shape when conversation turns to the virtue of being a good judge of character. She still takes people at face value, hopes for the best, and awaits developments, an attitude which doubtlessly invites a life full of surprises and tumult. Under the motto "I let myself in for that one," many promising friendships grind to a jolting halt, and for years she unquestioningly threw herself into piles of prosaic work, enabling her less industrious staff of advisers and managers to live very comfortably. But that was long ago and far away, her husband talked her out of that one.

At times she feels as disemboweled as the sadly misused suckling pigs, the only *faux pas* at her otherwise greatly enjoyable party. One thought persistently troubles her and she fights in vain to put it from her: How grave is the fact that she still hankers after her rose-colored blinkers? Just think about it: She's from Berlin, a town whose humor stems from predominant poverty and which is anchored in the firm and unshakable belief that situations which are already intolerable can only get worse. And, as stated, she's still besottedly sold on the idea that people can be good, even though she has more often than not experienced the opposite in her capacity as public property and doctors' subject. Sometimes she'd like to remove herself completely from human dependence, praying that the long period of familiarity is at an end, but being as unsuited for Zoroastrian complacency as she is, and lacking a trustworthy confidante, she falls into air pockets of despond and melancholy. Over and above all this, she feels that there are too many articulate explanations for the necessity of hate and too few woolly ones for that of affinity; she'd like to throw her arms around the prickly German writer who recently stepped down from his beloved political rostrum and exposed a fundamental yearning by saying: "The world is crying out for the soft sell."

•

What do the bleary-eyed mill owners do on the all too quickly dawning morning of the day after the night of the super party? They clean their smashed mill with the help of their extraordinarily friendly neighbors; then their ways part for the rest of the daylight hours. David pulls on his boots and goes off to supervise the building operations, while his wife takes her place at the electric piano with her daughter and Hansi, plugs her ears, and stares out at the drizzling rain as she tries to think of words with the suitable number of syllables to fit the phrases Hansi is suggesting on the keys. At one point she obeys a very human impulse and visits their sole functioning toilet, takes her position behind the still lockless door, and watches spellbound as two large paint-bespattered hands suddenly grip the door at both sides, lift it from its hinges, and carry it away. Despite her precarious position, she finds her voice, shrieks for all she's worth, and stays put. The hands reappear with the door immediately, hitch it back onto its hinges, and push it to. For several days she will make frequent forays to all parts of the house where painters are at work and peer challengingly into their faces, half hoping and half fearing to detect an expression of embarrassment or of advanced intimacy, but none is forthcoming.

That afternoon, two lawyers arrive. They take their places on kitchen chairs between the bed and the electric piano and begin by discussing the weather. This harmless time-honored opening gambit has a note of urgency about it on this occasion, because the wind is blowing rain through the vacant window frames with considerable force. The lawyers struggle back into the raincoats they've just shed and resume their seats, looking as though they're about to embark on a tricky nautical expedition. Right away they come to the point. The point is the mill owners' last will and testament. One lawyer has come from Zurich; he is lean and wiry and his skin has that cleanness and freshness about it that suggests a life free of alcohol and nicotine, full of exercise and fresh air and regular sleep. After some little maneuvering, he finds the desired position for his legs, but not for the rest of his body: the trunk and arms seem to jerk back and forth almost uncontrollably. His alert yellow-brown eyes dart from one face to the next, zoom to spots of extreme interest on the wooden floor, examine them exhaustively, then dart back to the faces with renewed energy. The second man is the local Austrian lawyer. His strong suit is a brilliantly bluffed show of awkwardness; his round, bright-blue eyes peer at the world in pure astonishment, his frequent bubbling bursts of laughter are carefree and cordial, and the way he sips at his big glass of whiskey with obvious enjoyment leads one to believe that his concentration is focused more on his palate than on the matter at hand. When he starts to speak, however, his words are rapid and devious and are accompanied by a series of snorts and grunts and wheezes, and it soon becomes clear that it would take an extraordinarily patient opponent to withstand the temptation to say yes to everything, if only to get him to stop.

For the moment the Zuricher is still, sipping his orange juice and stealing bright little peeps as the Austrian babbles something about ". . . the property alone, and then the division of the furnishings, of course, the Court of Chancery would have its say on every last chair." The lady of the mill doesn't attempt to listen too intently since she's incapable of understanding any form of officialese and knows that she'll lose the thread whether she concentrates or not; the words and their meaning tumble over each other and begin to balloon in her brain after a very short while, so she turns her attention to the clothesline hanging in the neighbors' garden: despite the rain it's full of brightly colored children's pants and sweaters. The colors delight her and she makes plans to buy canvas, brushes, oil paint, and turpentine, plans to fulfill the promise she made herself in the hospital —to paint again.

Her husband knows that absent look of hers when he sees it and now huddles forward on the edge of the bed the better to concentrate on the stream of legal chatter. From a great distance she hears the Zuricher's singsong accent as he soars at the end of a long speech and appears to address her husband: "In case of death on the part of the wife . . ." She wrests her eyes from the clothesline and its bright rain-soaked load; only now does she notice that her husband's hair has turned almost completely white. During the day he either wears a hat or his hair is full of dust anyway, and at night the paltry lighting in their improvised apartment has helped conceal the change that has taken place in the last six weeks. There are deep rings under his eyes too, and the tan of his skin disguises the transformation in his face only at first glance. He is still a strikingly handsome man, but the lines that surround his eyes and run from the nose to the corners of his mouth, causing the optimistic upward twists to wilt into a droop, bear witness to the effect the verdict has had on him.

The Zuricher's clear voice slices through her observations. "There's a further matter, which requires delicate handling," he says distinctly. The Austrian listens to the Swiss's point, and for once replies concisely, which surprises his colleague—for a moment it looks as if he might begin to purr. Stretching his neck like a Siamese cat that is being stroked in exactly the right spot, he murmurs a long and thoughtful "Yeees," to round things off. The Austrian promptly ruins everything by delivering a speech of considerable length and intricacy; the Swiss surprises everyone again by welcoming it with absolute accord, going so far as to say, "I am in complete agreement," therewith ending the discussion of the point in question. They both scribble in their notebooks, put check marks at the bottom of the pages, and turn them over.

David now rubs his right ear, lights a cigarette, and offers his opinion; the Swiss repeats the last four words of what David has said and adds a deliberating "Hmm" of his own. While this is going on, the Austrian fidgets with his spectacles and his glass, and, to Christina's delight, displays a fine sense of fun and fantasy by taking a page from his pad and folding it into a sailboat. This upsets the Swiss greatly. His eyeballs fairly spin around in their sockets as though freshly greased, coming to rest eventually on the dial of his wristwatch, which is equipped with every known method of measuring the passage of time. His studied perusal of the chronometer attracts the Austrian's attention and puts an end to his little game; he knits his brows and his round eyes appear to huddle together. Both the lawyers are now looking intently at the watch, one apparently earnestly checking the hour or the date and holding himself in check at the same time, the other watching with ill-concealed impatience to see just how long the impoliteness may last. David clears his throat and stretches his very long legs, his knees clicking as he does so. At this point Christina hammers on the electric piano. She bangs on the top notes, then in the bass, discovers that balled fists get you a whole lot more than just single fingers, discovers the knob that controls the volume too, and turns it up as far as it will go, fairly lifting the adult conversationalists from their seats. The Swiss decides there's nothing for it but to ignore the racket and shouts his next points bravely. In view of the circumstances, both lawyers seem tacitly to agree to bury their little hatchet and nod at each other with knowing smiles, rather like two doctors when they catch each other taking wild diagnostic shots in the dark. After two further sticky hours, the Austrian gets up and scratches himself, empties his glass, and rams a massive stack of papers violently into his shabby satchel. The Swiss rises too, rubs hands that are blue from the cold, and turns to the lady of the mill, saying, "Well, I think we've covered every point." He takes his orderly sheaf of transparent plastic folders and stows them carefully into various compartments in his attaché case. Together they clamber down the chicken-run ladder, leaving behind them a vaguely disquieted couple and a very happy, piano-thumping child.

In the evening, after the lawyers, Hansi, and the workers have all left, David and his wife lie in bed watching the flickering light of the candles and listening to the gurgling of their brook. Their daughter is asleep beside them. They lie there and give themselves up to their thoughts, murmuring a disconnected sentence now and then. His thoughts drift back to the street full of cabbage, lamb, and fish smells, to the zinc bathtub and the savings pot on the kitchen shelf, to memories of withering damp cold and a father who either ranted or said not a word. She remembers the toilet on the stairs, the dingy back courtyards with carpetbeaters thudding and the corners full of garbage cans, remembers drooling old men lunging at her from dark doorways, the smell of leather and shoemaker's glue in Stepfather's "Soling Establishment," the street with three tangents next to Wilmersdorf railway station, the prickly material of the sofa she slept on, the light in the stairway that burned for exactly three minutes, then switched itself off with an evil click. The stations they had encountered on their journey through poverty and luxury had had a gypsy-like quality of transience about them; they had set up camp in oases that had always seemed suspect from the word go, and that had been dependent on the shifting values of the open market of their freelance professions, relying on public praise or public condemnation, on the few precious moments of unqualified recognition.

They lie there, for the moment still stunned, in "their" room, in "their" mill, filled with mistrust and anxiety at the step they've taken, the ravine they've crossed in transforming from nomads into solid settlers, from gamblers to insurance-paying pedants, and hang on to the thought that they are now responsible, loving parents, being twisted around ten pudgy little fingers every minute of the day. Whatever other reasons there were for the step, they had wanted peace. More and more they abhor the thumbscrews of public malice, the butcher's hook onto which libel, envy, and greed slip so easily. More and more do they detest the pulverizing intrigues, the money-conscious cunning of their oh-so-friendly advisers. After one and a half decades of almost daily companionship, they want to escape from the escalating brutalization surrounding them and their success, want out of the cesspool of slander printed about them in heavy type with screeching exclamation marks. They still cherish a hope of shaking off the encroaching numbness, the desensitizing process that illness, the verdict, and overexposure in the media have brought with them.

For quite some time now they've approached each other with the care, shyness almost, of two people who know each other all too well. They dread the cliché, the dog-eared phrase, the verbal diarrhea that can stifle simple emotion. Above all, her greatest dread is: his coolness. And his: her fury. His coolness pours oil on the fire of her wrath, her eruptions quickly extinguish the level flame of his measured participation, drive him into remote retreat. They know the first rumblings of their harridan days when they hear them, know too, later, that they've maltreated their partnership, that love and hate are interchangeable; each needs the other's nearness and friendship. They also know that they alone are capable of hurting each other, and that all others, including close friends, are relegated to being just "people" when they themselves are harmonizing. When they are not, the friends are rallied to the battlefield of their gigantic egocentric dramas, only to be rudely elbowed into the wings or knocked clean from the stage should they dare to attempt to dictate the course of the plot, the intensity of which they are incapable of understanding.

Love and friendship are subject to two entirely different sets of rules, she thinks to herself, lying there; friendship must prove itself, love must be *there*. It may weather many a setback, many an onslaught, outlive wars even. "Sleep now," her husband says. "Sleep and forget."

Once again the verdict flares up: she thinks of the time shortly after it had been spoken when he came to the hospital carrying a cardboard box, sat down beside her bed, and was silent with her for some time. Then he opened the box and lifted out tiles, tiles for the bathrooms in the mill. They had plunged into the planning, dug in their heels when it had come to differences of opinion, agreed, argued, gone into raptures about colors, the designs for old-fashioned windows and door handles, until they'd succeeded in shoving the verdict aside, upstaged it, played the mill into the foreground.

He, who since his youth and the encounter with TB has regarded dying and death as a natural and acceptable component of living, to be approached with sublime fatalism, is often taken unawares and then stands impotent in the face of her panic-filled mania for life. Her shrewish willfullness and towering desperation seem suspect to him and greatly disturb his love and need for peace and contentment—except when they are working together. Because of this he tends to classify actions of hers which irritate him as "tantrums" and feminine lack of control. In short, he too is an adherent of the ancient masculine maxim that a man who shouts is "dynamic," a woman who screams "hysterical." A talk "man to man" is more valid to him, of more substance and durability, than one between man and woman, and there's no convincing him that human shortcomings or lack of character are universal and in no single case dependent on gender.

That same night I dreamed that a complete stranger to me,

an elderly lady, was squatting in a narrow room beneath a high window; her head rocked loosely to and fro on her shoulders, then fell bloodlessly to the floor. She felt around and finally found it, picked it up, and set it back on the dark frayed hole between her shoulders, seeming contented until she made a sudden, incautious movement and the head threatened to pitch forward and fall again.

I wake up covered with perspiration. My husband and daughter are sleeping peacefully. The brook is still gurgling, two lights go on in the farm next door: milking time. A cock crows some distance away, the bell at the level crossing rings, a little while later a freight train rumbles by.

In the evening Bertha arrives, in answer to a desperate cry of help from the floundering family. Forgotten the weeks of albatross waddling and the farewell note she'd scribbled in pencil when she'd stormed off and left us over a year and a half ago. Without Bertha the house is in disorder, is illegitimate and virtueless—not to mention the lack of regular nourishment. Bertha is: moat, drawbridge, and portcullis. Without her the hordes swarm in from the plains and scale the walls of the citadel.

She approaches. The family excitedly hurries over the wobbly planks to the front door, clutching candles and torches, listening with bated breath as the taxi chugs down the hill and stops in front of the mill. The back door opens and two red suitcases fall out into the mud, two umbrellas follow them, then a bag with a plastic window through which one can see David the cat performing somersaults that are remarkably agile for his age. Then a framed aquarelle picture of Bertha appears, finally Bertha herself. She awkwardly edges her way forward on the back seat saying, "God, oh, God" and "Goodness gracious me." Her hair is snow white and cropped and freshly set, battened down and fastened, her body has gained in corpulence, the albatross leg grown worse, her arthritis more evident, and her faith in human nature gone to the dogs once and for all, as she is soon to tell us.

After we've hugged each other and shed a few tears, Bertha says, "Well, then" and "So," instigates a short search of her suitcases, and comes up with her enormous old apron, which she puts on and ties around the middle. She distributes presents, notices deploringly that the lady of the mill has "not a gram of fat on her ribs," declares that her predecessors must have been "scum, riff-raff" and "persons," and that the mill is "very nice, I'm sure, but still in a hell of a mess." And then again, "So." After a welcoming glass of wine, Bertha gets red blotches on her face and sits with Christina on her lap and poses her habitual evening question: "What on earth shall we cook tomorrow?" then adds, "We'll cross that bridge when we come to it." Then she stands up, tucks David the cat under her arm, strokes Christina's hair, and proclaims her final "Time for the high road, so." We hurry after her eagerly, but have difficulty getting to sleep; we twist and turn in the delicious certainty that from tomorrow on we'll get breakfast, lunch, and dinner at rigidly appointed times. After the first, warning "You can slowly take your places," the next "It's served" will follow, and if there's a further delay, she'll look aloof and say, "Now it's ruined," and leave it at that. She'll answer the front door with her legs planted wide apart and send unwelcome callers scurrying for cover, she'll shout on the telephone because she always shouts on the telephone, and should Martin, the priest, be on the other end of the line, then the connection between Austria and Bavaria will be in serious danger. And of course she'll still say she must "go toilet," and this in a low voice, for toilet is improper and has no right to an article. She'll postpone her days off because "Now's not the time, too much going on," and when she does take them she'll call after an hour's absence, because "I was worried you wouldn't cope." She'll return from her vacation much earlier than was planned because "The old women got on me nerves," and will glower at our house guests with the charm of a CIA agent. She'll cook her extra-special dishes only for those intimate friends who have proved themselves beyond a doubt; others, who may possibly harbor the ambition to be admitted to the small circle of regular guests, will have their enthusiasm promptly dampened with a "Nothing but cold cuts today." Anyone who has once been referred to by Bertha as being a "good-fornothing nincompoop" may pay her compliments and increase the size of his tips until he's blue in the face, all to no avail. Bertha decided many a moon ago that we were naïve and too good-natured, and made it part of her job to govern, protect, and guide us.

•

During the last sessions the one-eyed monster unleashes his malice; silently he warms to his business, goes too far, and burns me badly. No one seems very surprised that my skin turns violet, swells and festers, and threatens to split the incision open again. "Ointment. And ten days' rest." The arm is put back in the sling, again the patient totters around like a wooden Indian. After ten sleepless nights she's terrified anew of the monster, and Bertha stalks past the laborers muttering, "Now it's going too far" and "Who'd have thought it possible."

•

I swear that I'd had not the slightest intention of blowing my top. I had been motherly-mild, had looked forward timidly, anxiously, to our daughter's first day at school. According to the local custom, the first day was short, beginning and ending in the church. Satchels and sandwiches weren't necessary. Our House of God is undoubtedly imposing, and it's as cold and dark as Siberia in winter. The organ remained mute on this occasion.

Like a duck that's missing one duckling, I hurry along the six rows of the assembled class, feebly trying to control my agitation. To my left: the father, quite composed. To my right: Bertha, with a pinched look about her that hollers, "What am I doing in a Catholic church at my time of life?" and murmuring, "Ah, just look at our little sweetheart," every now and again. I search my bag for the third time and finally find the right pair of spectacles, put them on, and see the ash-blond hair. It's throwing off reddish tints in the sunlight. She's chatting animatedly with the girl next to her, taking not the slightest notice of her hovering family, or of the repeated "Shhhs" the severe-looking teacher is hissing at her.

A red-faced elderly man comes hurrying in, arranging a sheaf of papers, takes up his position, lifts his eyes to the ceiling, and stays that way until the children grow quiet. Only when the silence is total and golden does he let his eyes slide almost scaldingly over the children's heads. Then he raises his sonorous voice, which is clearly on sure ground, used to authority and success, starts in with a sentence that contains the word "sinners," continues with another that warns his youthful audience that "the carefree days are over, the earnestness of life about to begin," then asserts that "your parents will surely be glad to get you out of the house and off to school." This much must be said for him: within a very short time and with a few carefully chosen phrases he manages to undermine the relationship the children thought they'd had with their parents, and makes it clear to them that school is not all the happy-go-lucky fun it's been cracked up to be. The little heads sink down between the pews, little hands clutch and scratch at little knees, a shiver passes through their ranks as though they've only just noticed how cold it is. The gentleman follows up his first triumph with a reminder that regular visits to this house on Sundays are imperative, this isn't only his own personal wish but an explicit command from on high—with the last two words his eyeballs roll up to the ceiling again. The little heads tilt back and follow the direction of his glance in dreadful anticipation, while their parents listen in a state of etherized stupor, or so it seems.

The ash-blonde child's mother feels a twitching in her legs. Arno Schmidt's "You want tolerance after 1,500 years?" comes spilling to the fore. She turns to her husband and snarls, in English, "Let's get out of here." He looks down at her reprovingly and grunts, "Behave yourself," which only serves to drive her farther up the baroque wall. She jumps up, squeezes her way along the pew, and stamps out—unceremoniously, as it turns out, since the flagstones are very old and uneven and she nearly sprains her ankle on her way to the door. Outside, she marches up and down in the autumnal sunshine, her head boiling, the rest of her freezing, and waits with a minimum of patience until her child is released from the claws of medieval dictatorship.

Martin once related that he'd asked his pupils what they thought the meaning of "original sin" was. "That one generation is as stupid as the next," one of the boys answered. "Right you are," Martin told him. Here as elsewhere: two priests, two vastly different worlds. "God made willfulness—who exiled it?" the mother fumes, almost out of her mind and shaking with God's homely cold.

We get into the car without a word and take home nothing but running noses and a torrent of disunity. Doors slam in the mill, and the mother is once again seized by speechless rage and bitter disappointment, a condition the verdict can apparently do nothing to change.

•

Our daughter's school books contain nice little pencil and tempera sketches of "family life." Mama is baking a cake as Papa comes home from work; he's tired, of course, but still thrilled to bits about the cake. Mama smiles and stirs her batter while Papa retires to his armchair with the paper. On the next page Mama laughs gaily as she waters the plants (here, school-book mamas don't go to work and never ever read, they're one and all illiterate, apparently) and says, "Papa will be home late today." The children look dashed and express heartrending regrets. Mama looks as though she'll pop a fuse with the intensity of her delight at this, and offers some stupefying solace.

The books also show that the children attend mixed classes but that the sexes are divided when it comes to handicrafts. "Why don't the boys learn how to sew and cook too?" I ask, which has Christina and her schoolchums rolling in the aisles. They simmer down and look pensive when I ask them how on earth poor Johann or Franz will get on in life if he doesn't find the right girl or can't afford a housekeeper. From the way Christina looks at me, it's clear that she's beginning to realize that her emancipated and professionally active mama bears scant similarity to the ones she knows from her books.

Her mama has hardly reconciled herself to these hard facts of school life when she's confronted with a new problem. She's awakened from a fitful sleep one night by her daughter; sobbing and trembling, Christina crawls into the big double bed and whispers, in the following order, "Fires of hell, Last Judgment, end of the world, deadly sin." Each of the jolting phrases intensifies her misery. After endless, patient, camouflaged questions as to where she had heard these things, it turns out that they've been part of the first lesson in religion. The Protestant calls the Catholic first thing in the morning.

Martin (shouting): "Yes, what's up?"

Mama (also shouting): "Do you give them the same nonsense?"

Martin: "Not a word. I'll come right away."

A few hours later he comes roaring through the fog and rain in his Volkswagen jalopy and spends the whole afternoon talking to Christina. In spite of his efforts to convert fear back to joy, the fires of hell flare with undiminished brilliance, sear their way through to alert infantile cells, breed neuroses and immovable guilt complexes, and although we've managed to get her exempted from the religion classes, Christina persists in chewing her nails and sucking her thumb in bed, fears the dark, and rears at the sound of thunder, things she'd never done until the first mention of purgatory.

Hell has many profiles. And yet again: two priests, two interpretations.

•

The news comes that Werner, the carpenter who'd been so obsessed with the mill and sang "The Pearl of Tyrol," is dead. Cancer. He'd been treated for sciatica for the past nine months. His doctor need not answer to anybody—everyone makes mistakes, it's only human. Not like pilots. If they're lucky enough to live through their mistakes, they face a jury.

The adhesions in the patient's belly are becoming less and less funny. They're talking of operating again. The seventh abdominal operation. The patient asks the new professor, "Can you guarantee that another operation would remove the trouble, once and for all?"

Pause. Little coughs. A look out of the window. "Well now ... You appear to be prone to adhesions, nearly everyone is after so many operations; for this reason it could happen that similar complications might occur at a later date."

"Worse ones?"

"One can't tell."

"So why operate?"

"Because at any minute you could suffer a complete stoppage of the bowels, and the drugs you're taking now to avoid this circumstance could lead to addiction."

"How would my hepatitis react to the anesthetic?"

"That's a point."

"And is it advisable to operate again so soon after the amputation?"

Pause. A wrinkled brow. He'd had nothing to do with the "cherry-size" item. Suddenly he realizes what I'm talking about. "Oh yes, of course. Well, that's a ... perhaps we should take X-rays first."

I'm given a room for the day. I'm in the same hospital in Salzburg, but in a different department. The new professor is not a gynecologist, he's the chief surgeon. He's small and round and has broad hands with short fingers. He sweeps into the room in his long smock and says, "You must go down to be X-rayed every hour; in between you can come back here and rest. By the way, I was in Berlin at the end of the war, I fought in the last battle." The war veterans exchange nods of recognition.

The window here is on the left, for the first time on the left. Through it I can see the mountains; their peaks are lost in clouds, diagonal streaks of snow mark their sides. Right in front of the window there's a cheerless modern building of little fantasy, and the corrugated-iron roofs of a number of construction huts. To the right, two of the small hospital roads meet, at the junction a red-and-white-framed convex mirror has been erected. It's like one of those distorting mirrors at a fairground; fat distended short-legged figures and flattened ambulances that look as though they've been in a bad crash slide across it and disappear.

The room contains a tall thin palisander cupboard, and across from the bed there's a triangular table with three legs, beside it two chairs. On the wall beside the window are two framed color photos, one of a fox, the other of a hedgehog. The curtains remind me of those that invariably adorn the windows of modernized village inns, stripes and dots, squares and oblongs, blue, brown, and gray-white. Depressing. The heavens are overcast, obliterated. To ward off the gloom settling over me, I swing my left arm, stretch it as high up as I can, bend it backward, and clutch my right elbow from behind my back. All of it works, each movement comes easily. My U-boat commander and Red Fluff have done a splendid job, and if on top of it they managed to prevent those few little bugs from slipping away . . .

The door opens and bangs against the outer wall, a black-haired creased little man comes in pushing an old wheelchair. "Come to get you," he says. I offer him a cigarette and the lighter's flame shows me his cracked and wizened face clearly for a few seconds; it's no bigger than a child's. I hear him clomping along behind me as we go down corridors, through doors, out onto the road, enter an elevator, out again and down another corridor. Finally we come to a pair of glass double doors; he pushes me through and stops the chair with a flourish that almost spills me forward on my face. The manic hubbub peculiar to hospitals the world over is at an impressive high, the X-ray department of this one appearing to be particularly turbulent. In direct contrast to the frenetic staff, the patients are sitting and lying listlessly in neat rows around the walls like sardines and look as though they've been there for a long, long time and have given up trying to remember why.

I'm pushed into an office where two telephones are ringing; nobody answers them and they eventually stop. Then a nurse comes in and wheels me over to an X-ray screen. The radiologist appears in due course, wearing the typical introverted expression that comes of looking into people instead of at them. I say "Good morning" to him over the top of the screen and he jumps like a startled rabbit. Obediently I choke down the vile-tasting gruel and obey the standard commands: "Breathe in, hold it, breathe out!" I'm trundled back and forth between my room and the X-ray department the whole morning, always doing exactly as I'm told. At one point in the proceedings the professor comes in and invites me down to his office. It's exactly like the other offices of this establishment, drab and colorless, not at all the restful harbor one would imagine a surgeon coming back to after hours of standing over an operating table. They surely deserve something better than this postwar furniture, the cheap glass-fronted bookcases, armchairs as resilient as cast iron and lamps like those of a waiting room in a small market town railway station.

Each of us exhausted for different reasons, we chat about exploding birth rates and overpopulation. "I'm a burden, you're a burden, perhaps the authorities should start handing out weapons, or let TB flare up again, it's less painful than the plague we're nurturing at the moment, I believe. How about it? If we have to kill ourselves off, why not choose a more humane method than cancer?" He shrugs his shoulders. The glass top of his desk is empty and gleaming; he wipes the edge of it, moves the wastepaper basket from the left to the right side of the desk, and says, "I think it's about time we were getting over there again."

I resume my stance behind the screen, comfortable now, expecting no surprises, when the radiologist reaches around and starts pressing my belly with his gloved hand, squeezing the gruel along my intestines. He peers at his magic mirror, presses and prods until I can stand the pain no longer. I give a rasping squawk and sag back against the slanting board behind me, then slide to the floor. I see their astonished faces gazing down at me in the blue half-light, the radiologist looking very dissatisfied with his dropout patient. The professor is called and he soon hurries in carrying a hypodermic at the ready. I lie on the thorny couch and hear them mumbling. "No one can live with adhesions like that," one of them says.

The hospital is asleep, the night shift brewing coffee as I stagger back to my room. The professor sits down on the bed and knits his short fingers together. "I'm one of those surgeons who likes to avoid operating where possible," he says. "However, in your case I see no alternative, and I believe we should proceed as soon as possible." I know I'll say yes and not come back. Not again. Not one after the other.

I make one last try. "All my veins are ruined. How could you do the anesthetic?"

"We'll find one that's good enough. And while we're about it, we ought to cauterize that fissure and remove the gall bladder."

"Would you mind sending what's left to my next of kin c.o.d.?"

He looks almost paternally concerned and says, "I wish I had better news for you."

David picks me up an hour later. "How was it?" he asks. "Another operation," I answer. We drive back along the almost deserted autobahn in silence. Mondsee glistens greenly through the low-hanging clouds, now and then a chalk-white sickle peeps through them and in our window. A light drizzle starts before we reach the Attersee, the windshield wipers hum comfortingly, I doze off, wake up with a start, doze off again. Memories of doctors start spinning around my half-drugged brain like blurred figures on a merry-go-round. They loom up, superimpose themselves over each other, squirm out of the cracks of walled-up storerooms, skip out of their place in chronology, march up, and state their case, some of them with monstrous self-importance, others with proud disdain, very few with plain candor.

The first to step forward from the whirling crowd is a dark militaristic orthopedist of French descent. He's got Christina's bad leg in his clutches; he takes a slender gold ball-point pen from the breast pocket of his smock and draws a line along her thin calf, saying in a sharp penetrating voice, "This is where I shall cut, then distend the Achilles' tendon." Christina's eyes lose all color from fright. "Please, Mama, please, Papa, please don't let him."

"I'll strangle the bastard," I yell. David stamps on the brakes. "What's up? Are you in pain?" He shakes me. "The specialist," I say, "the one who wanted to operate on Christina." David presses the cigarette lighter. "Yes," he says, "yes, I know." The lighter illuminates his long fingers.

The bastard retires and a university clinic professor with gold buttons on his white coat comes forward. The clinic was a crackerjack German one, he was its chief pediatrician. He had the tone and bearing of a field marshal, and any vestige of modesty he might have been blessed with at birth had been eroded by a lifetime's succession of submissive, imploring mothers—an incorrigible case of elephantine arrogance from the top of his broad and shining pate to the pointed tips of his custom-made Italian shoes. It had been 11:45 p.m., Christina was running a temperature of 103 degrees. We took her to the hospital, Gold Buttons made his entrance and, in a nasal voice, commanded, "She will remain here for observation." I tell him what the specialists in Bern had diagnosed as being the cause of the weakness in her leg. My concern about her present fever is such that my narrative is halting and probably very inelegant. This seems to amuse him, yes, there's no question, he seems to find me very entertaining. He raises his pale-blond eyebrows and lends me his jug-handle ear, feels the child's foot, lets it drop again carelessly, and says, "I am not of the same opinion as my Swiss colleagues." I wouldn't have been surprised had he added, "Over and out," and slammed down the field telephone. Even so I venture to ask, "And what in your opinion is the real cause?" He draws himself up, the gold buttons are in danger of popping. More nasally than ever he says, "That I don't know," as though I'd asked him where I might locate a toilet. I assume my best subordinate manner, make a hint of a curtsy, and ask, "May I stay with her?" Whoops—his eyebrows are back up again and his breathless "What?" almost has me kneeling to kiss his ring. I struggle for words and come up with: "A child needs its mother much more when it's sick than when it's healthy, and I might be able to relieve the night nurse a little." His look reminds me of some I had seen during my childhood; they'd usually been accompanied by the phrase "un-German conduct." My whimpering smallness warms him to the cockles, however, and he proclaims benevolently, "You may remain if you promise to behave." With this he marches out of the conference, revealing buttons at the back too. Three heavy golden ones.

There are glass cages instead of rooms. Children with bandaged heads, arms and legs in plaster casts, splints, infusion bottles, and tubes; they are sobbing, crying, screaming. "Mama," I hear. The night nurse is wearing clogs and mink eyelashes. She sits in her cubicle with her elbows propped on her desk, stirring a cup of coffee, filing her nails. She picks up the telephone and has a long conversation with Jupp, then with Wolfie, finally Peter. Peter takes longest. Her approach and the degree of warmth she invests in her voice vary with each partner. With Jupp she stands no nonsense, she's obviously got the upper hand; she sips her coffee noisily and munches her way through three biscuits as they converse, and there's no doubt, she really means it when she rasps, "You must be off your tiny rocker" and "This is the end of the line." Wolfie is another matter. He's out of a higher drawer altogether, the tone of the conversation is subdued, and Wolfie's principal interest appears to be politics. She squirms uncomfortably as she says, "Structural crisis," and, a while later, "Definitive statement." Her aghast expression and the perplexed "What did you say again?" followed by a hesitant "Oh yeah, parity," seem to suggest that whatever the basis of their relationship may be, she'd be a whole lot happier were Wolfie there in the flesh instead of on the telephone. With Peter the hormones start to simmer, now the tone becomes honey-sweet and breathy, pillow talk vibrates around the cubicle as she swallows syllables and purrs little sighs. After about half an hour she says, "Wait a minute," lays the receiver down on the desk, clip-clops out into the corridor, yells, "Quiet!" clip-clops back in again whistling "It's a Hard Day's Night," takes up the receiver, and effortlessly finds her way back into her TV-commercial-sexy voice. A little boy is sobbing desperately; his neck is in a cast and his hands are tied. A girl is pressing out high thin screams as though she were being tortured, others keep up a continuous chorus of "Mama."

At four o'clock in the morning this mama goes into the

cubicle and asks, "Aren't you ever going to attend to the children?" The nurse kicks the leg of a chair with a clog, barks, "What business is it of yours?" and glares at me defiantly. Children don't register complaints, and the professor must surely know why he hired her.

At six, the day shift moves in to the assault, chattering and giggling. One of them comes into our cage, says, "You'd better hurry up and get dressed, the professor will soon be here on his rounds," and before I realize what she's doing, thrusts a thermometer up to the hilt into Christina's rectum. "Are you out of your mind?" I shout at her. "Don't take so long if you put it in deep," she answers nonchalantly, "or do you think we want to stand around for three minutes with each one?" "That's it!" I say and start to dress Christina. We collide with Gold Buttons on our way out the door. He hasn't had much sleep either, of course, and his master's voice is not as vibrant as usual, but still the authority rings through. "What is the meaning of this?" His retinue's lips all form O's. "Sleepless nights we can get at home," the irate mother answers. "Impudence," one of the retinue says. "At your own responsibility," says another. "I only wish I thought you understood the meaning of the word," the mother babbles heatedly. "You may be able to get away with it with the children—and with the senile, and with all sick people. But not with me, not yet anyway." Gold Buttons looks as though he's about to rip off my epaulettes and have me court-martialed; as I turn on my heel, it's on the tip of my tongue to say "Heil Hitler."

At the exit a nurse comes running up breathlessly behind us. "Thank you," she stutters. "You're the first one that's ever said anything, it's like a concentration camp..."

I hear the children screaming in their glass cages for many a long night.

Nothing has changed, apparently. I still revere the memory of the professor who operated on my jaw without anesthesia when I was fourteen. "Pull yourself together, you brat!" he'd roared.

We don't appear to be really very fond of children, we folks to the north of the Alps—children don't contribute enough to the competitive ascent of the ladder, are more a hindrance than a help. What did that doctor in Bavaria say when he heard that she was still wetting the bed at the age of three? "Give her a good hard walloping, that's what she needs—a bit of discipline." And he was thirty at most, so he couldn't have learned his discipline from the Nazis.

The professor in Bern, the one who was born in Ticino, on the Italian border, is different. He has hands as soft as a chick's feathers, and his love of children shines from every pore. He laughs with them, cries with them, and when Christina was four and we discovered that her teeth were in a terrible state, he said, "We'll mend them while you're sleeping. One little sting and then you'll go into a wonderful sleep." Turning to us, he said, "She must know neither pain nor fear, not yet."

Here's a face that belongs to an allergy specialist: "Take cortisone three times a day for the next month," he instructed me. I go back to him after a few days with my eyes puffed and swollen and looking as though I'd gone three rounds with Muhammad Ali. "Look what it does to me," I wail. He smiles, appears to be highly amused. One shouldn't let these little incidents get one down, it's true, but in view of the Hippocratic oath they all happily took, it's hard to grasp sometimes, or at least it used to be—for me, anyway. "Stars don't get any younger either, you know," his receptionist said sweetly as I left his office in despair.

Two doctors who looked after me for film-insurance companies come padding up the conveyor belt: one poured penicillin into me intravenously through something that looked like a horn; the other took out his pocket knife and stabbed a huge carbuncle I had on an unmentionable place. As the pus shot up to the hotel room ceiling, his knife slipped and injured me in an even more unmentionable spot. He nevertheless pronounced me fit to shoot the next day—can't afford a delay, otherwise your premium will go up and the production company will whine, things like this get talked about and nobody'll give you a job any more, the bread line's just around the corner, the show must go on. "She's a real trouper," they say when you crawl onto the set on all fours.

A couple of my dentists deserve special mention, not so much for their expertise as for the entertainment they provided. There was a certain Dr. Wagenheber—or was it Wegenhaber? I received a warm recommendation from a friend to place myself in his hands. His apartment was already very individualistic, I remember, with a series of nude ladies in corny, less than elegant poses in place of wallpaper, Japanese tables, and hosts of Moroccan-leather cushions. He was beefy and blond, with freckles, and he went for my teeth in a big way. His bill could be described as big too, powerful even, but I'm used to that, it comes of all the zeros the press hangs on to our reported salaries. With his highly original technique he introduced me to pains and swellings that even I had never encountered before, and just as I was considering which method of suicide to choose, the police arrived. They were very polite, although they looked highly distraught, and said that they required information which they thought I might be in a position to provide. After hemming and hawing and hopping from one foot to the other, they came out with it: the apothecaries downtown were all swimming in prescriptions for morphine which were made out in my name. My tall husband loped off to our lawyer, the lawyer loped off to Wegenhaber—big surprise, he'd left for Africa. It turned out that he'd been supplying a cozy little circle of pushers with dope and had made the mistake of believing that my NAME would protect me, or rather, him, from obnoxious inquiries. I do hope he's found true happiness in Africa. Anyway, David and I spent a jumpy sort of time after this as, and one can understand it, dope peddlers are not fond of people who sing, and can turn ugly, at least that's what the policemen said as they decided to patrol our house for the rest of the year.

There was yet another with special priority for a solid seat in my memory. He came from the same town in southern Germany, which would seem to be a breeding ground for original dentists, and he pulled one of my incisors because, beneath it, there was an "acute apical abscess"; this was the first title he gave it, later it became "a granuloma in the roots," and later still "a bucket of pus." That it didn't belong there was clear even to me. He reached for the laughing gas, which proved to be not my cup of tea, and I vomited immediately. We got down and cleaned up the mess together, then he administered Novocain, which put me into a state of allergic shock. As my face started to inflate, he looked nonplused and yelled, "Pull yourself together!" He did get the tooth out in the end, but not, unhappily, the apical abscess. Just how he managed one without the other is a secret he kept closely guarded, but he was a master woodcarver—his waiting room, which was strangely always empty of patients, was full of delightful dwarfs he'd made himself: jolly ones, sad ones, standing ones, and sitting ones, some with aprons and others lying propped up on their elbows and beaming, dwarfs with wheelbarrows, rakes, and scythes.

A third dentist in Germany was telling me a funny story one day while drilling and laughed so much that he slipped and bored a hole right through my cheek. He went on laughing and said it was nothing to get upset about, but the incident did play a decisive part in persuading me henceforth to get on a plane and go to Switzerland when in need of dental care. There I met a gentle Englishman who had studied in the States and married a Zurich girl, and we've been together ever since. In three operations, each lasting from six to eight hours, he straightened out the mess a Russian with the butt of his machine gun and a bevy of German dentists with their original techniques had made of my jaw. The Englishman takes his time, and even deadens the gums with a special cream before giving the injection; up till now he has never said, "Pull yourself together." He doesn't have the conventional inquisition chair either; no, one lies flat out on a comfortable green couch which he can raise or lower at will, one feels like drifting off into a refreshing sleep the moment one gets on it. In the twelve years I've been going to him, I've grown really fond of him, as much as one can grow fond of one's dentist. He probably wouldn't say the same about me, because apart from the normal complications which seem to be part and parcel of my physical condition, a wisdom tooth raised Cain on a Sunday last June, and, while everyone else in Zurich was sailing on the lake or sitting beside it licking ice cream or sipping Campari-and-soda, he had to pull the tooth.

Just before we turn into our exit on the autobahn, a German liver specialist leers at me through the windshield. He had some newfangled machine called a "liver scan," or "radio-isotope examiner," and I lay under it one day and heard his secretary call the local newspaper from the next room to tell them the great news. The evening edition carried a detailed report of my visit along with the sad communiqué that the doctor had been obliged to advise me to go on a diet.

How could I ever forget Dr. Mehl? The unforgettable Justus Erasmus Mehl, M.D. His brother-in-law owned an apothecary which was handily situated next door to Mehl's office, and somehow I could never get rid of the feeling that this had some direct connection with the numerous prescriptions for pills, tablets, suppositories, and potions Mehl gave me. The alarming thing about Mehl's treatment was that, instead of feeling better after gulping all the medication, I felt lousier by the hour and my looks deteriorated accordingly. Then one day I bumped into an old friend who had studied medicine in his youth and I told him my tale of woe. I'd hardly mentioned the names of all the various things I was taking when he began behaving very oddly —for a moment I thought he was going into a spell of epilepsy. Gradually he brought his jerking limbs back under control and explained to me very carefully that I was in the process of committing a singularly tortuous form of suicide, and that even an East Prussian stallion's life expectancy would be radically reduced were it to undergo such a cure, for while one type of pill raised the blood pressure, another lowered it, some tablets were for water retention and others against, these were sedatives and those energizers, and should I continue to take them all at the same time, he told me, my metabolism would shortly give up the ghost. No sooner had I slung the whole medicine cabinet onto the rubbish heap and severed my relationship with Dr. Mehl than I felt right as rain again, but, foolhardy as I am, I gossiped to someone about Mehl and his methods and duly received a registered letter from his lawyer warning me against further calumny. Mehl was fashionable and "in," went to all the right parties, and had earned a name for himself as a raconteur and shaggy-dog storyteller, and was especially favored by the ladies. So there I had my warning, was forbidden to take the Lord Mehl's name in vain; the letter ended by informing me that one more word about Dr. Mehl could lead me into serious trouble—into court, instead of an early grave, one might say.

I took it very much to heart and stuck the letter behind my make-up mirror. I'd learned my lesson, there are some people you just can't fool around with, they have codes of honor and strong feelings about reputation, not only worship at the iniquitous shrine of Mammon, but also prize esteem and respect, characteristics they have in common with many actors, in fact. Only actors give one a lift, can even be instructive, and hardly ever endanger one's life.

To wind up the cavalcade, a Bulgarian anesthetist comes knocking on the window. In broken German he'd told me that he'd got a job in a private clinic shortly after escaping from the East and arriving in West Germany. The clinic dealt mainly with accident cases and was conveniently located near a busy and dangerous stretch of the highway. The head of the clinic, a surgeon, was also an alcoholic but had good friends on the town council, including the mayor. On his very first day, the Bulgarian witnessed a sad happening: the surgeon aimed a nail at a patient's broken hip, missed, and drove it into his bladder instead. Needless to say, the patient made a spontaneous *exitus*, but the surgeon kept his nerve, remained in full command of the situation, and extracted the expensive gold nail from the deceased's bladder, remarking that it would be sinful to waste it. A week later he clobbered his wife, who assisted at the operations for reasons of economy, with a handful of bloody towels; she gave as good as she got, and soon an earnest battle was raging over the anesthetized patient. The Bulgarian tried to mediate, but was hit on the head by a flying clamp and had to retire to attend to his own wounds. This patient never regained consciousness either. By the end of the week, the Bulgarian felt the time to go had come, and as he walked down the drive, the surgeon was in the act of laying the foundation stone to a new wing which would provide the clinic with fifty additional beds.

The rain drizzles to a stop. Traunstein-Nefertiti's nose is protruding from a wisp of cloud that resembles a chiffon scarf. Beneath her the silver-gray lake lies tranquilly reflecting her contours, like a hand mirror that she's laid aside. With a nod the patient turns her head toward the next village, in which lives a doctor who is honestly concerned with helping his fellow human beings; day in and day out he can be seen driving along the narrow country lanes, returning gray in the face and aged and unapproachable if one of his patients has died, even when the patient had clearly been without hope. It's his holy ambition to keep them alive and out of pain. He has tried to persuade her that verdicts are vastly overrated, that the reprieve could still arrive, and that her intestines and adhesions are a bit of a laugh, have a touch of feminine caprice about them. They played this game for many months until one day they looked at each other over a glass of cider and agreed that they knew that they knew nothing. Since then they have had a respectful, affable relationship.

16

.

It's a slow starter, this spring of the year nineteenhundredand-
seventyfive, one that leaves itself time and seems to smile ironi-
cally and seductively at haste, hate, yes, even at death itself. The
author is obsessed on these shyly inviting spring days, obsessed
with her obdurate, mysterious passion to live; she ties it up like
a bundle of rags, but there, in the center, as at the center of a
typhoon, the stifled outrage pulses on, the outrage she feels
about her verdict.

This particular May morning is the thirtieth anniversary of the
day on which her fatherland lost the Second World War and
she ran for her life through the streets of Berlin in a soldier's
uniform, clutching her hand grenades as she dodged the Russian
snipers. She concedes: she's still running.

This May morning is also the sixteenth anniversary of the day
she and David met for the first time on a street in London. Next
week, Christina will celebrate her birthday, her seventh.

May 16, 1975
Crinkled, mealy clouds are coming in from the west. The warm
wall of air pressure we call *Föhn* is holding them back from the
south. Nefertiti is lying back sunning herself in a blaze of azure
blue, her pursed upper lip kissing a baby lamb of a cloud. Below
her the lake seems to have shrunk to a puddle in the thinness of
the *Föhn* air, the "Sleeping Greek" and other peaks are so close

that they appear to be advancing on the hollow and the mill. To the north and the east though, everything is normal and green and flat, willing and waiting.

Nineteen gay Chinese lanterns are swinging in the courtyard. For the umpteenth time a number is called out and some lucky child has hit the raffle jackpot. Now there's a sack race, then blindman's buff. Every mouth and every shirt front bear evidence of ice cream and chocolate cake, every eye is gleaming and every cheek glowing apple red—no, there's a girl who's pale as a sheet and about to bring it all up again. Rudi and Elsa are squabbling and both are crying because she won the car he'd had his eye on and all he got was a necklace. Bertha, waddling and very albatrossy today, passes Solomonic judgment: swap.

I celebrated my seventh in the "Soling Establishment," next to the stove that stank of oil; I sat on the gluey three-legged stool behind the counter and Stepfather said, as always, "Watch yourself when you stand up, otherwise you'll get tangled in the lathes." And the eternal leather dust and the draft from the door, which the "casual customers" never shut properly. "Must have been born in a tent," my mother always said as she slammed it behind them. And the hatred I felt for my gentle, ever-coughing stepfather since Mother had married him, set up a "proper home," and taken me away from my grandfather. Every sandwich tasted of leather and glue and varnish and dust, even the ones I took to school in my satchel. It was cold on my seventh, very little snow, but cold, and the outside walls of the shop had damp green spots on them. I sat there brooding, thinking that I ought to be feeling happier, but not succeeding. They'd given me a "practical" present, a scratchy woolen dress, gray.

•

My daughter Christina: If I were obliged to write you a letter now that you would be able to read only at some future date, what could and should I say to you? Everything I know. It's not much, but we promised never to lie to each other, never ever.

To start with, I would admit to you that, from the beginning,

· 373 ·

your mother was never apathetic, and that this attitude was responsible for many a bruise and gash. Should I then advise you to be different?

I regret very much that you don't appear to have inherited any strong feeling for music. Music is the path along which speech cannot follow, it's the hollow, or the lofty refuge where one can allow one's bruises to heal in safety; one needs a place, for not even a rhino will come to the end of his life without having collected a bruise or two, and you don't have that sort of skin to begin with.

Would you prefer me to start by telling you about anti-human beings, or shall I talk about beauty? My grandfather, or your great-grandfather, never spoke to me of anything but beauty, so I learned nothing from him about people, whether anti- or fellow human beings: he excluded them from our life together, ignored them with an iron will. I discovered them later, when I was on my own, and for this reason, I suppose, my skin blemished very easily. I would like to warn you against the imposing façade of worldliness, behind which the desert of human vanity stretches endlessly, and against a certain breed of people who resemble those birds one sees pictures of that pick a crocodile's teeth while he's asleep. The birds have a useful function in nature, are not solely here to scavenge, whereas these people scavenge strength, thought, joy, love, beauty, and goodness, and have no other purpose in life at all. They are the barracudas of humanity, and usually move in schools.

I dread the day when you will cry for the first time, not just because of one, but because of many people, for that is the day on which you will come to know the sting of hopelessness. It will pass, slowly, and will always be in danger of recurring, but it can be compensated for by beauty. By the beauty one experiences in painting, for instance—you don't have to be a master, but never give it up, your painting, please, the pictures you paint now would have made many an impressionist weep with joy.

As a typical descendant of your great-grandfather's, nothing seemed as exciting to me when I was a girl as a mountain that had never been scaled; I thought of it as the one place that still might bear God's unspoiled traces. I loved this thought, and I loved Grandfather. He in his turn loved me, beauty, and success. In that order. He loved success for the simple reason that it protected one against anti-human beings—or so he believed.

While we're about the warnings: you inherited one very dangerous characteristic from me, the capability of being devoted to one single person. I implore you to keep a check on this capacity for unconditional love; love offers no protection and can wound you as nothing else, the wounds go deep and you mustn't bleed to death. Very few have the grace to accept and treasure the gift of love, valuing it as little as they value the gift of life: the hunter's ardor is cooled by the sight of the captured prey.

You are beautiful. I will say it again, loud and clearly: You are beautiful. It mustn't happen that some toffee-nosed teenager or a spritely roué surprises and bowls you over with this banal statement one day. And the compliment requires no return favors, certainly not physical ones, unless, of course, that's what you have in mind. Always remember one thing: you do the choosing, never allow yourself to be chosen. Something else: don't say yes from exhaustion. This last I learned from my one-time teacher and our common present friend, Else Bongers. She said it when I was already sixteen, too late to undo the things I'd already done, and too soon for me to be able to grasp the full wisdom and use it to advantage.

Seek the company of people to whom you can divulge the quality of your truth. There is an individual truth, one which I'm afraid is humblingly subjective, and there is a gigantic, cosmos-encompassing one which you can lose yourself in. All other truths are subject to changes in fashion, dependent on some form of dictatorship, and have colors with the steadfastness of a chameleon. Be careful that you don't lose your truth between courtesy and the necessity for the occasional white lie, and don't let that many-headed serpent called cynicism persuade you that it is the true and only wisdom. There is a Christian alternative which overburdens us all, and we tend to use the burden as an excuse to neglect the alternative. I believe that the only possible reason for our being here is to serve in some form or another but that the form is not always readily found or recognized. And I've noticed that those who refuse to serve often wind up as slaves.

One of the most absurd things about human beings is that they refuse to accept the brevity of life, and brief it is, whether you live to be a hundred or not. Try not to have idols: they are interchangeable and lead to a wantonness that is easily mistaken for love.

There will be days when you will want to hug the whole world, and others when you will want to crawl under the nearest stone. You'll never be alone in feeling this way, although to know it is small comfort—aches and pains cannot be shared, not even toothaches, as you've already learned. The feeling will go away again, but you must give it time, don't fight it too hard or it might devour you. And look for a profession that gives you real pleasure; if it pleases you no more, change it.

Your children will leave you one day and you must help them to be able to go with a clear conscience. What remains is work. A man, another person, can leave you or you him; what remains is work. And should you feel the need to write one day, it's a matter of complete indifference whether you write about yourself or about others—this is another of those hypocritical farces the anti-human beings indulge in, maintaining that only those who thrust their egos behind them are worthy of respect. This alleged uninterest in oneself is nothing but chickenheartedness and dishonesty. One more thing: it's good to know failure, now and then. One must learn to take it with the same equanimity that one needs to manage success. And if you have to make mistakes, make them good and big, don't be middling in anything if you can help it.

Don't pay too much attention when there's talk of "happiness." Happiness is a specter, a soap bubble, a photo caption. You have already gathered that we as a family come under the heading of happiness in public opinion, we stand for happiness as we flash our smiles at the cameras. And what's usually the story behind it? You're itching to get back to your game, I'm invariably in some pain, and your father was due at the theater in Salzburg long ago and is jiggling the car keys impatiently behind his back. "Happiness" is a sort of medal society pins on your breast for doing nothing, honoring the coincidence.

To get back to beauty: it's everywhere, just as suffering is everywhere. And people turn a blind eye to both.

Perhaps you won't.